THE FLOWER ARRANGER

JJ ELLIS

AGORA BOOKS

ABOUT THE AUTHOR

JJ Ellis was born and raised in Yorkshire in northern England although now lives near London. The author's interest in Japan was sparked when a family member won a trip there by singing in Japanese at an exhibition in the UK. Several visits followed — to Tokyo and further flung places such as Ishigaki and Iriomote — as Ellis developed the idea for *The Flower Arranger*. Two more crime novels featuring the team of Tanaka and Blain are planned.

THE
FLOWER
ARRANGER

First published in Great Britain in 2019 by Agora Books

Agora Books is a division of Peters Fraser + Dunlop Ltd

55 New Oxford Street, London WC1A 1BS

Printed and bound in Great Britain by Clays Ltd, Elcograf S.p.A.

To Scarlett,
who followed her dream to Japan.

PROLOGUE

He cut off the leaf with the precision and care of a surgeon. Someone who took pride in his work. What was taken away was just as important as what remained.

To do the flowers justice, to do the whole arrangement justice, the spaces — the emptiness, the *Ma* or negative space — had to be calculated in exactly the way his mother had shown him all those years ago.

He worked quickly but methodically. Those who saw him doing this probably wouldn't believe he was capable of it. The nerdy salaryman with no friends. Just one of tens of thousands in the Akasaka district of Minato, working too-long hours with little purpose. Scurrying back like a plague of rats, heads down, masks muzzling mouths, through the metro tunnels to their single room apartments in identikit suburbs.

Some days that would be him. But not today. Today was a special day.

This location was perfect. A traditional Japanese room in an isolated building, without western frills and — importantly — with a large *tokonoma* alcove to display his arrangement.

His mother had always told him that the flowers themselves were just as important as the way they were arranged and framed. So, for this most special of occasions, he'd collected some of the most beautiful flowers he knew of — from deep in the jungle rainforest of Iriomote island. The others on the guided tour were too busy looking at waterfalls or wiping sweat from their foreheads to notice him leaving the trail. They didn't see him snipping specimens of the Okinawa Sekkoku, the wild Okinawan orchid — critically endangered, he knew. But he had just borrowed some of their beauty, not destroyed it. More branches of the *Dendrobium okinawense* with their distinctive white-pink five-petal flowers would grow back to replace the ones he'd taken.

He held up one of the flowers to admire it. Its asymmetrical nature was in itself a thing of beauty, something his mother had delighted in pointing out to him. The five petals would, to an untrained eye, seem unbalanced. Between the first and fifth petal there was almost a semi-circle of empty space — nature's own answer to *Ma* — as though two or three of the petals had already been plucked before their time.

If his arrangement in the *tokonoma* was a tribute to the beauty of the mother he remembered, then the music playing in the background — the same song repeating over and over — well, that was something for his father. *Ikebana*, the art of flower-arranging, was supposed to be silent. But he always played this same song.

It was a song that had been used, abused in his view and in the view of its composer, in an American film. But it was a pure song, a song that — with its strange structure, its soaring vocal that never reached a chorus, never repeated — was the perfect accompaniment to his flower arrangement. A complement to the haunting beauty of these rare orchids.

Everything felt right. Everything felt ready. The Ray-Ban

Wayfarers, carefully repaired after the unfortunate incident at the concert, shielding his eyes. The black shirt and trousers were newly ironed and pressed.

Standing guard, the two snakes he'd collected on his jungle trip.

There was one thing he wasn't sure about. The mascot he liked to take to concerts, that he was known for and that he'd even allowed some of his idols to touch. The comforter his father had given him to sleep with each night.

He placed it in the alcove, to the right of the flowers and twigs.

The candy-coloured clown.

The song began again. But he didn't mime as the actor had in the film. He sang in perfect tune, matching the multi-octave purity of his hero's voice. His father's hero's voice. The other Man in Black. The one who wasn't Johnny Cash.

And now he knew what was wrong with the arrangement. He'd always known. It wasn't the striped male doll with the made-up laughing face. It was the *Ma* — the negative space in the centre of the arrangement.

It needed to be filled.

There was only one thing beautiful enough to fill it and — finally — she was here with him.

Ready, if not willing, to play her role.

CHAPTER ONE

She looked at the reflection of her face in the Ginza line train's window, crushed up against the salarymen rushing home. Her mid-1980s Johnny Marr-esque hairstyle, and her dark suit, made her look almost indistinguishable from the Japanese young men she was sardined in with. Blending in wasn't deliberate, although the attempt to mimic her guitar hero was. Still, her naturally olive skin, elfin looks, and the haircut had its advantages. Most Japanese edged away from westerners on the metro trains, or ostentatiously donned their face masks if they weren't already wearing them. Her Japanese friends claimed it wasn't racism, just embarrassment at the thought they might have to exercise their limited English. But it didn't happen to Blain. And if any of those Japanese dared to talk to her, they got a reply in a perfect accent with perfect grammar, reinforcing her Nippon-esque qualities.

The stations ticked down to Ueno, where she had to change. She read the *kanji* with the ease of a native, and when the display flicked to Roman lettering, she already knew where she was. But each passing station seemed to add to the crush.

The Hibiya line would be quieter. Just three stops, then another day was over and she could relax.

The Master bowed. Blain bowed back and smiled.

'The usual, Holly-san?'

Blain gave a slight nod, her grin widening. Just getting to the café was like reaching a haven, and as she sat at her favourite corner table and breathed in the meaty fumes of bowls of food being readied by the Master and his girlfriend behind the counter, she could feel herself finally relax. She loosened her dark tie.

Another shit day over at last. And as it was Friday, another shit week gone too. There were plenty of women like herself back in England who would do anything to have her job. One of the only western journalists working for a Japanese newspaper in Tokyo. Spending her time interviewing sugar-sweet teenage pop stars, with their starey, over made-up eyes and jaw-defying smiles. But Blain wanted something harder, more substantial.

The Master gently placed the bowl of chicken katsu in front of her.

'This will take away all your troubles, Holly-san.'

Blain felt her saliva glands pumping. 'The best in all of Tokyo.'

'Ha! You cannot say that. There are too many restaurants to try. Tokyo is big.' The Master wiped his hands on his apron then spread his arms wide. 'Bigger than big. The city that never ends.' Then he drew close to her left ear. 'Any success yet?'

He knew that Blain was constantly nagging her news

editor on the *Tōkei Shimbun* to give her a chance on the crime beat, usually the preserve of the older, male reporters. She shrugged and shook her head.

'Don't leave too quickly tonight,' the Master continued to whisper. 'There is someone who comes here most Friday nights who it will be useful for you to meet. Three people gathering together can create wisdom, and the man I want you to meet is a wise man.' The Master winked.

Blain's interest was piqued, but she was too hungry to think too much about it. She dived into the katsu bowl with the relish of someone who hadn't eaten for days.

The food had a homely feel. And as the warmth spread through her body, Blain smiled wryly to herself about her latest assignment.

If she'd been doing the job for a newspaper back in England, then it might have been more to her liking. An exposé of the Japanese J-pop idol culture, and the way the four girls — the new members of Hello Happy Princess, the latest girl group to be emblazoned in giant neon signs in Shinjuku and Shibuya — had twirled their slightly too-short schoolgirl dresses. The way the eyes of the middle-aged *Otaku*, their nerdy fans or followers, followed each twirl, hoping no doubt for a furtive glimpse of underwear.

But her leather-faced news editor, Akihiro Yamamoto-san had been quite clear that he didn't want any scandal. Groups like Hello Happy Princess were big news amongst the *Tōkei Shimbun*'s readership because of their embodiment of school-girl innocence. Their *kawaii* cute faces, and perhaps even their too-short skirts, would feature prominently in a colour photograph that would be the main attraction, rather than Blain's words. Yamamoto-san wanted a cute story to go with a cute photograph of the latest recruits to Hello Happy Princess after the previous members 'graduated' — the euphemistic term for the churn as the teenagers hit their twenties and became too old, replaced with these new models. So, Blain could write nothing tainted. Nothing questioning.

Blain had watched the procession of fans stream past the four girls. Each was allowed just a few seconds with their idols before heavy-set minders behind moved them on. If one of the *Otaku* took liberties, asked for a kiss, or held onto a hand for too long, they would be bundled out.

There was one point where she really thought she might have a harder story. The minders seemed to be trying to move in on one of the *Otaku* who was getting over-friendly. He was thrusting a dirty clown doll towards the main singer as they lined up for the meet and greet. Blain watched the girl recoil, momentarily lose her sugar-sweet, wide-eyed smile, and, at almost the same moment, one of the heavies moved in to pull the man back. The man retreated, holding his hands up, one clutching his doll mascot, but, in the mêlée, his sunglasses had been knocked to the floor. Blain had watched his narrow, ferret face contort in anger and thought for a moment he might resist the bouncers and that she might get a better story than Yamamoto-san wanted. But instead, the man simply picked up the now-broken sunglasses and exited the gathering.

Blain left too, wondering briefly if she should follow him all the way to Shinjuku station, where he seemed to be heading. But then he turned down a side-street in the red-light area, and she gave up her half-hearted chase, knowing her priority was Yamamoto-san's story for the morning edition.

Her bowl of katsu was finished, and Blain refreshed her palate with a cup of the matcha green tea.

When the café door swung open and a late-thirty-something man entered, Blain somehow knew this was who the Master wanted her to meet.

As the man took off his raincoat and sat down, the Master sidled up to him. They began a low-voiced conversation, with both occasionally looking at Blain and smiling. The reporter felt she was being appraised.

Then the Master raised his eyes and beckoned her over.

'This is Holly-san, the reporter I was talking to you about, Tanaka-san. Holly, I'd like you to meet Inspector Tetsu Tanaka, head of the Tokyo Metropolitan Police Department's new Gaikoku-jin Unit. I think you may find sharing information between the two of you mutually beneficial.'

CHAPTER TWO

Inspector Tetsu Tanaka — Tanaka Keibu — surveyed the Frenchman across his desk. The man was in silhouette against Tanaka's favourite window. On less frenetic days here at the Keijibu, Tokyo's criminal investigation department headquarters, its serene view over the Imperial Palace grounds often helped bring inspiration to his more mundane investigations.

But this case was anything but mundane.

The man — who'd introduced himself as Pascal Durand — was frantically chewing his fingernails, then running his hand through his hair again and again.

'I don't understand,' he was saying to Tanaka.

'What don't you understand, Mr Durand?'

'I just want some help to put out an appeal to find my daughter. I didn't ask to talk to a detective. Why's it a criminal matter?'

Tanaka leant back in his chair and folded his arms across his stomach. 'It isn't at the moment, Mr Durand. Let's hope it won't become one. It's simply that I'm in charge of liaising with foreigners. No one here speaks French, but as I speak reasonably fluent English, as do you, we felt it was the best approach.' Tanaka made a play of tidying the papers on his desk. He opened a random file and thumbed through it, just to keep his hands occupied.

The detective wasn't being entirely honest. What the man had told him so far had already disturbed him. Not least, the fact that the man had managed to lose his daughter in the teeming metropolis that was Tokyo. How could anyone be so careless, so negligent? Tanaka and his wife, Miho, had lost their own daughter, never seeing her blossom like the cherry trees coming into bloom all over the capital.

Never seeing Misaki reach her potential. Never knowing her. Just that photograph of her as a baby in the *tokonoma*. That fleeting moment of joy. The photograph his sons and their friends always wanted to talk about until they saw the looks of devastation on their parents' faces. She would have been seventeen now. The same age as Durand's missing daughter.

Tanaka swallowed hard and tried to push the thoughts from his head. 'It's difficult for you when you're in a totally alien country,' he continued. 'All the shop signs not only in a foreign language, but in a different alphabet. It's easy to become confused...'

He held up a page from the *Tōkei Shimbun* to make his point, outlining the newspaper advertisement characters with his finger. It was a new newspaper, not really Tanaka's style — given to him by the young female reporter he'd met and chatted to on Friday evening at the café next to Minami-Senju station. He preferred something a little more cerebral and probing than the mix of celebrity and business news it seemed to offer.

'It's easy to panic. I felt the same when I first went to London.'

'London? What's that got to do with anything? I just want some sort of appeal to go out for my daughter to contact me.'

Tanaka didn't answer immediately. Instead, he rose from the desk and walked behind the man, looking out through the window. This was his favourite time of year, the Imperial Palace gardens covered in a riot of pinks and whites from the *sakura* trees. A Sunday such as this would usually be spent picnicking under the blooms with Miho and the boys. It was a centuries-old tradition — the *Hanami* festival. A sacred time of year, when weather forecasters tracked the cherry blossom front up from Okinawa at the start of the year, here to Tokyo by April, and then on to the North and Hokkaido. Maybe once he'd finished at the office, Miho, Takumi, Sora, and he would have time to go to the Meiji shrine, near Harajuku, to pay their respects. To remember the fifth member of their little family, who couldn't be with them.

And it was the cherry blossom festival that had been the reason for the timing of the visit to Tokyo by the Frenchman and his daughter. Now it had gone wrong. But how wrong? Tanaka furrowed his brow. It was at odds with *Hanami*. He turned away from the window again, moved a couple of paces next to the man, and placed his arm gently on his shoulder — a form of physical contact Japanese would usually shun, but it was Tanaka's role to empathise with foreigners.

'As I was saying, I've never been to your country, France, but I have lived and worked abroad. I served an attachment with the police service in England. I remember my feelings of confusion, of being overwhelmed, when I first arrived.'

'I'm not confused at all. My daughter has gone missing. I just want the help of the police to find her.'

'It's only been four hours, Mr Durand. Your daughter has

not contacted you for four hours. That's really not a long time at all. She is seventeen; in Japan, she would no longer be considered a child. Please let's keep things in proportion.'

Durand's face coloured.

'That's all very well for you to say. It's not your daughter who's gone missing.'

Tanaka wasn't going to enter into an argument. The man had a point. 'All right,' he said, sitting down at the desk again. 'Let's go through exactly what's happened and how you and Marie-Louise came to be parted. If she still doesn't contact you, or return to your hotel of her own accord, in a few hours we will issue an appeal in the media.'

He watched the man slump forward, the tension momentarily eased. But while Tanaka had succeeded in calming the father down, privately he was worried. Very worried. Because this wasn't the first girl to disappear from a teenage fashion shop. And the other, a Swede, still had not been found, several weeks later. As yet, they had no leads.

Tanaka finally got the story from the man in some semblance of order. The girl wore Lolita clothing — a name that made Tanaka shudder — but one that Durand said was completely innocent. Indeed, it was this innocence that characterised the fashion subculture, originating in Japan and now — according to the Frenchman — an obsession for many western girls. They dressed in Victorian-influenced, voluminous cupcake prints. 'Little Bo Peep' was how Durand described her. The girl — Marie-Louise — had won a fashion competition at Tokyo Ultra, an annual Parisian exhibition of Japanese culture. The prize: two return tickets to Japan. Her father had come as her chaperone. To look after her. To protect her. He didn't seem to have done a particularly good job.

The crucial time had been at the Closet Child second-hand fashion shop in Ikebukuro — a commercial and entertainment district in the Toshima area of Tokyo, at the northwest corner of the circular Yamanote line.

Tanaka tapped his finger at the station on his wall poster of the metro map.

'You say you left her for about an hour while she looked through the dresses in this shop.'

'Yes. She seemed quite happy. I'd been trailing round the fashion boutiques already for two days. I'd had enough. I just wanted some time on my own.'

Tanaka gave a cynical laugh then realised it was inappropriate and tried to turn it into a cough. He wanted to empathise but couldn't. Durand's problem was one he would have loved to have had — indulging his daughter in a fashion shop for teenagers. Instead, it would be the obsessions of teenage boys that he would have to deal with in a few years' time. Baseball, girls, and computer games, if he was lucky. Drinks, drugs, or worse if he wasn't.

'So what did you do?'

'Sorry?'

Tanaka noticed Durand's fingernail-chewing had begun again.

'When you went off for an hour. What did you do?'

'I just went for a beer.' Tanaka noticed the man's eyes dart to the right, as he frantically began hand-combing his hair again. He was lying.

'And so an hour later, you came back as arranged?'

'Yes. An hour or so. Yes.'

'An hour… *or so*?'

'Look, an hour. That's what I said. That's what we'd agreed. But she wasn't there. I tried ringing her mobile. No answer. I tried asking the sales staff if they'd seen her. They couldn't understand me. I was frantic with worry.'

'Of course. That's understandable. So what did you do?'

'What could I do? I thought maybe she was angry I was late and...'

'*Late?*' asked Tanaka. 'Sorry, I'm not following you completely. I thought you said you came back after an hour, as arranged?'

'Well... maybe I was a few minutes late. So eventually I went back to the hotel...'

'The Shiba Park?'

'Yes, the Shiba Park Hotel, in Daimon. Four nights' accommodation there was included in her prize.'

'And she wasn't there?'

'No. And the reception staff hadn't seen her, the room key was still on the hook, and there was no message. I'm frightened, Inspector Tanaka. Very, very frightened.'

This time Tanaka didn't attempt to offer any words of reassurance. 'I can understand your concern. We will — as you say — put out an appeal.' He twirled a paper clip between his finger and thumb then drew in a long breath. 'It would help us if you could cast your mind back over the hours and days leading up to this. Did you notice anything suspicious on your previous two days in Tokyo? Did Marie-Louise seem her normal self? Had you and your daughter rowed at all?'

'Rowed? No... not really.'

'Not *really?*' The man was hiding something, Tanaka was sure. First the lie over where he'd been while the girl had been looking at clothes in Ikebukuro. Now his reluctance to talk about some disagreement, however minor.

'Okay, we'd had a few cross words,' Durand finally admitted. 'My bank card wouldn't work in the cash machine. I'd run out of money, and, although I'd warned my bank I was coming to Japan, for some reason the card had been stopped. I tried machine after machine, even in the post office. But no luck.'

'Why did that provoke an argument?'

'Because I'd given Marie-Louise 200 euros in Japanese yen for spending money. She was going to use it towards buying her dream dress from Angelic Pretty in Harajuku. It was what she was most looking forward to about the trip.'

'And?' prompted Tanaka.

'And I asked for it back. I had no other money and no way of getting any out from the bank. It was the only way we were going to survive for the remaining two days of the holiday. We're due to fly back to Paris tomorrow. So that's why we were in the second-hand shop, rather than buying her dream dress new from the shop in Harajuku. I'd ruined her dream.'

Tanaka rubbed his chin thoughtfully. 'I don't think you should blame yourself for that, Mr Durand. What about the other part of my question? Did anything else unusual or suspicious happen in the three days you've been in Tokyo so far?'

Durand frowned. Then after a moment's thought his eyes and jaw opened simultaneously. 'Yes, there was. Yesterday, in Odaiba. At the Hello Kitty store.'

'Hello Kitty? Why did Marie-Louise want to go there? It's usually for younger girls, isn't it?'

'I know. But this was some J-pop star doing an appearance there. I don't remember her name, but I might have it back at the hotel on our itinerary. But I agree it was very weird. The audience were in two very distinct groups — I thought it was odd at the time. Teenage girls and boys — too old for Hello Kitty — and then loads and loads of middle-aged men with cameras. It was bizarre.'

Tanaka shrugged. 'Plenty of aspects of Japanese culture can appear bizarre, Mr Durand. Especially to westerners. But in what way was it suspicious?'

'Well, one of these men wanted a picture of Marie-Louise. She was dressed in a Lolita outfit. It happened before I had a chance to intervene; I was only half paying attention anyway. J-pop's not my sort of thing...'

Tanaka smiled encouragingly at the man.

'...so I was over at the side, in the café area. But I saw him take the photo, and then he seemed to hand something to her.'

'What?'

'I don't know. I was too far away to see clearly. And Marie-Louise was very evasive about it afterwards.'

Inwardly, Tanaka sighed. He could see his planned visit to the shrine disappearing before his very eyes — they would have to follow up all this information immediately, before the trail went cold.

'Do you have a photo of Marie-Louise with you? Preferably two photos — one in her Lolita outfit, and one in normal clothing.'

The man pulled out his smartphone and started jabbing at it. 'No. *Merde*. As I thought. I don't have much storage space on my phone. So I downloaded all the photos to my laptop last night. Then I deleted them off the phone. They're at the hotel.'

Tanaka tried not to let his annoyance show. His interrogation of the man had already delayed things. There would now be another half-hour's delay before they could put out the appeal, along with the necessary photo.

'I'll get a patrol car to take you back to the hotel. When you get there, find a relevant photo. I'll come and meet you there in half an hour's time, and we'll then email the photo back to HQ to go with the appeal.'

Durand began to rise from his chair, as Tanaka continued.

'I'll also send my deputy to the Closet Child store to talk to them and check whether they have any CCTV images which may help. After that, you and I should go to this Hello Kitty store in Odaiba — I think that is where we are likely to have most luck.'

'Thank you,' said the Frenchman.

'One other thing. This man who approached Marie-Louise at the Hello Kitty store. Was there anything distinctive about him?'

'I don't know. Most Japanese men look the same to me.' Tanaka ignored the man's unreconstructed racism. 'He *was* dressed slightly oddly. All in black, and a slightly old-fashioned style.'

'What about his face? His build?'

'Slim build, taller than most Japanese men. I didn't really get a good look at his face. He was wearing dark glasses... Oh, and he was carrying something in his other hand. Again, I didn't get a good look. It almost looked like some sort of doll. Perhaps he'd bought a present at the store for one of his children?'

Perhaps, thought Tanaka. But more likely, perhaps not. The man sounded like an *Otaku*.

Tanaka stood up and offered the Frenchman his hand. 'I'm sure we will soon find your daughter, Mr Durand.'

It was reassurance without any basis.

Hollow.

And Tanaka regretted saying it almost as soon as the words passed his lips.

CHAPTER THREE

Blain entered her Hello Happy Princess piece into the news system's pending stories folder. Within a few minutes, Yamamoto-san's username locked the file as he started to edit it. A couple of minutes later, a top line message asked her to approach the newsdesk.

'This is a good piece, Holly-san,' Yamamoto said in his thick regional accent which Blain struggled to understand — her brain catching up with his words a second or two later, like a simultaneous interpreter. 'But I've removed the paragraph about the argument with the *Otaku*. You know why.'

Blain forced herself to mentally count to ten. From the corner of her eye she saw Hasegawa-san — the deputy news editor — barely suppressing a grin. It was simply a game to them.

'You know best, Yamamoto-san,' she said, giving a slight bow. 'I will trust your judgement, of course.'

'Cut the crap, Blain,' said Yamamoto, pressing the send button to mark the file ready for the sub-editors and design-

ers. 'You're good, but you're not as good as you think you are.'
As he delivered the words, he grinned at her.

Blain knew this was her chance. While he was in a good
mood. While he was thinking he'd got one over on her.

'Do you have a moment for a short chat, Yamamoto-san?'

The news editor fixed her with a hard glare. 'Is it just going
to be a re-run of our usual "chats", Blain?'

She shrugged. 'I'd still like to talk to you. I have a possible
new contact.'

Yamamoto gestured with his eyes to Hasegawa, signalling
to his Number Two he needed to take charge of the newsdesk
for a few minutes. Then he led Blain through to his glazed side
office. The news editor perched on the table and indicated
Blain should take the low sofa. It was an old trick — one she'd
had played on her in the UK when she was just starting out in
newspapers, before the move to Japan. Before it all went
wrong back home. She wasn't going to fall for it. Instead, she
leant against the closed door — ensuring her eyeline was level
with Yamamoto's.

He cleared his throat. 'So, Holly-san. This isn't going to be
your usual whining?'

'Well…'

'Ah.' Yamamoto folded his arms across his chest. 'I see it *is*
going to be.'

'You know how much I want to do the police beat.'

'We've been through this before, Holly. You're too valuable
on show business for me to lose.'

'Couldn't you at least give me a trial, Yamamoto-san? Or a
temporary posting? Or allow me one day a week doing crime?'
She brought her hands together in front of her face in a pray-
ing, pleading motion. *'Onegai itashimasu.'*

Yamamoto appeared unmoved. 'The only way a good
crime reporter can get stories is by developing his or her

contacts — in other words, by buttering up the detectives. That can't be achieved one day a week. What about this new contact you say you have? Perhaps he's someone we can pass on to the senior crime reporters.'

Blain bit her lip. It was very tempting to tell Yamamoto to stuff his job. But she knew she would struggle to get another with as many potential opportunities.

'It's a personal link. Arranged by a friend of mine. The detective is the head of the Gaikoku-jin Unit at the TMPD.'

'And why do you think he would offer scoops to you?'

'I don't know that he will. But there's only any chance of that if I'm allowed to develop my relationship with him further. And for that I need time.' Yamamoto had closed his eyes now. She didn't think he was ignoring her. She hoped it meant he was giving her proposal serious consideration. 'If you do not enter the tiger's cave, you cannot catch its cub,' she said.

Yamamoto bent double with laughter. 'Ha! You think you are so Japanese you can use our proverbs on me, do you, Blain? Let me throw one back to you, one that is relevant to what you're asking. You've heard of the expression "One who chases two hares won't catch even one"?'

Blain nodded.

'That applies to you. I respect your work on show business. We even give you by-lines.'

'Occasionally.'

Yamamoto sighed. 'All right. Here's what I'll agree to, but as soon as — in my view — it has a negative effect on your show business reporting, the arrangement comes to an end. One shift a week you can trail one of our police reporters. But not at the Tokyo Metropolitan Police Department. That would be too rarefied a start. If you're doing this, I want you to be giving something back. You have a good knowledge of

Japanese youth culture especially the JK.' Blain frowned, wondering what he was driving at. 'You know, the *joshi kosei*, the high-school girls phenomenon. Even if you don't always understand or agree with it.'

'I don't ever agree with it, Yamamoto-san.'

Yamamoto gave a thin smile. 'Nevertheless, your knowledge of the subject could be useful for the Fourth District. One shift a week you can spend at Shinjuku police station, which houses the press club for the Fourth District. The area, as I'm sure you're aware, includes Kabukicho. The town of no sleep. The red-light area. Plenty of JK girl bars. You might find some stories there. You might be able to help with some stories. But there is one condition.'

'What?'

Yamamoto's smile turned sly. 'You still do your regular five shifts a week here on show business. The shift in Shinjuku is an extra one. And you won't get paid any extra for it. Are you still interested?'

It wouldn't make use of her new contact, the inspector in the Gaikoku-jin Unit introduced to her by the Master at Café Muse. It wasn't really much of a foothold on the crime beat. But it was something. It was the best offer that Yamamoto would make: turn it down, and Blain knew she wouldn't get another chance.

She gave a low bow. 'Of course. I'm very grateful, Yamamoto-san. I won't let you down.'

CHAPTER FOUR

Tanaka busied himself over the next few minutes getting in place what he'd promised to do for Durand. But in truth, it was as important for the reputation of the Keijibu as for the safety of the Frenchman's daughter. Japan had one of the world's lowest crime rates, but Tanaka knew this told only half the story. The headline figures had little to do with the efficiency of the police, who, in Tanaka's experience, were hopelessly mired in bureaucracy and institutional inertia. Most of the reasons for it lay deep-rooted in Japanese society — their non-violence and respect for one another. That was how he, Tetsu Tanaka, had been brought up. And it was how he was bringing his children up. He hoped his sons would never show a lack of respect towards women as some Japanese men did. It was that lack of respect which troubled him. He wondered if it lay at the root of this case.

He picked up the phone and dialled his deputy.

'Izumi-kun!' he barked. 'My office, now.'

His estimate of half an hour to meet the Frenchman was optimistic in the extreme. But it would do Mr Durand good to sweat a bit, perhaps it might encourage him to tell the whole truth this time. That's what Tanaka hoped to get on the mono-rail journey to Odaiba.

Katsuhiko Izumi came rushing breathlessly into Tanaka's office. His boss was normally mild-mannered, but he would have been able to tell from the tone of the phone call that Tanaka was stressed.

'Tanaka-san!' Izumi bowed towards his superior. 'You wanted me, Keibu?'

'I need you to go to Ikebukuro,' Tanaka said. He noticed Izumi's breath was still laboured from his run up the stairs. Izumi was a reliable if unremarkable officer, diligent but not a lateral thinker. His main failing was a tendency to spend too long, and eat too much, in the local *Yoshinoya* — the fast-food chain of Japanese cuisine. Izumi had been ordering too many *gyudon* — beef bowls with rice. It gave him the appearance of a slimline sumo wrestler. And that wasn't very slim.

Tanaka outlined to his assistant inspector what he wanted him to do, and, at the same time, began an email to all Tokyo police precincts for them to put out an alert for Marie-Louise Durand. All it needed for completion was the photos, which he could attach when he got to Pascal Durand's hotel.

Picking up his lightweight raincoat, he headed for the metro station and his rendezvous at the Shiba Park Hotel.

Tanaka and Durand said little on the twenty-minute walk from the hotel to Takeshiba station by the waterfront, to catch the Yurikamome monorail train to Odaiba. It was one of Tanaka's least favourite parts of the city — an artificial island originally built to protect Edo, the capital of the Tokugawa shogunate, now modern-day Tokyo. In the nineties it was supposed to have become a showcase for ultra-chic living, but then came the collapse of Japan's bubble economy and Odaiba's near ruin. It had only been saved by being turned into a kind of giant funfair, complete with big wheel, toy warehouses, and artificial beach. To Tanaka that's exactly what it was. Artificial, and an eyesore.

But the first part of the journey took them over something Tanaka loved, the Rainbow Bridge, or Reinbo Burijji. He, the children, and Miho loved the view of the bridge at night from the Tokyo Tower, illuminated as it was in red, white, and green to give a rainbow effect. And it was no less impressive viewed here from the Yurikamome line during the daylight.

Tanaka turned to Durand now. The Frenchman was ashenfaced, fidgeting, his legs knocking together in some static dance, as though he needed the toilet. But Tanaka knew what he really needed. His daughter back, safe and well.

'Have you told Marie-Louise's mother yet, Mr Durand?'

'No. I haven't yet. I don't want to worry her unnecessarily.' Tanaka frowned at the man. Durand held his arms out, palms outwards. 'I know I should, and I will, of course. But she's thousands of kilometres away and if — as I hope — it's all a big mistake and Marie-Louise turns up, well...'

The man's voice trailed off. The excuse sounded exactly as feeble as it was. 'Have you checked your phone to see if she's tried to get in touch?'

The Frenchman reached into his pocket and pulled out his smartphone.

'Of course. I'm constantly looking at it. But no. There's been nothing,' he said, peering hopelessly at the screen.

'We're trying to get a trace on your daughter's phone. Is she in the habit of turning it off to save the battery?'

Durand shrugged. 'No. Not as far as I know.'

'Well, the last time we know, she used it was about the time you last saw her in Ikebukuro. That's where my deputy is at the moment. Checking in the fashion shop. If we're lucky they may have CCTV images. And the street level surveillance in that area is very good.'

'Street level surveillance?' Durand appeared nonplussed.

'Yes. We'll be able to find out if anyone followed you... to the *bar*.'

Tanaka emphasised the final word of his sentence and challenged Durand's gaze. The Frenchman sighed and turned away.

'Okay, I'd better come clean with you,' he said.

'Come clean?' asked Tanaka, feigning innocence. 'About what?' He had a good idea what was coming. Durand's eyes had given him away at police HQ just over an hour before.

'I wasn't completely honest about going to the bar. I didn't. I went to one of the porn video rental places. You know, the ones with the single booths. It's been doing my head in following Marie-Louise round to these fashion shops all day. I needed a bit of "me time". That's why I haven't told my wife yet. She doesn't have to know that bit, does she?'

'No.' Tanaka replied. 'Not unless...'

'Unless what...?'

'Unless it becomes relevant, Mr Durand.'

They lapsed into silence as Tanaka let the implications sink in.

They had looped round the Rainbow Bridge now and on to Odaiba itself. Tanaka glanced to his left, out of the train window, and gazed up at the Ferris wheel. Rusting and under-used. And behind it, the curiously named Palette Town — where the two men were heading. Tanaka knew it as a soulless mall, parts of which were in the process of being demolished. Not before time, he thought.

'By the way,' said Durand, interrupting the detective's

musing, 'I looked up the name of that J-pop star. It was Sayumi Michishige, from Morning Musume.'

Tanaka nodded. He knew the name. Plenty of teenage Japanese girls were fans, with pictures covering their bedroom walls. Unfortunately, that often held true for middle-aged, single males too. They were one of the biggest J-pop idol groups — revered by teens and *Otaku* alike.

When they arrived, the overwhelming impression Tanaka got from the Hello Kitty store was pinkness. Not the beautiful pink of the Imperial Palace's cherry blossom trees. No, this was the sickly, Day-Glo pink of millions of young girls' bedrooms. Even the staff member he was talking to was dressed in the same shade of pink. Bright pink jumpsuit and, on her head, a ludicrous Hello Kitty headdress.

He showed her a photo of Marie-Louise.

The salesgirl nodded enthusiastically, the headdress' whiskers oscillating madly, and began speaking rapidly in Japanese.

Tanaka translated for Durand.

'She recognises her. Very *kawaii* she says, very cute girl. And yes, she did see a man taking her photo. Marie-Louise posed for several in fact. They had to ask them to move to one side because they were disturbing Sayumi Michishige's performance. So you must have just caught the end of it, when he was handing over... well whatever he was handing over.'

'But does she know who the man was?'

'She thinks we may be in luck,' replied Tanaka. 'He may be part of the Hello Kitty store fan club and would therefore get advance notice of all the events here.'

The salesgirl had disappeared now, into a back room.

'She'll only be a moment — just checking the database.'

Tanaka could see renewed hope etched on Durand's face.

The girl returned and immediately started apologising to Tanaka in Japanese, accompanied by repeated low bows. Tanaka listened to her account with mounting frustration.

'What's wrong?' asked Durand, clearly picking up on the tone of the conversation, despite not understanding what was being said.

Tanaka gave a long sigh. 'The girl recognised the man from previous events, although she didn't know his name. So she checked the database where all fan club invitees should be listed with their photographs.'

'And?' asked Durand.

'She couldn't find his photograph, and therefore can't give us a name. I'm sorry, Mr Durand. We are no nearer to finding your daughter.'

Despite their security precautions, and the fact that all of the audience should have been known to them, the man who had interacted with Marie-Louise seemed to have managed to gain entry to the event without giving his name. It could, Tanaka tried to tell himself, simply be the result of an over-sight. It might be nothing significant. Tanaka's training, however, told him that nothing like this was ever insignificant. If this was the man who'd abducted Marie-Louise — if indeed she *had* been abducted — he seemed to have successfully covered his tracks.

CHAPTER FIVE

He was taking a risk coming to the index tree. It was showing its age — supported by cedar posts, its trunk protected by a canvas blanket. But it was always one of the earliest to blossom here in the capital city. *Kaika* — the first bloom — had already been reported: he'd seen it on the news that morning.

The girl's skin was unblemished by the sun, almost as though she must have deliberately stayed out of its rays, and he was keeping her out of the harmful ultraviolet now. Keeping her in the safe room he'd built. He couldn't bring her here, of course, so he'd taken a high definition photograph of her face on his smartphone, so he could match the colours.

Petals to skin.

Skin to petals.

He pictured her in his head. She was from the north of Europe. Blonde hair. Startling blue eyes. Eyes so blue you wouldn't find them in Japan — not even in Hokkaido, where occasionally blue-eyed Japanese people were found. Skin so white it was almost like an albino's. And she was his — captured to create a fleeting moment of haunting beauty.

He held up the photograph against the blossom. It wasn't an exact match, but he could adjust her skin tone to blend with the almost pure white flowers with their pink tinges. The Somei Yoshino variety of cherry tree — its blooms opening before the leaves came out, so that the tree, old though it was, looked almost pure white from top to bottom.

He looked around, waiting for his moment. What he was doing wasn't really appropriate in the grounds of a shrine. But he'd already clapped his hands together. He'd said his prayer. And when no one was looking, he broke off one of the youngest branches from the elderly tree, secreting it in his bag, carefully wrapping the tissue paper round the blooms to try to protect them.

White. Perfectly white with a tinge of pink. From top to bottom.

That was how the tree looked.

And that was how the girl would look.

Once he'd finished his arrangement.

CHAPTER SIX

S hinjuku Police Station was a squat cuboid of a building,
next to Nishi Shinjuku metro station. Twelve storeys of
grey, rectangular cement, some ten minutes from the narrow
streets of the red-light area — towered over by neighbouring
office blocks which stretched even higher into the Tokyo
skyline. Blain wondered if she'd fall at the first hurdle when
she saw the police officer standing guard in front. She had to
get past him to get into the building, and her rendezvous with
the *Tōkei Shimbun*'s Shinkjuku crime reporter, Asato
Tokichiro. The guard peered at her suspiciously, but, when
she said she was a reporter in faultless Japanese and showed
her ID, he let her through.

Blain took the lift to one of the upper floors and then made
her way to the press club via the directions she'd memorised
from Yamamoto. Her near-photographic memory sometimes
freaked people out — at school, she'd been nicknamed The
Human Encyclopaedia by one of her teachers.

The press club was a large square room filled with desks
for each of the major Tokyo and national newspapers and for

the radio and TV stations. Most of the desks were occupied, although some of the occupants didn't seem to be. Her eyes lighthoused over the nameplates. Tokichiro-san appeared to be taking a power nap at his desk — and he wasn't the only one. His workstation, though, was particularly messy, strewn with discarded snack bags and plastic drink bottles.

As she approached, his female neighbour — from the *Asahi Shimbun* — rolled her eyes. 'I've tried to wake him up to stop him snoring. You're welcome to have a go. Too much sake at lunchtime.' Blain could smell the fumes on his breath. The grunting rhythm was interrupted by periods when he didn't seem to breathe at all, like a truffle-hunting pig that had finally reached its prize. 'Or we could try to move him to the sleeping room.' The *Asahi* reporter pointed to a curtained-off *tatami* room in the corner of the press club. 'Whatever, please do something.'

Blain first shook the giant of a man by his shoulders but failed to disturb the rhythm of snores. So, she shouted in his ear. 'Tokichiro-san! It's Holly Blain here. Your new trainee police reporter.'

A final huge snort, and the reporter shook himself awake, looking disoriented and confused. 'There's no need to shout. I was just thinking up an intro to a story.' He eyed Blain suspiciously and sniffed deeply. Then he spat whatever he'd sucked from his nostrils or sinuses into the waste bin. 'Yamamoto didn't say you were a woman... well, *girl*. You're not going to be much use in Kabukicho. Well, not unless you want a job in a hostess bar.' He sniggered at his own feeble joke, as the *Asahi* reporter next to him shook her head.

'I'm sure you'll be able to show me the ropes,' said Blain.

Tokichiro-san snorted. 'There are some S&M places I could take you to, if that's what you mean.'

'No, it's not,' replied Blain, her expression deadpan. She'd known when she'd pushed for a break on the crime beat that this was what she'd have to put up with. Blatant sexism. In fact, seeing the female *Asahi* reporter was itself a surprise. As her eyes scanned the room, she realised that the two of them were the exceptions — every other reporter here was male.

Tokichiro had started putting on his raincoat and wiped his mouth with its sleeve. 'Nothing better than a quick tour to start with, then. An insider's guide to Kabukicho.' His eyes appraised Blain's body from head to toe, a lupine hunger showing in them. 'It will give me especial pleasure to show a girl round the fleshpots of Shinjuku.' Then he peered closely at her face. 'You *are* a girl, aren't you?'

Throughout the tour, Blain feigned ignorance of what Tokichiro was showing her: the host and hostess bars, the schoolgirl cafés such as they were — although Akihabara, as Tokichiro explained, was the main centre for the dubious *joshi kosei* activities, despite what Yamamoto had said. What Tokichiro didn't know — and Blain wasn't about to tell him — was that she already knew Kabukicho better than the back of her hand. She'd walked these streets before, been shown these streets before, the seedy and seductive cheek by jowl in a multi-colour of neon. Her guide had an even more intimate knowledge than the veteran crime reporter: she was a hostess at one of the clubs herself. And Haruka wasn't just Blain's guide, she was her girlfriend.

Tokichiro's guided tour ended in an *izakaya* in one of Kabuki-cho's narrow alleys, with him regaling her of various sordid tales and the odd crime story while ordering repeated beers at

Blain's expense. He seemed disappointed when — after about an hour — she said she had to go.

'Do you need me to walk you back to the office?' The offer was half-hearted, and Blain could read the secret delight on his face when she declined. She wasn't going back to the office.

The doorman at the Valentine's Dream club didn't register surprise that a woman wanted to enter. Blain's androgynous looks, in the low lighting of the club, meant she would blend in with the salarymen inside. And he knew Blain — and she knew him.

'I'm not staying for long, Kioshi-san.' She gave a low bow. 'I just want to say hello.'

'Of course, Holly-san. You know the rules, though. If she is with a customer, you must not interrupt. But it's quiet so far this evening. I think it will be fine.'

Blain felt a frisson of excitement as she walked along the narrow corridor into the club. Was this what it was like for the male customers? The mystery of unknowing, of hoping, of who would be there — which beauty you'd be buying drinks for. A yearning for something that usually stayed out of reach, and then the hangover of guilt and shame when they realised they'd spent tens — even hundreds — of thousands of their hard-earned yen on an unattainable dream.

But for Holly Blain, it had been attainable. She thought of Haruka singing, breathily, in her ear as Blain played guitar. It was a memory that made her warm, excited.

Her girlfriend was perched on a barstool, chatting to a couple of the other hostesses — one looked European, possibly Russian judging by her Slavic cheekbones, the other south-east Asian — possibly Thai or Vietnamese. Valentine's

Dream — unlike some hostess bars — had a mixed recruitment policy.

Around the club, with its dim light panels substituting for rice paper screens, there was a smattering of clients — Blain counted two or three salarymen with girls pouring their drinks at the low, Japanese style tables. Kioshi-san had been right, it was nearly empty. Blain knew that wouldn't last. Later in the evening, the club would be packed: Haruka would be unavailable. Most nights she would be too tired afterwards to pay Blain a visit — occasionally though, she did, and, for Blain, those visits were like a sprinkling of fresh morning dew on her face.

The Russian, Svetlana, smiled seductively at her as she approached the bar. Svetlana always made it clear that if Haruka and Blain ever ceased to be an item, she would willingly take the Japanese girl's place in the young English-woman's bed. She nudged Haruka. 'Your *boy*friend's here.' It was their standing joke — the emphasis on the first syllable. In the mirror, Blain sometimes *did* look like a boy.

'Ho... lee...!' exclaimed Haruka, drawing out the syllables of her name, and pulling her into a hug. 'Why have you come now? I have to work soon. You know this.' Blain pulled Haruka's face towards hers and kissed her. A long, lover's kiss, provoking whoops of delight from Svetlana.

'Hot girls. Wow! You should get on stage — or get a room.'

Blain pulled back to admire Haruka. 'I was working just round the corner. I thought I'd drop in to see you. The band's playing tonight...'

'You and your western pop music,' said Haruka. 'So, you don't want me to come to visit later. That's what you're saying, isn't it, Holly? You'll be too tired after pretending to be a pop star in some dive in Koenji.'

Blain shrugged. 'You know me too well.'

Haruka asked the bartender for two iced teas, gave one to Blain, and then pulled her over to a dark corner of the club. 'So why were you in Kabukicho, other than to come and see me?' Haruka had taken one of Blain's hands in her own and was slowly caressing her fingers. To Blain, the delicate touch, Haruka's silky soft skin, was how she imagined the touch of an angel would feel.

'I've been allowed to do the crime beat.'

'Oh Holly. At last! You've wanted that for so long. I'm so proud of you.' Haruka pulled her into a hug. Blain could feel the girl's ribs under her skin, the sides of her small breasts. Blain didn't want to pull away, but she did.

'It's only a trial. And it's only one day a week. And there's a downside.'

'What?' asked Haruka, her face creasing in alarm.

'It's in addition to my normal week. On one of my days off.'

'Oh Holly. That's not fair. You don't want to spend your time with me.' Haruka pouted in mock indignation — much as Blain imagined she would if one of the salarymen deigned not to buy her a drink or decided he wanted to be with another girl for the evening.

Instead of answering with words, Blain guided Haruka's head towards her for another kiss.

The music club was indeed in Koenji, as Haruka had guessed. Blain had to divert to the apartment to get her guitar, tune it, and hope that it stayed in tune in its hard case during the metro journey. The diversion to see Haruka had made her late.

Once she reached Higashi-Koenji station, she ran towards the club and down the steps. They shook beneath her feet as she thundered down — not from her running but from the thumping bass lines of the band's opening number. *Already late*. She pushed her way through the bar area and into the live room, immediately hit by a twin assault on her senses — a wall of sound, and the thick fug of choking cigarette smoke.

Working in a smoky atmosphere never seemed to worry Haruka at the hostess club, but Blain hated it. There was no choice, though. There were moves to introduce a smoking ban in time for the 2020 Tokyo Olympics, but, so far, the smoking lobby had resisted it.

Blain leapt on to the stage, ignoring the disapproving looks from the other band members. She didn't have time to set up her effects pedal for this first number — she'd just have to play it straight. Plugging the lead into the house amp and flipping the guitar strap over her shoulder, she waited for the right moment to join in. Her guitar parts were the glitter — the icing on the cake. Rhythmic lead guitar, or arpeggio-like rhythm — whichever way you wanted to look at it. The guitar, a cheap Rickenbacker copy, was strung in Nashville tuning — the four thicker, bassier strings replaced by narrow strings from a 12-string set and tuned an octave higher. It was magical: a guitar transformed into something else. And when Blain started to play and the guitar chimed in almost like a peal of bells, she was in jangle heaven. In her own head, she was a star.

Tanaka realised the reporter couldn't see him — the stage lights blinding her to the details of the members of the audience. He'd tried to attract her attention when she'd rushed on stage, but she was too preoccupied with being late. In any case, she looked to be in her own world, her own zone — concentrating on her job, her music, rather than trying to impress those watching. The detective felt totally out of place. Most of the crowd was mid-twenties, or younger, even though the music itself felt like it had been brought in a time machine from the eighties. After they'd swapped business cards in the café near Minami Senju station, Tanaka had realised that she'd given him the wrong one: it was the one for her band, with Twitter, Facebook, and Soundcloud links — rather than her reporter's card for the *Tōkei Shimbun*. Then he realised her gig tonight would involve just a small metro detour. So, he'd dropped in to see her instead. Now he was beginning to regret it. Her own guitar parts were about the only thing he could bear to listen to. The rest of it was far too loud, far too bassy for Tanaka's taste.

After around six songs, the singer announced a break — they would be back with another set in about thirty minutes' time. As the house lights went up, Tanaka rubbed his eyes, trying to adjust to the brightness. Blain seemed to be involved in an animated discussion with the other band members — from the few shouted words he heard, it seemed to be about her late arrival. He needed to attract her attention: he wanted to talk to her and didn't want to have to subject his ears to the rest of the band's set.

Finally, the argument — or heated disagreement — seemed to clear and Blain was on her own, fiddling with various effects pedals and leads. Tanaka approached the stage.

'Blain-san, I know you must be busy. But do you have a moment to talk?'

The reporter looked up at him. The initial anger at the interruption evaporated from her face when she saw who it was, replaced by a look of mild puzzlement.

'Of course, Tanaka-san. Just give me two seconds to finish

this. Then we can go outside. I'll meet you on the steps in a couple of minutes.'

The sweaty warmth of the club was immediately replaced by a slap of cold air as Tanaka opened the exit door. Spring and the cherry blossom were finally here, but the late March night still had the power to constrict the pores on Tanaka's face and cloud the breath in front of his eyes. But at least it was fresh air — a relief after the smokiness of the bar.

He sat on a step about halfway up the flight to ground level, carefully arranging his overcoat under himself to try to prevent the cold entering his bones, his hands thrust into his pockets. Tanaka didn't usually trust reporters or try to trade information. But the Master at Café Muse had vouched for Blain, and he himself had warmed to the young woman who dressed like a salaryman. Her knowledge of Tokyo youth culture and particularly the Lolita fashion scene could help Tanaka. And he needed help. Marie-Louise Durand's father would be constantly on his back — and so far, Tanaka and Izumi's efforts had drawn a blank. Pascal Durand could make trouble for Tanaka at TMPD headquarters: Tanaka knew that too well. He might have been pigeon-holed in the Gaikoku-jin liaison unit because of his perceived 'foreignness' thanks to his mixed race, but it was a pigeon hole Tanaka rather liked. But this current case was proving complicated — and worrying.

He looked down at his watch. Five minutes had passed. Perhaps Blain had forgotten; she clearly had other things on her mind, and maybe it had been unfair of Tanaka to track her down here. But, as he thought this, the club door opened, and there she was, bounding up the steps towards him. She sat next to him on the steps, seemingly oblivious to the ice-cold concrete, still on the adrenaline high of the gig.

'Sorry. A loose connection with my effects box and I had to sort it. I'm in enough trouble as it is for turning up late. Did you catch any of it?'

Tanaka nodded.

'Not really your thing?'

He shrugged. 'I appreciated your guitar playing, Blain-san. When I could hear it, that is. For my tastes, the bass guitar and drums are too loud. Perhaps you need a quieter, more delicate band?'

Blain laughed. 'You're right. I want to start one. But this is extra pin money for me. I'm not really a fully-fledged member. They pay me a small amount as a session musician for each gig and each part on their recorded tracks. It's not fully me. Anyway, why are you here? I didn't expect to bump into you again so soon.'

'It's not an accidental meeting. I need your help on a case. Would you be willing to help me?' Tanaka had expected to get an enthusiastic response. It wasn't often that a reporter was given an inside track by a detective. But he saw the shadow of a frown cloud her face.

'I have been given a little break on crime,' she said. 'In the Fourth District. Helping the *Tōkei Shimbun*'s reporter in the Shinjuku police station press club.'

'I sense a "but"?'

Blain nodded. 'The problem is it's only one day a week. The rest of the time I'm doing showbiz.'

Tanaka clasped his hands and rubbed his thumbs together, one on top of the other, as though to work out the cold. 'It's your show business contacts and knowledge I need in connection with a crime case. Well, perhaps it's more accurate to say a *potential* crime. Two western girls have gone missing. One French. One Swedish. Both very much into this whole *kawaii* culture.'

The female reporter turned to him and held his gaze. 'I'd like to help if I can. Of course I would. Please tell me more, Tanaka-san.'

Normally the buzz of a gig would keep Blain awake for at least an hour as she chewed over in her head what she could, or should, have played better. Added to that, there was everything that Tanaka had told her. The excitement that — if she could persuade Yamamoto-san — she might actually get to work on her first crime story. But she was so exhausted, she fell into a deep sleep as soon as she laid her head on the buckwheat husk-filled pillow.

CHAPTER SEVEN

The bitterness of the dawn air felt much like the cold of the previous night to Tanaka. Cherry trees may have announced spring's arrival, but winter didn't seem ready to release its grip just yet. A searchlight cut through the gloom — trained on the vast chasm of the Shinagawa Incineration Plant's refuse bunker. To Tanaka, it looked like something from a *Star Wars* film — a huge hole, filled with garbage. And there — suspended a metre or so above the pile — hung the grab bucket of the crane, its jaws full of various detritus. Like a giant feeding animal with a voracious appetite, Tanaka knew the beast would normally grab its load, then empty its jaws into the hopper that led to the furnaces. But the whole operation had been shut down, and Tanaka and his colleagues summoned, because of something one of the control room operators had seen on the live video feed: a body in the jaws of the grab bucket.

Not just *any* body. Even from the grainy video pictures, the operator had been able to tell the body was that of a young — probably teenage — girl. And that — from her pale, almost white, Caucasian skin — she was a foreigner. From her striking blonde hair, almost luminescent under the spotlight's beam, Tanaka had a very good idea who she might be. Elin Granqvist. The eighteen-year-old who'd disappeared some weeks ago from a fashion shop. Or at least, who'd last been seen at a fashion shop — just like the French girl, Marie-Louise Durand. Her head was lolling back over the edge of the bucket, being buffeted by the giant fans — used, Tanaka had been told, to ensure the stench from the rubbish stayed within the confines of the bunker. As he watched her head now, he saw a flower drop from her ear onto the pile of rubbish below.

'Turn the fans off immediately,' he yelled to the yellow-jacketed, white-helmeted garbage operative.

'But then the smell, Inspector, it will—'

'Do it. Now,' ordered Tanaka. Sergeant Katsuhiko Izumi at his side would be surprised by his forcefulness. Rudeness, even. But evidence was being destroyed and lost. 'Izumi-kun,' he barked, turning to his deputy. 'You saw that flower fall from her head. We need that recovered.' He pointed to the peak of the trash mountain, where the flower could still be seen — its purity at odds with the jumble of foul-smelling waste.

Izumi gave a small bow. 'Of course, Tanaka-san. But you surely don't expect me to go down there and get it?'

'I don't care how you do it, Izumi,' sighed Tanaka. He'd been shouting to make himself heard above the roar of the fans but now realised they'd been switched off, and everyone was looking at him thanks to his raised voice. He lowered it to a whisper. 'Just get it done, Sergeant.' Then he turned back to the garbage officer. 'I need your most skilful crane operator to carefully bring the load up to ground level, without disturbing the body any further. Will that be possible?'

The garbage official gave a small bow and then stroked his

bearded chin while peering at the crane's grab bucket. 'I would hope so, Inspector. The bucket has been suspended like that for nearly an hour now, since the video operator spotted the body and we alerted the Tokyo Metropolitan Police Department. The body hasn't fallen yet, although moving it further is, of course, another matter.'

'I want to oversee the procedure,' said Tanaka. He looked up to the top of the crane, peering through the gloom to see if he could see anyone inside the control pod.

'The operator is no longer up there.'

'Where's he gone?' shouted Tanaka.

'No, you misunderstand me, Inspector. What I meant was that the cranes are no longer operated by a driver. We do everything remotely, from the video control room. We can ensure that you sit next to the operator in the control room while he moves the bucket, if that is your wish. You will be able to watch on the live video feed.'

Tanaka didn't answer but just nodded his head.

When they reached the control room, various technicians were gathered round one of the screens watching one of their colleagues — overseen by Sergeant Izumi — apparently 'fishing' for the flower that had dropped from the girl's head. The man was using a giant extendable litter picker, pivoting it on the edge of the pit so that he didn't have to brace its weight. The assembled throng gave a small cheer when they saw the picker's teeth close round the flower. Tanaka just hoped it wasn't being damaged. It reminded him of the toy grabber in the Hello Kitty store he'd visited with Durand on Odaiba the previous day. When Durand had excused himself to go to the toilet, Tanaka had had a go at the game. He'd managed to win some strange looking animal that was apparently a 'Hello

Kitty Panda' — a hybrid that seemed to be neither truly feline, nor ursine. Whatever, Takumi and Sora had both fought over it when he'd got home — Miho's solution was that they had to share its care, with each looking after the toy on alternate days.

The chief operative, who'd been outside with the detectives by the garbage bunker, drew up a chair next to one of the other operatives. This man, in turn, was staring fixedly at a video feed of the currently unmoving crane grab bucket.

'This is Hitoshi Ito.' The man rose from his seat and bowed towards Tanaka. 'Ito, this is Inspector Tetsu Tanaka from the Gaikoku-jin Unit of the Tokyo Police. Inspector Tanaka wants to oversee the recovery of the body. We need to do this very carefully.'

'*Hai*! Of course, Kacho.'

Tanaka lowered himself into the chair. 'I want to make sure as little of that bucketful of rubbish is lost as possible. Will we be able to work out where the garbage has come from? Which wards and which parts of those wards?'

'That will be difficult, Inspector. Most of the garbage comes from the Shinagawa ward. But our plant can deal with the amount of rubbish produced by 600,000 people per day. Shinagawa's population is less than 400,000. So we often take in rubbish from neighbouring wards. For example, Meguro.'

'What about more central Tokyo? Minato or Shibuya?'

'It's possible, too. But less likely. We can sift through the garbage in the grab bucket. We might find receipts or paper bags with shop names. That might help. But only if this garbage all came from the same lorry load. By now, it will have been mixed up. And you saw the fans working. Paper, for example, is easily blown away.'

Tanaka frowned. He could see that line of inquiry was

fraught with problems. 'So, are we ready to bring the body up?'

As the operator was about to move the joystick, Tanaka's mobile bleeped. He held his hand up, indicating the operator should do nothing for the moment, as he read the message. He'd asked for a trained police forensic investigator to attend the scene. He was used to such requests being turned down. His bosses at the TMPD were obviously as worried about this latest case as he was — if his assumptions about the identity of the body were correct. For once they'd agreed to his request. The investigator would be arriving in the next few minutes.

Once the grab bucket was above ground, Tanaka ordered the operator to move it to the side of the bunker and lower it, without opening its teeth and depositing the contents. He didn't want the process of releasing the jaws to cause more damage to the girl's body.

In the few minutes before the forensic investigator arrived, Tanaka busied himself getting the crime scene in order. Strictly speaking, the body should have been left where it was, in the waste bunker. But there it would have been virtually inaccessible. It was too dangerous. So instead, Tanaka instructed Izumi to get the uniformed officers to erect a tent to keep out the elements and seal off the area. As all this was happening, Tanaka made his own visual appraisal of the body.

The control room operator had offered to zoom in on the girl's face a few minutes earlier, but Tanaka demurred. He would get a better sense from a first-hand visual inspection. He turned up the collar of his raincoat and hunkered his head down inside, his hands thrust into his pockets. Almost as though he wanted to protect as much of his own exposed skin as possible — as though whatever malevolence had struck this girl down, might strike him too. It was an irrational thought, but one he couldn't dispel as he walked towards the resting grab bucket.

Immediately, he knew his assumption that this was the missing Swedish girl was correct. Her face, lolling back, staring unseeing at the steel grey Tokyo sky, was undamaged and instantly recognisable from the missing posters that Tanaka had ensured had been prominently displayed in her favourite haunts — such as Takeshita-dōri in Harajuku. Such pale skin, Tanaka almost wanted to reach out and touch it. Once he'd snapped on a pair of protective gloves, he did touch the body — very, very gently, just easing down her eyelids to give the appearance of a girl asleep, rather than — as he suspected — one who had been brutally killed.

The question was, how had that killing happened? He carefully moved some of the rubbish to one side — discarded bento boxes, throwaway chopsticks, broken bits of plastic. Some of this should have been sorted better according to each ward's stringent garbage collection policy. But then Tanaka chided himself for such an irrelevant thought.

The teeth of the grab bucket had clearly caused some injuries. Had she been thrown into the rubbish pit alive? If so, surely, she would have fought back? There would be bruising, grab marks. He couldn't see any. The only blemish on her near pure-white face was a mole on her left cheek.

A lock of her white-blonde hair covered the right side of her neck. Tanaka gently brushed it aside, almost as he might do in a tender moment shared with Miho. That was when he saw it. A scabbed over scar. But it didn't look to be from a forceful, traumatic, or accidental injury. Instead, the cut that had caused the wound looked clean, precise, deliberate.

· · ·

Inspector Megumi Nishimura came from the new breed of Japanese police recruits, and she looked as though she had just stepped straight out of a business meeting — rather than been woken in the early hours to attend an unexplained death. As one of the new recruits, she'd been favoured with forensic training, something Tanaka had been denied — he was probably already seen as too long in the tooth in his early forties. The idea was to try to combat the low rate of post-mortems in Japan — itself borne of the shortage of forensic scientists and pathologists at universities.

But although Nishimura had the necessary expertise, Tanaka wasn't convinced she was dressed for the occasion. Her slim-fitting business suit accentuated her narrow waist, the wide collar of her pale open neck shirt looked like it had been ironed flat to the lapels of the suit. And — in common with many Japanese women in work environments, to Tanaka's dismay — she was wearing stilettos.

'Tanaka-san. I hope this is something important to get me out of bed at such a ridiculous hour on a Sunday morning.'

Tanaka flicked his eyes towards the girl's body.

'She fell in?' asked Nishimura.

'I don't think so, no. She's a Swedish girl, who'd been missing for several weeks. In my view, it's a suspicious death. I want to press for a full autopsy.'

'I appreciate your keenness, Tanaka-san, but let me be the judge of whether that is necessary. Surely our first assumption must be that this was an accident, unless the evidence proves otherwise.'

Tanaka wondered about mentioning the strange cut to the neck vein. After examining it, he'd pushed the girl's hair back to the position in which he'd found it, so it wasn't immediately obvious. It would be a good test of Nishimura's observation skills. And — by keeping silent — Tanaka could allow the young investigator to think it was her own discovery.

The forensic officer — hands covered by protective gloves, and mouth and nose masked — set about her external examination, speaking aloud for Tanaka's benefit, even though the information she was giving was already known to him.

'So,' she said, her voice muffled by the mask, 'Caucasian female, possibly Scandinavian judging from her appearance. Age — perhaps late teens. Clothed, in typical teenage *kawaii* fashion.' She moved some of the looser detritus from the lower portion of the body. 'Crush wounds to the abdomen. Too difficult to assess from an external examination whether these are pre- or post-mortem injuries, however there are no other obvious signs of trauma to the lower body or abdomen.' She moved to the girl's head. 'The flesh looks particularly pale, but this may simply be a product of genetics and the fact that she is most probably from a northern climate where there is less ultraviolet exposure.' Nishimura paused, as though she was thinking. 'But that might be worth further examination at the mortuary.'

She opened the girl's eyelids, looked into the eyes, and then closed them again with a reverence similar to that Tanaka had shown. Then she pressed her finger into the girl's cheek, then her neck. As she made the latter movement, the lock of hair Tanaka had carefully replaced moved away again. 'Hmm. No bruising or other damage to the neck to indicate strangulation. No abnormal petechiae in the eyeballs or skin.' But then she peered more closely at the neck wound. 'That *is* interesting. Did you spot this, Tanaka-san?' She held up the strands of the girl's white-blonde hair, with one hand, and beckoned Tanaka closer with the other.

'Interesting,' mused Tanaka. 'No, I hadn't spotted that, I'm afraid.' The lie sprung from his mouth surprisingly easily: *uso mo hōben — circumstances may justify an untruth*, he thought. Tanaka considered himself a scrupulously honest detective, but he wanted Nishimura onside — he needed her support if he was to get a full autopsy. The best way of doing that was to let her believe she had discovered something he hadn't. 'What do you think it means, Nishimura-san? Could it be related to the cause of death?'

A frown creased Nishimura's face. She sighed deeply. 'The wound is to the external jugular vein. It brings deoxygenated blood back from the head to the heart, via the superior vena cava.'

'And?' prompted Tanaka.

'Well, I am suspicious about the pallor of the girl's skin. That injury may give us an answer.'

'How so?'

'There's no indication of force having been used. My conclusion would be therefore that the girl did it herself.'

'So, you're saying this is a suicide?' This wasn't proceeding in the way Tanaka either expected or wanted. The Japanese police had something of a reputation for jumping on suicide as a cause of death too easily — there was less paperwork involved. It was something that sickened Tanaka and was perhaps one explanation for the country's spectacularly low murder rate compared to other developed countries.

'Not necessarily. But for me, the likelihood is this may have been a self-inflicted death. The girl is clearly obsessed with fashion, you would agree with that, Tanaka-san?'

'Yes, but—'

'One possibility is that she wanted her skin even paler than it is now. I believe it's a desirable quality amongst some teenage western girls, certainly those obsessed with Japanese culture, as this one seems to have been.' Tanaka found himself clutching his neck in horror as the forensic investigator

continued to expound her hypothesis. 'In the Middle Ages —
in Europe — there was the same sort of rabid desire for pale
skin. It was thought to distinguish the refined classes from the
ruddy-faced peasants. I believe this girl had been blood-
letting. The jugular vein was a favourite for that in those
times. Deliberately reducing her blood sufficiency for
cosmetic reasons. To increase her paleness.'

Tanaka couldn't help but let out a small snort.

'I take it, Tanaka-san, that you don't think much of this
hypothesis?'

Tanaka realised his efforts to keep Nishimura onside were
in danger of being undone by his failure to disguise his scepti-
cism — he needed to change his tone. 'No, you misunderstand
me, Nishimura-san. I was merely expressing amazement that
young girls would do this sort of thing. I have never heard of
it. Have you ever come across it before yourself? And how do
we explain how she ended up in the rubbish collection pit at
the Shinagawa Incineration Plant?'

'The last part of your question is — to some extent — easy
to answer. If she had regularly been blood-letting, perhaps for
nights out or events where she wanted to look particularly
pale, then she would have been at risk of fainting. She may
have fainted and fallen into the rubbish pit. Or somehow
fallen from a bridge into a rubbish lorry as it was passing.'

Tanaka breathed in slowly, the foul smell of the rubbish
plant filling his lungs. 'That is, I suppose, one possibility. But it
seems to me highly implausible. Why did the girl disappear for
weeks on end before her death? If she was prone to this
supposed self-harm, why didn't any of her friends — or even
her parents — tell us about it? And surely, to take blood from
her own neck so neatly, would be nigh on impossible?'

Nishimura looked slightly crestfallen. 'It was just a theory,
Tanaka-san. And there are no other visible signs of injuries.'

'I appreciate that is the case from this superficial external visual examination, Nishimura-san. That is why we need a full autopsy. This is a suspicious death of a missing person, whether your theory is true or not. Until there is a thorough examination of the cadaver, how can we possibly rule out foul play?'

The younger officer stood staring at the girl's body for a moment. 'I don't disagree with you, Tanaka-san, but you are well aware of the difficulties of obtaining permission from headquarters for such an autopsy. First, we need to examine the body back at the lab. I will do that to the best of my abilities.'

'I think you also need to do toxicology tests. I still cannot believe this was a suicide or self-harm gone wrong. It doesn't fit with the facts. Yet from what we can see from her clothed body, there are no signs of a struggle. One explanation for there being no struggle is that the girl was unable to struggle. In other words, that she was drugged.'

CHAPTER EIGHT

He was sad there had been mistakes, but there were some compensations. The room was secure, it was comfortable, but he'd always known that while the two of them were there it was more dangerous.

They would talk, they would plan. They couldn't escape, of course, unless he made an error, unless he dropped his guard. But the chances of him doing that had been greater while there were the two of them.

Now there was just the French girl, he felt safer. The trouble was, she was too young, just as the Swedish girl had been. Too vulnerable. He'd been attracted to her fresh beauty, much as he and his mother had been to the pristine, rare white orchids from Okinawa that formed the centrepiece of so many of her flower arrangements. If you picked something, no matter how rare, how protected, you were only really borrowing it. Yes, you could water and feed it, but once picked it would die. But even if something died, new life would emerge to replace it. That was the way of the world. That was how new beauty emerged. He wasn't the world's best handyman, but when he started to fit out the room, he knew enough. And with no family to support, he could put parts of his salary away and occasionally employ tradesmen. If you knew where to look, you could find people who wanted to be paid in cash, who wouldn't ask too many questions. If they did, then his answers had the ring of truth.

Why do you need a toilet and shower down here, in a windowless room?

You know how it is. I want to rent it out to make some extra money, but I don't want the neighbours complaining to the planning department. I'll put the windows in last of all.

Why do we need to bring all the building materials in through the garage?

The same reason. I don't want the neighbours causing problems with the planning department. I'm paying you in cash.

Why are you only making the improvements on this side of the cellar?

The other side will be the bedroom. I'm doing that later, when I've saved up some more.

This staircase is much narrower than standard, and why haven't you built the opening to the ground floor yet?

I'm not opening it up until the end. I don't want the authorities discovering it.

If they asked too many questions, he'd stop using them. He'd left one side of the basement in its original state, the two parts separated by a roughly constructed breeze-block wall. He knew it didn't meet the stringent building control standards, and, that if a really big earthquake hit, it wouldn't be sufficiently strong. But that was a one-in-fifty-year event, one-in-a-hundred maybe. Everything would be ready by then. He'd have achieved what he'd set out to achieve. The last part, the wide sliding bookcase covering the narrow staircase void that you had to turn sideways to descend down, that was something he did himself. The bookcase itself was from one of those flat-pack furniture warehouses. Other than its extra depth, it was fairly standard. Where it was special was its control mechanism. That was where his knowledge of computers, of electronics, finally came into its own. He was confident no one would work it out. All the time he was doing this, he told himself this wasn't serious. He was only pretending. Other than when he was working, or attending idols concerts, he had the time. Because he wasn't married, and because the house had been left to him — and he didn't have to rent — he had the money. No wife, no children, no parents to support or help.

No parents. He shouldn't think about that.

He told himself a lot of people would do the things he was doing if they had the money and the time.

And he was just pretending, wasn't he?

But as time passed, as his subterranean room neared completion, he realised he wasn't pretending at all.

He was serious.

And if something — someone — was picked and plucked, then new life would bloom as a replacement. Just as each day the world turned, each and every moment new life was created. It was something magical. Something he had to capture. It was his mission. It had been — ever since that day he'd won the school prize and there was no one left to congratulate him.

CHAPTER NINE

Blain couldn't understand why Tanaka had missed their lunchtime meeting at Café Muse. He'd fixed it on the steps of the 2000 Volts music club the previous evening, when he'd talked about picking her brains on *kawaii* youth culture. But she'd waited for more than half an hour at the café for him. No message, no excuse, nothing. When she tried his office at the Tokyo Metropolitan Police Department all they would tell her was that he was busy on a case and unavailable. It was odd — especially when he'd gone out of his way to meet her at the club the night before.

One of the tricks of the trade she'd been shown when she was training on the *Tōkei Shimbun* was the art of cultivating contacts by visiting and giving gifts, often unannounced and in the evening. For the police, she'd been told, this was particularly valuable. But you had to find a way to be invited into their homes — sometimes by using underhand methods.

Instead of writing the show business story she was meant to that afternoon, Blain used whatever contacts the *Tōkei Shimbun* had to find out more about Inspector Tetsu Tanaka.

She'd also spoken to the Master at Café Muse. With a little surreptitious digging, she'd managed to find Tanaka's address, and the names and ages of his family. Now she was primed to try to get inside his life — to find out more about his missing girls case from the source.

First, Blain armed herself with a cool-bag filled with frozen plastic blocks from the work freezer. Then she walked to Shimbashi station to get the JR Yamanote line — Tokyo's answer to London's Circle line, and a lot more efficient — for the 15-minute ride to Nippori, north of Ueno. She knew the Ueno area well from playing in live bars there before she'd managed to get a regular slot with the band. The area of Tanaka's home she knew less well. It was an old house at the back of Yanaka Ginza — a so-called *shitamachi* area of Tokyo, a traditional area relatively untouched by Japan's economic miracle of the seventies and eighties, narrow streets, small shops, and crammed-together houses.

Blain's first destination was in Yanaka Ginza itself — an ice cream shop. There, she bought a large tub of a new variety she'd seen had become particularly popular at this time of year — especially amongst schoolchildren. *Sakura* ice cream. A vanilla-based ice, with added *sakura* powder, and a layer of cherry and lemon syrup over the top. Now she was armed.

After a couple of false starts, Blain finally located Tanaka's house, an unassuming building, less than fifteen feet wide. At one time, this would have been one of the typical wooden *shitamachi* houses, cheek by jowl with its neighbours. Now it was still tightly packed in but was uniform Tokyo concrete grey — and, no doubt, constructed to withstand the city's frequent earthquakes.

Blain rang the bell at the front door.

A small, neat Japanese woman answered. Younger looking than Blain was expecting and certainly younger than Tanaka looked.

'Mrs Tanaka?'

'Yes?' The woman eyed Blain suspiciously, without fully opening the door.

'Is your husband at home? I am a journalist contact of his. He wanted to get some information from me about a case he's working on. And I've brought him a present.'

The woman made as if to take the bag containing the ice cream, without actually inviting Blain inside. Which rather defeated the object.

'He's not here at the moment, I'm afraid. I don't know when he'll be back.'

Just then, two smaller faces appeared around Mrs Tanaka's legs. 'Who is it Mama?' asked one of the boys.

Blain saw her opportunity. 'I'm a friend of your father's. I've brought him a present. A tub of the new *sakura*-flavoured ice cream.'

As the two boys excitedly shouted 'Ice cream! Ice cream!', Mrs Tanaka tried to shoo them out of the way, leaving the door unattended for a moment.

Blain pushed her way inside. 'Do you have a freezer, Mrs Tanaka? I can put it in there for you while you look after the children.' The reporter was already over the threshold and had eased her shoes off.

'It's through there, in the kitchen,' pointed the flustered woman. Blain hurried through before she could change her mind.

'Can't we have some ice cream, Mama?' pleaded the younger son as the family trooped after her.

'No, Takumi.'

The older son joined in. 'Please, Mama.'

'I said no, Sora.'

Blain opened the freezer door, then paused. 'I'm sure it would be okay for them to have some, if you don't mind, Mrs Tanaka. There's plenty to go round.'

The woman threw her hands up in the air and then smiled at Blain. 'Oh, I suppose so. They'll never be quiet otherwise. Do you want to join us? You can wait for my husband. There was a big development in one of his cases today, though, so I'm not sure when he'll be back.'

'Was it the missing foreign girls?' asked Blain. 'That was what he wanted to talk to me about. I'm the show business reporter for the *Tōkei Shimbun* — he wanted my help about *kawaii* fashion and culture. I think both the girls were last seen—'

Miho Tanaka suddenly put her finger to her lips and gestured with her eyes towards her two children, sitting patiently at the table waiting for their ice cream.

'Which girls, Mama?' asked Sora.

'Never you mind, nosy boy.'

The reporter realised her error and changed the subject. 'Do you have some bowls and spoons for the ice cream, Mrs Tanaka?' asked Blain.

'Yes, of course.' She reached into a kitchen cupboard to get out the bowls and then into a drawer for the spoons. 'And I'll make us some green tea. My husband always says it's a strange mixture, but I love ice cream washed down with hot green tea.'

'Me too,' laughed Blain. Her ice cream ruse had worked, just as Yamamoto-san had said it would. She'd been accepted into the bosom of Tanaka's little family. But what was this important new development in the missing girls case that his wife had mentioned? For the girls themselves, it didn't sound good. But for a reporter like her, it was what she craved — the possibility of getting a head-start on the rival Tokyo and national newspaper crime reporters, and the chance of arguing her case to Yamamoto that she should transfer to the crime beat full-time.

CHAPTER TEN

Tanaka had only had the briefest of conversations with Miho earlier in the day to say he was likely to be late. On the mortuary slab in front of him was the reason why: the body of the Swedish teenager, Elin Granqvist. The dead girl — now divested of her clothing — was being examined minutely by police forensic specialist Inspector Megumi Nishimura. Tanaka found it hard to look at the body without imagining an older version of Misaki taking the girl's place on the metal table. He tried to banish the thought from his head.

'Have you discovered anything further, Nishimura-san?' Nishimura's examination had already been going on for some hours — Tanaka had spent the intervening period breaking the news to Elin's parents, who'd been in Tokyo conducting their own freelance search for their daughter. They were understandably distraught, broken, numbed — but through all that, Tanaka had detected a disdain for the Japanese police, something he himself occasionally shared. He felt a huge weight of personal responsibility here: Tanaka and his colleagues should have found her before she met her end. He was determined Marie-Louise Durand would not meet the same fate. He wasn't looking forward to bringing Mr and Mrs Granqvist to the mortuary for the formal identification process.

'I've taken the samples for the toxicology test, but even though I've asked for the express service—'

Tanaka gave a low bow. 'Thank you, Nishimura-san.'

Nishimura gave a smaller return bow in acknowledgement. 'Even though I've asked for the express service, which is a special favour for you, Tanaka-san, the results still won't be back until tomorrow at the earliest. Other than that, there is not much further I can add that wasn't evident to us at the incinerator plant.'

'So, no other signs of trauma to the body?'

'That would be sufficient to indicate a cause of death, no. My conclusions are still the same. However, there is one thing which may be of interest.'

Tanaka raised his eyebrows. 'What?'

'There are some abrasions around her right ankle, here.' Nishimura pointed to the lower portion of the girl's right limb. Tanaka peered closely. For a moment, the tell-tale tang of the mortuary's disinfectant was replaced by something more floral — whatever perfume Inspector Nishimura was wearing. It smelled like the same brand that Miho used. 'It's not immediately obvious,' continued Nishimura, 'but there are some signs of soreness. The skin isn't actually broken, but it is inflamed, as though it's been rubbing — possibly straining — against something. And look.' Nishimura waved her hand in a semi-circle around the dead girl's ankle. Tanaka could see a faint red mark encircling the leg.

'What do you think it is?'

'It may indicate the girl was restrained in some way. That

she had something attached to her leg, possibly to prevent her escaping from somewhere.'

'In that case, your conclusions do seem to have changed,' said Tanaka.

'I don't think it's enough,' said the young forensic investigator. 'But let's see what the toxicology report says. If there is anything remotely suspicious then, yes, I will support you in your efforts to get a full autopsy, Tanaka-san.'

Tanaka's face clouded with anger when he walked into his home's kitchen. It was supposed to be his family sanctuary — his escape from the pressures of work. Now the reporter from the *Tōkei Shimbun* had invaded that space and seemed to be sitting down to eat with Miho and his two young sons.

Miho immediately jumped up to greet him, and Tanaka tried to disguise his anger for her sake.

'Tetsu-kun. Welcome back. You know Holly Blain, I believe. She brought some ice cream as a present for you.'

'It's *sakura* flavour, Otou-san,' giggled Takumi. 'We've left a bit for you.'

'You'll have to be quick though, Otou-san,' added Sora. 'It's yummy.'

Tanaka's mood softened. It was kind of Blain to bring the ice cream, even though he saw the gift for what it was — an excuse to get into his home. But then he was equally guilty — he'd missed their lunch date which he'd requested, without giving her any warning of his absence.

He allowed Miho to take off his coat and then sat down at the table, as Sora scooped a portion of the sickly pink ice cream into a bowl, and Takumi tried to pour him a tea, spilling it on the table in the process.

'Thank you, my son.' He ruffled the younger boy's hair.

Then he turned to Blain. 'So, Holly-san. I am sorry that I missed our meeting. There was a development in the case I was talking to you about which meant I couldn't leave work, and I was too wrapped up in things to call and warn you.'

Although Blain was sitting, she attempted a small bow. 'I understand, Tanaka-san. And I am sorry to be here when you want to greet your family after a difficult day at work. I just brought the gift for you, and your wife kindly insisted I should wait to see you in person.' Then she laughed. 'Unfortunately, there is not much of your gift left. Some little people have eaten most of it.' Takumi and Sora giggled. 'I can leave you now, if you wish.'

Tanaka shook his head. 'I will finish this, then we can have our chat, Holly-san.'

After a few minutes, Tanaka ushered Blain through to the lounge. It was a traditional Japanese room, and Miho brought a small jug of warm sake through and placed it on the low table, along with two cups. She bowed and left the room, almost as though she was a lowly serving woman rather than Tanaka's wife.

Blain initially took up the traditional kneeling — or *seiza* — position on the *tatami* mat floor, but noticing that Tanaka was sitting cross-legged, she switched to the more comfortable position of both legs to one side. It wasn't that she couldn't maintain the *seiza* posture — unlike many foreigners she could, and for several hours. She just wanted to reflect the detective's own informality and put him at ease.

'So, is there anything you can tell me about this "new development", Tanaka-san?' As she asked the question, her eyes were drawn to a photograph of what looked like Tanaka and his wife cradling a baby that seemed to have pride of place in their *tokonoma* alcove.

Tanaka frowned. The reporter realised he had noticed her staring at the photograph. It didn't seem to be something he welcomed. Nevertheless, he answered her question. 'You know that really I can only release information to full members of the press club, Holly-san. You put me in a difficult position.'

'But I thought you wanted my help. For my contacts and knowledge about teenage Japanese culture?'

'That's true. It would be useful. But anything I tell you has to be off the record for the moment. You cannot attribute it to me. And before doing a story, you need to wait until we have given an official press release to the full members of the press club.'

'At Tokyo Metropolitan Police Headquarters?'

'Of course. If the members of the press club see that I've been giving information directly to a reporter from District 4, and a part-time reporter at that, then they will make trouble for me with my superiors. The relationship between the press and police in Japan, and in particular in Tokyo, is a very delicate balance. I'm sure you are aware of that, Holly-san.'

'But you want my help?'

'Yes.'

'So surely, if a fish has a heart for the water, the water will have heart for the fish. Isn't that a case of what we have here?' In other words, thought Blain, you scratch my back and I'll scratch yours.

Tanaka gave a slow nod.

'So, totally off the record,' continued Blain, 'what is the new development?'

'You must understand and abide by the conditions I have

laid down, Holly-san. I can help you, but you cannot write the story until you have my say-so.'

Blain nodded.

'Alright then. I am very sorry to say that one of the missing girls, the Swede, Elin Granqvist, has been found dead. You cannot say that officially, because the body has not been formally identified by the parents and won't be until tomorrow. Nevertheless, it is true.'

Blain felt a mounting sense of excitement which she tried to dispel. Death should not be exciting. It was tragic. The girl's parents would be beside themselves, broken. They would almost certainly never recover. It would haunt them forever. But she was a journalist, not a parent. For her, this was a chance to make her mark as a crime reporter. She knew it was cynical — but it was just the way it was.

'How did she die?' she asked, trying not to betray her eagerness. Trying not to sound too crass.

'We don't know that conclusively. We are carrying out toxicology tests on her body.'

'Where and when was she found?'

'Her body was found in the refuse bunker of the Shinagawa Incineration Plant.' Blain felt an immediate mental recoil. Her stomach tightened. A young girl, with so much of her life in front of her, excited no doubt to be in a foreign country, especially one as alluring and magical as Japan. Then her adventure ends in death, dumped in a refuse pit.

'Do you know how she got there?'

'No.'

'Could she have fallen in accidentally?'

'Personally, I think that is unlikely. We need to wait for the results of the toxicology tests.'

'Do you have any reason to suspect she was drugged?'

'No, except there were few if any signs of a struggle on her body. No bruises. No cuts or injuries. Except...'

Tanaka paused. Blain could tell he was weighing up whether or not to trust her.

'I give you my word that this is off the record,' she said.

'This bit has to be more than off the record. You must not, for the time being, use it in any report. It is background information only. You will be the only reporter I will release this to. If these aspects escape and become widely known, I will know who to blame. And that would be the end of our relationship, Holly-san.'

Blain nodded.

'There were two significant, and slightly strange, areas of trauma to the girl's body. One was barely visible — mild abrasions encircling her right ankle. Our best guess is that it indicates she was somehow restrained by her leg over some period of time. Possibly held captive somewhere, although that is of course speculation. The second traumatic incident was to her jugular vein.'

'In her neck?'

'Precisely. We believe that she may have lost significant amounts of blood from that wound.'

'So, she bled to death after being knifed in the neck?'

'It wasn't a knife wound. And I don't necessarily think it was inflicted — or even self-inflicted — with the intention to kill. It was — possibly — merely to draw blood.'

Blain felt her pulse thunder in her ears. This was astonishing, macabre. Some sort of vampire-killer was possibly on the loose in Tokyo — choosing teenage western girls as his victims. This wasn't just a story that would make the lead in Japanese newspapers — this was a major international exclusive. She wanted to keep her part of the deal. To keep it all off record. To not report the details the detective had made clear should not — as yet — be reported. But the story was too good. Her career could hinge on it. All bets were off.

As the conversation ended, and they stood up to leave the room, Blain moved towards the *tokonoma*. She was about to pick up the photograph of the baby and its parents, when Tanaka's voice rang out.

'Do not touch that, Miss Blain.' There was an icy anger in his voice, and he'd switched to English and used her surname. She immediately drew her hands away, as though she'd been burnt, turning towards Tanaka and mouthing 'sorry'.

But it wasn't anger she saw in his eyes. Just a faraway, glazed look.

Full of sadness.

Full of longing and loss.

CHAPTER ELEVEN

The next day, Tanaka got up early. Not just because he had a busy day ahead, but because he wanted to get the first editions of the morning newspapers — particularly the *Tōkei Shimbun*. When he found a copy at the news kiosk, he stood under a street lamp and quickly scanned through. He was already regretting telling the reporter as much as he had. After all, she'd simply used an old trick to get into his home. If she was capable of using subterfuge for that, then she was capable of ignoring Tanaka's warning not to run the story before the press club at TMPD had been informed. She was capable of ignoring his instructions not to include the details about the neck wound, blood loss, and possible leg shackling. He doubted, though, that she would have been able to write and file the story in time to make the morning newspaper. His quick scan of the paper confirmed that — there was no mention of the case. Tanaka quickly scanned the other papers to see if anyone else — Izumi, or Nishimura, for example — had leaked anything to other reporters. But all the main editions had nothing on the story.

That would change the next day. The press conference at TMPD was scheduled for 2pm. Before that, Tanaka would have to get the parents to formally identify the body — something he wasn't looking forward to.

Tanaka was also waiting for an update call on his mobile from Izumi. He'd delegated to his sergeant the task of organising uniformed teams to take around photos of Elin Granqvist to some of her known haunts — teenage fashion shops, Takeshita-dori in Harajuku, and that sort of thing. They'd done it before, of course, at the time of Elin's disappearance. But at that stage, Tanaka had been unable to call on many resources. Now — with at least the possibility they were dealing with a murder inquiry — Tanaka's request to get a decent number of uniformed officers involved had been more warmly received.

His phone vibrated in his pocket, soon after he'd stuffed the newspapers he'd bought into his workbag. It was Izumi.

'I hope you have something good for me, Izumi-kun.'

'*Hai*, Tanaka-san. Something very interesting. Can you meet me at the police box in Kabukicho?'

Tanaka looked at his watch. Just come up to quarter past six in the morning. It would take him around forty minutes to get to Shinjuku and the red-light area. 'I was just about to get some breakfast, Izumi. Do you want me to bring you something?'

'We can go to breakfast when you get to Kabukicho, Tanaka-san. You will be very interested in what I've found.'

Kabukicho early in the morning looked at its seediest worst. The colourful neon signs, that at night lent the area an air of excitement, were all turned off. Most places were shut now, apart from a few cafés trying to catch some of the morning breakfast trade. The only other signs of life were street cleaners and the odd drunk who'd no doubt spent too many of his hard-earned yen in one of the many dubious establishments Kabukicho hosted.

'You're being very mysterious about this, Izumi-kun. Why wouldn't you tell me what it was about over the phone?'

'Because I was in the Kabukicho police box. Many of the officers there have close contacts with the businesses around here, as you can probably guess, Tanaka-san. I didn't want anyone saying anything inadvertently — or otherwise.'

'So what have you got?'

'Well, as you know, uniforms were showing the Swedish girl's photo around again yesterday evening, in the places you suggested. One of the officers was in Akihabara. There are some JK bars there.'

'Get to the point, Izumi-kun.'

'In one of the bars, one of the salarymen recognised the photo. He said he'd seen the girl working as a hostess in Kabukicho.'

'But she was only seventeen,' said Tanaka. 'She was too young to work as a hostess.'

Sergeant Izumi shrugged. 'I'm only reporting back what I was told. That's why I thought we should pay the bar a visit.'

'Which bar? And why would anyone be here at this time of the morning?'

'The Aphrodite-Go-Go. It has a mixed recruitment policy. International and Japanese girls.'

'Okay. But what about the second part of my question?'

'I asked around at the Kabukicho police box, without mentioning which club or what it was about. Apparently, some of the bar owners use their venues to sleep in too. Just in case they get an unfriendly visit from an unfriendly Yakuza member. To protect their clubs.'

Tanaka shrugged. He didn't know the ins-and-outs of the hostess club business. And he had no burning desire to find out. But he had to admit Izumi's lead was worth chasing up.

The entrance to Aphrodite-Go-Go was locked and shuttered. As Izumi kept his finger pressed on the doorbell, Tanaka couldn't help but doubt this assumption that the owner might be inside sleeping. So, he was mildly surprised when — after a couple of minutes ringing and banging — someone started barking through the entry phone speaker.

'Who is it?' a rough male voice yelled. 'We're closed. And I'm asleep. Or at least I was until you fuckers woke me up.'

'It's the police,' Izumi shouted back. 'Open up immediately.'

After a couple of minutes, the shutter motor whirred into action. An unshaven man in a dirty white vest stood at the door with his arms folded, as though he was unwilling to let anyone past. 'What do you lot want at this ungodly time?' he said, squinting at the two detectives through heavy-lidded eyes. 'And where's your ID?'

Tanaka held up his identity card. 'Inspector Tetsu Tanaka of the Gaikoku-jin Unit of the Tokyo Metropolitan Police Department. This is my deputy, Sergeant Izumi. We'd like to come inside and talk to you about a girl who we believe worked here briefly. Would that be okay, Mr...?'

'Tomahito. Ikari Tomahito. I'm the owner.' The man raised his hands in the air, almost as though he was surrendering. Tanaka realised after a moment he was merely doing his stretching exercises. 'Look, you've woken me up. Can't you come back later? Perhaps this evening? Then I'll have had a sleep and will be more willing to help. But everything is above board here — we check all identities and ages. No underage girls, no illegal workers.'

'We're not interested in that, Tomahito-san. But we do want to talk to you — now. Presumably I don't have to spell out what failing to cooperate with a police inquiry will mean for you.'

The club owner scowled, then stood back and allowed the two detectives to enter.

The interior of the club stank — an unappetising mixture of stale cigarettes and alcohol with faint notes of both women's perfume and men's sweat. But the furnishings, Tanaka noted, were relatively new. The club had a well-to-do air. The detective was sure it wasn't the seediest of its sort.

'Do either of you want a coffee?' the owner asked.

Tanaka shook his head. 'We've both just had breakfast. We'd like to get straight down to business.'

Tomahito sighed, slumped down on a red velvet sofa, and indicated to the two detectives to do the same.

'What can I do for you two gentlemen?'

Tanaka reached into his bag and pulled out the missing person's photo for Elin Granqvist. 'Do you recognise this girl?'

Tomahito held the photo in his hands, squinting at it. Then he placed it down on the table in front of him, rose, and walked towards the bar. There he picked up his spectacles and turned on a bank of spotlights directly above the two detectives. Tanaka found himself blinking under the harsh glare.

The owner sat down again and reappraised the photo. 'Yes. The Swedish girl. I can't remember her name. She only did a couple of shifts and didn't seem to like it. She didn't turn up for her third shift. I remember her because she was quite young-looking. I was suspicious she wasn't the minimum age to work as a hostess. But she had the necessary papers.'

'Then they must have been faked,' said Izumi. 'She was only seventeen.'

The bar owner whistled through his teeth. 'Well I can't do

much about that, then, can I? I did what I was required to do in checking her papers. Everything tallied. Her passport, everything. Is that what this is about? Are you accusing me of deliberately employing underage girls? That's a very serious accusation, and you'd better be sure you know what you're doing.'

'Is that a threat, Tomahito-san?' Tanaka glared at the man. He didn't like the business he was in, and he didn't like him. 'I think it is you who needs to watch his step. The girl *was* underage, and, what's more, she clearly *looked* underage. It also may interest you to know that she is now dead.'

'Dead? *Masaka!* So young, too. Well, I am very sorry to hear that, but it had nothing to do with me or the Aphrodite-Go-Go club. How did she die?'

'That is something of a mystery at the moment, Tomahito-san. It is an unexplained death. But it's also a *suspicious* death.'

'Where did she die? Where was she found?'

Tanaka paused for a moment before answering, wondering whether he should give the information to the man. There didn't seem any harm in it, and, in any case, after the 2pm press briefing, it would become common knowledge. 'At the Shinagawa Incineration Plant. Her body was found in the grab bucket of the refuse tip.'

'Poor girl. I don't know there's anything more I can help you with, though. As I say, she did two shifts here only, then didn't turn up for her next one.'

'You didn't think to inform anyone that she'd gone missing?' asked Izumi.

The man shrugged. 'If I did that every time a girl quit without warning, I would be ringing the police every other day. There's a high turnover in this business.'

'Weren't you suspicious she hadn't asked for her pay?' asked Tanaka.

'She wasn't due any,' said the man. 'Usually the first week's pay goes on insurances, the cost of our identity checks, and a deposit against this sort of thing happening. They only start earning from the second week onwards. Well, except for tips.'

'Tell me more about the shifts she *did* work,' instructed Tanaka. 'Was she popular? Who was she with?'

'Look, I'm not being funny, but it really would be better if you came back this evening. I'm not even sure I was here on her two work days. I certainly don't remember anything about them. Who she was with, whether she was popular. Nothing at all. I don't remember any complaints either. If you come back this evening, I promise you there will be girls here who will remember her. They've probably got better memories than me too. I'm getting on a bit. But, by then, I can check my calendar to see if I was working, I can get out all the paperwork we have on the girl, and you will be able to talk to whoever you want. Is that a deal? It will also allow me to have more than the single hour of sleep I've had so far, so I'll be in a better mood.'

Tanaka sighed and started to rise from his seat. 'Very well, Tomahito-san. Please do not warn anyone about our impending visit, though. We don't want anyone to start constructing stories. We urgently need to get to the bottom of the matter. There is a chance that someone she met here could have been involved in her death. If that is the case, your other girls could be in danger too.'

CHAPTER TWELVE

She had her story now. She had her lever to force Yamamoto-san to give her a full-time slot on the crime beat. And she hadn't — so far — had to give anything in return to Inspector Tanaka.

They were back in Yamamoto's office. 'So, you're saying everyone else will have the story by 2pm this afternoon,' he said.

'Yes, but I don't think they will have as many details as I have.'

'Well, you know our policy, Holly-san. You will have to give your information to a senior crime reporter. To our reporter in the TMPD press club. He is the only one authorised to talk to the police about a serious pan-Tokyo story like this one. Who is your contact, anyway? Where did you get your information?'

'The information was given to me strictly off the record, Yamamoto-san.' She eyeballed her news editor. There was no way she was giving up on this one — no way she was going to hand it over to anyone else. 'And on the strict understanding that I should be the reporter who writes the story.'

Yamamoto sucked his teeth. Then he snorted and shook his head. 'Don't try to play me for a fool, Blain. It's me, and me alone, who decides which reporter writes which story.'

Blain gathered up her pad and pen from the desk and began to rise from her chair.

'Where do you think you're going?'

'Back to my desk. To get back to my show business duties.'

'You'll damn well give me that information first.'

'With respect, Yamamoto-san, if you want the TMPD press club reporter to handle the story, let him go ahead and do it. He can find his own sources and his own information. I can guarantee his story won't be as good as mine, but, as you say, that is entirely your choice.'

Yamamoto glared at her. There was almost hatred in his eyes. This was a pivotal moment; he could sack her — or back her. Blain had really left him no choice. Despite her bluster, she very much hoped it was the latter option. She didn't want to lose her job. If she was fired from the *Tōkei Shimbun*, she almost certainly wouldn't get another job as a reporter in Japan. She would be damaged goods.

The news editor sighed, then his face softened. For all his stern words, Blain knew that he thought she was a good reporter. He liked her. But was that enough? 'You, young lady, play a dangerous game. No Japanese reporter would dare to defy me like you've just done, certainly not a female Japanese reporter. You're very lucky too because it just so happens that our TMPD press club head reporter is off sick at the moment, and we've been having to fill in behind him on a daily basis. Someone's already been allocated today, but I can always think of an excuse to bring him back to head office. I'll make sure you get all the necessary accreditation. But it will be for today only and this story only. Muck it up, and that's your chance gone. Is that a deal?'

Blain bowed lower than she'd ever bowed before. What she really wanted to do was rush up to Yamamoto-san and squeeze him into a tight hug. But he wouldn't have appreciated that.

'And now you need to tell me what information you've gleaned, and we need to work out how to make best use of it.'

CHAPTER THIRTEEN

JANUARY 1992, SHINAGAWA, TOKYO

He tried to remember the one thing that made it clear to him that something was wrong.

Otou-san was home for Christmas. That was nice, as it didn't usually happen. Usually, he had to work. But he didn't seem very happy. He just listened to his sad records alone in the music room, again and again.

The boy didn't get any of the Christmas presents he'd asked for. That made him sad — and angry. He'd wanted a Super Famicom console. His best friend got one, and he didn't. He was shocked by the level of hatred he felt towards his parents — it was like an anger burning inside.

Instead, his mother had made him a hand-coloured wall chart of all the Nintendo characters like Mario. Each day, he tore a bit of it off to spite her.

But the one thing that really drove home to him that something was wrong was when the television disappeared. The television that he'd hoped to be playing on with his new Nintendo console.

'Everyone has got a TV. Why have you taken ours away?' His mother wouldn't look him in the eye. 'I hate you, Okaa-san,' he spat. 'Where is Otou-san?'

'He's in bed. He's not very well. You're not to disturb him.'

The boy ignored his mother. He was going to have it out with his father. He hadn't got the console he'd asked for for Christmas, and now the television had gone too. What was he supposed to do all day? How was he going to entertain himself?

He pulled the rice screen bedroom door back, without asking his father's permission. The depressing music — the American singer — was blaring over and over on a loop. But his father wasn't listening. He was lying on his back, fully-clothed, snoring, a half-empty sake bottle still clutched in his hands. The bedroom stank of alcohol. Some of it had spilled onto the bed, and his father hadn't bothered to put the top back on the bottle. The boy retrieved the cap from the side of the futon, and then screwed it back on, fighting back the feelings of nausea and shame.

His father still snored, on and on. Oblivious. Oblivious to everything that was going wrong. The boy was so angry with him. What on earth was happening? He started shaking the man, trying to wake him. Then pummelling him in his anger. Finally, he knelt at the foot of the futon and the tears began to fall. That was where his mother found him.

CHAPTER FOURTEEN

Tanaka wasn't particularly looking forward to briefing his boss, Superintendent Obi Yoshitake, but he'd been ordered to see him before the press conference. The reporters at the press club had already started asking awkward questions, simply as a result of Tanaka calling the gathering. Yoshitake would be standing alongside him. For Tanaka, that wasn't necessarily a blessing. The superintendent had always blocked Tanaka's career path, and it was he who had pigeon-holed him in the Gaikoku-jin Unit. For Yoshitake, Tanaka was too cerebral. He was a graduate entrant to the criminal division and hadn't done the legwork in uniform that Yoshitake considered necessary. More than that, Tanaka was only half-Japanese. It showed in his face, where the American genes of his ex-serviceman father fought with those of his Japanese mother. The result: neither one nor quite the other. Miho always joked that it made Tanaka even more conscious of his Japanese side — as if he was always trying to prove himself.

Tanaka bowed low in front of his superior. 'You wanted to see me, Yoshitake-san?'

'Yes. Come in, Tanaka. Shut the door behind you. Sit down.' Yoshitake offered Tanaka a cigarette, even though he knew the inspector didn't smoke. He did it every time they met. The superintendent blew a smoke ring and watched it rise on the thermal current towards the top of the office, until it widened to such an extent it broke up and dissipated. 'What's this I hear about you going in all gung-ho at the Aphrodite-Go-Go in Kabukicho?'

'Has someone made a complaint, Yoshitake-san? There was no justification if so. We were perfectly polite.'

'I'm sure you were, Tanaka. You're always too polite. Word gets around, that's all. Watch yourself there. It's controlled by the Yakuza. The Yamaguchi-gumi. You need to watch your step.'

'I thought the Yamaguchi-gumi's influence had waned since the split, Yoshitake-san?' In 2015, factions of the Yamaguchi-gumi in Kobe and Osaka had broken away from the main group.

'They are still perfectly powerful, Tanaka. You would do well to remember that. Anyway, it sounded like her involvement in the club was something and nothing.'

'I'm not sure we should dismiss it so lightly. She was underage.'

'But there for only two shifts.'

'Two shifts would be long enough to meet a killer.'

'Don't get ahead of yourself, Tanaka, or let your not inconsiderable brain allow you to conjure up situations that aren't actually there. We don't know this is a murder yet, do we?'

Tanaka settled himself into a chair opposite his superior and gave him a précis of the case. He wasn't entirely sure of the purpose of this given that the superintendent seemed to have already been briefed by someone else. Izumi? Possibly, although he tended to be loyal to Tanaka. More likely, Yoshi-take or one of his underlings would have been talking to Inspector Nishimura. But that still didn't explain how the superintendent was already aware of his Aphrodite-Go-Go visit. Perhaps he was a customer. Tanaka had to bite his tongue to prevent himself laughing out loud at this thought.

'Alright, Tanaka. It seems as though you're on top of things, up to a point. We've got one dead girl already, though. We don't want the French girl to go the same way. That wouldn't be very auspicious for your illustrious career, would it? And I think we should keep certain things back from the press at this briefing. Let's not alarm them with all this blood-letting business. Nishimura is probably just getting carried away with herself. And the possibility of the girl having been held captive... I'm not sure we want that broadcast to all and sundry at the moment. There are questions of national image involved in all this, Tanaka. People more senior than I are taking a close interest, so don't mess things up. I'll be with you up there on the platform, but I can't very well kick you if you start to go off message. So, make sure you don't. Alright?'

Generally, dealing with the press didn't make Tanaka nervous. But Yoshitake's warnings had unnerved him. Not least because the information that his superintendent insisted they hold back had already been divulged by Tanaka to the English reporter, Blain. He'd have to try to have a word with her. If he could offer some other carrot, there might be a chance of those details still not making it into print.

He followed Yoshitake into the room. The superintendent had chosen to wear full uniform, even though — as a member of the criminal division — it wasn't required. His boss liked to make an impression. Tanaka was dressed in his usual suit, indistinguishable from similar ones worn by millions of Tokyo businessmen.

Tanaka felt his throat constrict. He saw Blain sitting in the front row of the press club. What was *she* doing here? She wasn't even a member. Tanaka just hoped that her questions — if she asked any — wouldn't allude to the details that Yoshitake had insisted should be kept out of the investigation. Otherwise, Tanaka could envisage a long spell in Traffic coming up, sooner rather than later.

'Welcome, gentleman — oh and ladies, or should that be lady?' said Yoshitake to the assembled reporters. Tanaka saw him peering suspiciously at Blain — he wouldn't be used to female reporters, and he wouldn't recognise her. Tanaka just willed her not to step out of line. 'Inspector Tanaka and myself will be very grateful for any help you can give us publicising the case of the death of this Swedish girl, Elin Granqvist. Inspector Tanaka as Head of the Gaikoku-jin Unit will be giving today's briefing, although I'll stay here and both of us are happy to answer any of your questions, as far as we're able. So, Inspector Tanaka...'

Tanaka found he had to clear his throat before he started. Even then, he was conscious that, at any moment, he could lapse into a coughing fit. To him, his voice sounded croaky, lacking in authority, unconfident. Everything he didn't want to portray in front of Yoshitake.

He gave a succinct summary of the case so far, and the minutes passed a little like a dream — as though Tanaka was having an out-of-body experience — as though he could watch himself looking like an incompetent fool.

But he seemed to have got away with it. Yoshitake even smiled encouragingly when he'd finished. 'Thank you,

Inspector Tanaka. Now obviously a lot of that was already in the press release we gave you earlier, but we're happy to answer questions as far as we're able. Gentlemen... and lady.' Tanaka almost wished his boss hadn't extended the invitation to ask a question to the only female in the room — even though he felt sure she would ask one. She was a newcomer. She would want to make a good impression.

A hand was raised at the back of the room. Yoshitake nodded towards the reporter. It was a veteran crime hack from the *Yomiuri Shimbun*. 'Do we know where the girl had been in the weeks she was missing?'

'We're not sure, no,' said Tanaka. 'But we have some leads we're working on.' It was a vacuous, useless answer. Tanaka almost felt his face burn with embarrassment as he replied.

'How does a girl's body end up in the rubbish pit of a large metropolitan incinerator plant without anyone noticing until the crane operator has grabbed her in his bucket? Surely someone must have witnessed something before this?' The question came from another veteran — the crime reporter for the *Asahi Shimbun*.

'I agree, it seems unusual,' said Tanaka. 'We are working with the local uniform division in Shinagawa ward to try to trace where the refuse lorries that made that delivery did their round. But as you can imagine, everything at the plant is soon mixed up. I don't hold out much hope for that line of inquiry.'

There were a few mutters around the room. Then Blain put her hand up, and Yoshitake gestured that she could pose her question. Tanaka was on tenterhooks, willing her not to place him in an embarrassing position.

'Holly Blain from the *Tōkei Shimbun*.'

'Are you a member of the press club, Blain-san?' asked the superintendent.

'Our usual reporter is off sick, superintendent. I've been given temporary membership. What I'd like to know is what we're looking at here. Is it murder, suicide, what? If it's a suicide, then — with respect — it seems a little strange that you are holding this press conference. She wouldn't be the first western girl to find Tokyo too overwhelming, to have her dreams shattered.'

'That's a fair question,' said Tanaka. His main feeling was one of relief. Holly-san had neither given any of the extra details of the inquiry away, nor had she revealed that she already knew Tanaka — and had already been given her own private briefings. He gave mental thanks for that. 'There are some aspects of the case which lead us to conclude that this is an unnatural death, and that we *may* be dealing with a murder. However, that's not conclusive. We're awaiting toxicology reports on the body. We may be able to tell you more after that.'

'We've time for one more question only, I'm afraid,' said the superintendent.

The Kyoto News reporter put his hand up. 'Are you saying she was poisoned or drugged?'

'The tests are simply routine,' answered Tanaka. 'We've let you know all we can at this stage. I'm sure you understand why we have to keep some matters out of the public eye.'

'Thank you, Inspector Tanaka,' said Yoshitake. 'We will of course keep the press informed by regular updates and press releases, when we deem that necessary. But for now, that's all.'

Yoshitake trooped off the podium, with Tanaka following. He wasn't sure how his superior would react. Tanaka kept pace with his boss for a few strides as he marched back to his office.

After a few paces, Yoshitake stopped and held Tanaka's

gaze. 'I think we got away with that one, Tanaka, but, in the coming days, we won't get such an easy ride. We need some rapid progress in this case. Make sure you achieve that.'

Tanaka bowed low. The threatening nature of the superintendent's words was undisguised.

CHAPTER FIFTEEN

If Tanaka hadn't been looking forward to the press briefing, then the formal identification of the body by Elin Granqvist's parents was something he was actually dreading. He found himself taking rapid, deep breaths as he led them into the mortuary room. He had to fight down the feelings of nausea — the worry that this could be his sons' bleak futures if his or Miho's parenting skills faltered, or if they themselves chose the wrong path. Did he — as a detective — work hours that were too long and irregular? Was he letting his family down as a result? But then long hours were ingrained in Japanese culture. And children, from a very young age, were taught to be independent — often travelling on complicated metro and train routes to get to school, journeys that would even leave some adults scratching their heads. His thoughts, in any case, should not be on his own family and himself at a time like this. They should be with the Granqvists — but he almost found it too painful to think about their loss.

When Elin's face was uncovered after her body had been removed from the cooler, her father made the tiniest nod of his head to confirm it was his daughter. In her mother's eyes, Tanaka could detect a look of hatred — directed, he thought, towards himself. Their child had gone missing, thousands of miles away from home in a foreign country. Tanaka had let them down — failing to find her before her life was taken away. He had to make sure the same didn't happen to Marie-Louise Durand.

'Are we going in mob-handed, Tanaka-san?'

'I wouldn't put it quite like that, Izumi-kun. But I will make sure we have a couple of uniformed officers as back-up, should things get awkward.' They were discussing their tactics for the evening return to Aphrodite-Go-Go.

'I would suggest, then, Inspector, that those officers either come from headquarters, or an area other than District 4.'

'You seem to have a low opinion of the officers responsible for Kabukicho, Izumi. But yes, you may be right.' Tanaka wondered again about something that had always troubled him in regard to Izumi. The Aphrodite-Go-Go was linked to the Yakuza — Yoshitake had confirmed as much. Had Izumi really got his tip about it from the unnamed salaryman in Akihabara who'd recognised Elin Granqvist's photo as that of a hostess he'd seen working there? The thing that raised a doubt in Tanaka's mind was something he'd seen once on Izumi's arm. Or rather hadn't seen. Relaxing after one of their recent cases, Tanaka had treated his deputy to a session at one of Tokyo's *onsen* bath houses. One of the better ones. Yet Izumi had seemed reluctant. It was only when Izumi joined him in the hot spa that Tanaka realised why. He had something that looked like a bandage covering his arm. Tanaka had asked his Number Two if he'd hurt himself.

'What do you mean, Tanaka-san?' Izumi had replied.

Tanaka had gestured with his eyes to Izumi's right upper arm, to what appeared to be a bandage or strapping. His sergeant had clutched his left hand to the covering in panic, as though it might have slipped.

'Oh that. Just something from my childhood. A stupid schoolboy prank. But you know the rules about tattoos.'

Tanaka did. He also knew why those rules were in place. Because of the links between tattoos and gangsters. He didn't pry any further at that time — but he remembered he still hadn't had that close look at Izumi's personal file he'd promised himself. He hoped there were no skeletons there — skeletons that had now provided his sergeant with information about a Yakuza-controlled hostess club.

Tanaka had hoped after the formalities of the identification with Elin Granqvist's parents that Inspector Nishimura might have progressed with the toxicology tests. He'd eventually tracked her down, only to be disappointed. The test results still wouldn't be available until the following day.

Tanaka might suspect that Elin had been murdered, but he didn't *know* it. Despite the uniformed back-up, they would — as Superintendent Yoshitake had warned — still need to proceed carefully when they returned to the hostess club.

Tanaka had counselled the club owner, Ikari Tomahito, not to advertise the fact that the police were paying a return visit in the evening. He'd clearly ignored the warning — he'd also made himself scarce, delegating everything to his assistant manager, a woman of indeterminate age called Michiko Ito. She had a hard face: one that, Tanaka surmised, had once been beautiful, but had seen the surgeon's knife in more recent times, skin pulled back too tightly like you often saw with ageing American film stars of both genders. In this environment, the plastic surgery may not have been simply aimed at defying the ravages of time. Tanaka had known of several cases where girls in this industry — perhaps after becoming too demanding — had had their looks 're-arranged'. He dropped his gaze before the woman started to wonder why he was looking at her so closely.

'Tomahito-san said you would be coming back,' she said. 'We have got all the girl's records together and worked out who was on shift at the same time as her.' All this was said without a smile or almost any facial expression. Tanaka wasn't even sure if her face could convey emotion, so taut was the skin. 'Shall we go into the office first, and you can look through all the documents, then you can talk to the girls?' Tanaka looked around the club. There was a smattering of businessmen tête-à-tête with hostesses, but most of the girls were sitting at the bar chatting amongst themselves. One — who looked Slavic, possibly Russian — caught his eye, and beckoned him with an elegant finger. As though he was the latest punter about to be divested of a considerable amount of yen.

'Sergeant Izumi can go through the paperwork with you,' he said to the assistant manager. 'Can't you Izumi? I will begin by interviewing the girls. You say some of the ones here worked on the same shifts as the Swedish girl?'

The woman nodded. 'Dagmara. The dark-haired Polish girl — the tall one by the bar. Start with her. She will introduce you to the others.'

As Izumi went with the assistant manager to the back office, Tanaka approached the Polish girl. She smiled warmly at him, and he realised she had assumed he was reacting to her invitation to draw close. She hadn't realised he was the police officer the girls had no doubt been warned about.

'Have you come to buy me a glass of champagne, darling?' she asked.

Tanaka suddenly felt embarrassed under her gaze of appraisal. He dropped his eyes and almost mumbled his answer. 'No. I am Inspector Tetsu Tanaka of the Tokyo Metropolitan Police Department's Gaikoku-jin Unit.' Tanaka raised his eyes at the same time as producing his ID. There was no doubt the girl was beautiful. If he had been truly Japanese, his embarrassment would not be so obvious on his face. With his paler skin, he could feel it reddening. He wasn't always at his most confident with women. In fact, it was strange how easy he felt in the English reporter's company — perhaps that was because she was more like a tomboy, and, in some way, he felt protective of her. The fact that she was trying to make her way in a man's world, in a foreign country. 'We are investigating the death of Elin Granqvist, a Swedish girl who worked here for a couple of shifts. I believe you worked with her on those evenings.'

'That's correct, Inspector.' Dagmara's Japanese was almost perfectly accented — with the merest hint of her underlying native Polish tones. 'Why don't we go and sit in the corner over there, and I will tell you what I can. Though it's not much. As it doesn't look as though you'll be buying me a drink, would you like one? On the house, of course.'

Tanaka gave a small bow of thanks. 'An iced tea, please. I cannot drink alcohol while on duty.' It wasn't a rule he always stuck to — but he was certainly going to abide by it in an establishment like this. He couldn't afford to drop his guard.

The detective moved over to the corner seat. He watched

Dagmara collect the drinks then walk towards him. She flicked her head at a strikingly pretty Caucasian girl who was sitting at the other end of the bar. The girl rose from her seat and followed her.

'This is Courtney, Inspector,' said Dagmara, as the two girls sat at right-angles to him on the L-shaped sofa. 'She's from Sydney. Courtney — Inspector Tetsu... Sorry, Inspector, I forget your second name.'

'Tanaka. Inspector Tetsu Tanaka.'

'The inspector is asking about the Swedish girl who worked here a few weeks ago, Courtney. Michiko-san says we were the only girls who worked on both her shifts.' Then she trained her eyes on Tanaka. He dropped his gaze, found he was staring at Dagmara's braless chest and quickly raised his eyes again. The Polish girl smirked, as though she could sense his discomfort. 'What was it you wanted, Inspector?' There was a seductive tone to her voice — no doubt well-practised, thought Tanaka. As though it wasn't just information that was on offer.

'I want to know anything you can tell me about Elin Granqvist. Who she drank with. The salarymen she met. Did she make arrangements, that you know of, to see any of them outside the club? Did she mention any problems with her life in Tokyo? That sort of thing.'

'We wouldn't necessarily have all that information,' replied Dagmara.

'But did you notice who she was with?'

'I did,' said Courtney.

'Really?' exclaimed Dagmara. 'You never said before.'

'I'd not seen him before, and I've not seen him since. But he was with Elin both nights. The second night, he seemed agitated that she was with someone else. I think he might have slipped Michiko-san some money to intervene and move her away from the Japanese businessman she was with.'

'Was that businessman angry at having to change girls? What did he look like?'

'I don't think so, particularly,' said Courtney. 'And he looked... well, like a middle-aged, well-to-do, Japanese businessman. That's not very helpful, is it? But there was nothing very special about him.'

'Had you seen him before? Have you seen him since? Do you know his name?'

'He's a regular, yes.' Then Courtney lowered her eyes. 'I don't know his name. The management won't have a record either, unless for any reason he failed to pay a bar bill. They only keep details of *gaijin* who visit. There's a history of trouble with *gaijin* in hostess clubs — they often think that by paying lots of money, more is on offer than is actually the case.'

'What about the other man — the one who saw her both nights?' asked Dagmara. She seemed to be doing Tanaka's job for him.

'He was Japanese too, so again there would be no record of his name. Unless he got into any arguments or failed to pay. You'd need to ask Michiko-san about that.'

'Can you describe him?' asked Tanaka. 'What did he look like, what was he wearing, approximately how old was he?'

Courtney's fresh-faced, college-girl expression lit up. 'Yes, he did look different to the usual businessmen we get in here. He was a bit younger. Maybe in his thirties. And more awkward. He didn't seem very confident.'

Dagmara nudged her colleague with her elbow. 'You must have been paying him a lot of attention to notice so much. Are you sure you weren't jealous of the Swedish girl?'

The Pole received an icy glare for this interruption. 'She's dead, Dagmara. I just want to help the inspector.'

'Sorry.'

'What was he wearing, Courtney-san? And can you describe his appearance in more detail?' prompted Tanaka.

'He was dressed all in black. That's not so unusual. But what was unusual was it was a very old-fashioned look and very American. He looked like an American pop-star from the 1950s or 1960s. Very like one of them.'

'Elvis Presley, perhaps?' asked Tanaka.

'No. Oh, the name's gone. I'm too young. I think he had a revival a few years ago. Wasn't he in a group with some other big stars? He was well known for always wearing black. Wasn't he even called The Man In Black?'

'That would be Johnny Cash,' said Tanaka. He wasn't sure this run through the big names of American pop was really helping.

Courtney frowned. 'No, no. Not him. He had a really famous song.' Courtney started to try to sing the riff the song began with. 'Dum, dum, dum, dum, dummmm… dum, dum, dum, dum, dum, dum, dum, dum.' Tanaka was perplexed. 'You must know the one. He always wore sunglasses, even inside. This man was the same. He looked a bit odd. And he never took his sunglasses off.'

It was the sunglasses that were the trigger. Then the hummed riff made sense. *Pretty Woman.* Or, more correctly, *Oh, Pretty Woman.* Tanaka vaguely remembered it from his boyhood as a favourite of his late American serviceman father. He'd played it often when the family were stationed on Ishigaki, one of the southerly Okinawan islands.

Now Tanaka knew the singer.

The 'Big O'.

Roy Orbison.

. . .

Once they were back in the office, Tanaka and Izumi compared notes. 'What did you discover, Izumi, if anything?'

'The girl was definitely using false documents — or at least, the passport photocopy the club have on record has a false date of birth. According to that, she was twenty-two — five years older than her actual age. But she gave a false address in Tokyo too.'

'Do you think these were her own faked documents, or do you think the club arranged it all — possibly faked it all?'

'It's impossible to tell, Tanaka-san. But the club is covered and in the clear. As far as they were concerned, the girl was indeed twenty-two. Plenty of girls in their twenties still look like seventeen-year-olds and vice versa. The assistant manager made a point of underlining this — and I can't say I disagree with her. What about you — did you discover anything by talking to the girls?'

'Only that there was one particular customer who seemed besotted with Elin. Well, I assume he was besotted. He was certainly entranced enough that he gave an underhand payment to the assistant manager to make sure he could spend a second night in her company.'

'Why would he need to do that?' asked Izumi.

'Because another businessman — on the second shift she worked — had already in effect booked her services. The man in question paid the assistant manager money to invent some excuse to get the girl away from the other businessman. I'm not sure what it was.'

'So that gives us two potential suspects.'

'Exactly,' said Tanaka, stroking his chin. 'The man who was spurned, or rather who had the girl taken away from him, and this other man who spent two evenings with Elin.'

'Was there any suggestion he left the club with her?'

Tanaka gave a long sigh. 'No.'

'I did learn another couple of interesting things from Michiko-san. In fact, I think she took a shine to me.'

'You're a married man,' laughed Tanaka. 'Don't get too carried away.'

Izumi grinned. 'I simply used my charm, Inspector. Anyway, she told me that occasionally — when a particularly attractive girl joins the club — word gets round. To other agencies, if you get my drift.'

'The Yakuza?'

'Exactly. As we know, the Yakuza have moved away from some of their traditional money-making activities in recent years. Now they concentrate on playing the stock market, making money out of inflated stock prices on shell companies, that sort of thing. But Michiko-san, speaking strictly off the record, said there is some traditional work that still goes on.'

Tanaka tried to resist the temptation to lock his eyes onto Izumi's suit-sleeve covered upper right arm.

'Like what?' he asked.

'Vice. Porn films. The usual thing.'

'With European girls?'

'Sometimes, yes. Underground stuff. Under-the-counter stuff. Sometimes involving violence.'

'And is there any suggestion that Elin got caught up in this?'

'No, Tanaka-san. But it's worth chasing up, isn't it?'

'Of course, Izumi-kun. Good work. I'd like you to get onto that right away. Did you manage to find out anything else?'

'Oh yes. One name of interest on one of their lists.'

'Lists?'

'They don't keep records of their Japanese clients. That would be an invasion of privacy, apparently. But they do keep a list of their foreign clients, the *gaijin*. And one name stuck out.'

'Whose?' asked Tanaka, although he already had a very good idea what Izumi was about to say. And the next utterance from Izumi's mouth proved him right.

'A Frenchman by the name of Durand. Pascal Durand.'

CHAPTER SIXTEEN

B lain had already written a short story based on the press
briefing and was finalising the next day's newspaper
report — negotiating with Yamamoto what she should and
shouldn't include — when she got the call from Haruka. She
was intrigued when her lover's name flashed up on her
mobile. Haruka didn't usually try to contact her at work.

'Holly, darling. Are you busy?'

'Yes. But I can spare a few seconds.' She saw Yamamoto
giving her an evil look. Taking personal calls at work was
strictly forbidden. The difficulty with journalists was that they
were always on the phone, chasing leads, checking in with
contacts. It was a rule that was very difficult for the management to police.

'I have something interesting for you, to do with work,'
said Haruka.

Blain felt a flutter in her stomach. There was only one
story Haruka knew she was working on — the missing girls.
And Haruka wouldn't yet know that one had been found dead.
'I'm listening,' said Blain.

'Your friend has just been to a hostess club.'

Blain frowned. 'My friend?'

'The police inspector you were talking about.' Blain suddenly had visions of a sad, secret life for Tanaka, frequenting hostess clubs. And then she felt a spike of jealousy. She didn't mind Haruka fawning over businessmen she didn't know — but a police inspector she did know was quite a different matter. The next moment, Haruka dispelled her fears. 'Don't worry,' she laughed. 'He wasn't a customer here. He was at another club in Kabukicho discussing your missing girls case.'

Blain's ears pricked up. 'Which club — and how did you find out?'

'The Aphrodite-Go-Go. It's got a mixed recruitment policy like here at Valentine's. So, some of the girls who work here, work there, and vice versa. There's an Australian girl I'm quite friendly with at this other club. She told me one of the missing girls has been found dead. Did you know that?'

'Yes. The police announced it at a press conference this afternoon. But why was Inspector Tanaka at the club? I don't understand.' She also worried that Haruka must have been gossiping about the case — even though, as a result, it had turned up helpful information.

'Because of the dead girl,' said Haruka. 'She worked at this other hostess club.' Blain heard, as much as felt, her own instinctive sharp intake of breath. 'My Australian friend knew her. She only did two shifts, then she never came back.'

Blain could sense Yamamoto hovering on her shoulder. She turned and cupped her hand over the mobile.

'We need that copy urgently, Holly-san,' he said. 'I hope that's not a personal call.'

She could see him trying to peer at the phone display that she'd covered with her hand.

'No, it's not. It's a new angle on the story. I'll meet the deadline for the copy. I said I would.'

Yamamoto shuffled off, grumpily.

She held the phone up to her ear again with one hand and picked up her pen and notebook with the other. 'This is fantastic, Haruka. Is your Australian friend happy to be quoted?'

'No. She would lose her job. Just use the information. No direct quotes, no names. You understand, Holly.'

Blain found her journalistic instincts fighting with her loyalty to her girlfriend. 'Okay, agreed.'

Her pen almost tore the notebook's pages as she frantically scribbled a full shorthand note of what Haruka had gleaned from her Australian contact. This was a proper scoop. None of the other papers would have anything like this.

'And what did this man look like?'

'That's the one thing the police asked her to keep quiet about.'

'Oh, come on, Haruka-chan. We're a team. You must have asked her. You can trust me.'

'No, Holly-chan. I'm sorry. My friend gave her word to the detective that she wouldn't mention the exact appearance of the man to anyone.'

Blain chewed the end of her pen in frustration. But it was no good — all the Australian friend had been willing to tell Haruka was that the man was approximately in his early thirties and looked more like an *Otaku* than a businessman. It was enough of a hook for Blain. Now she could still omit the details Tanaka wanted omitting, without rendering her story useless. She set to work finishing the story on her computer. After this, Yamamoto wouldn't be able to deny her a shot at being a crime reporter. This was possibly the best story the *Tōkei Shimbun* would get all year.

CHAPTER SEVENTEEN

It was like a punch to the gut for Tanaka as he saw the front-page splash the next morning at the metro newspaper kiosk. His career disappearing in front of his eyes. How on earth would he explain this to Superintendent Yoshitake?

'OTAKU' SOUGHT OVER HOSTESS DEATH
WORLD EXCLUSIVE

By Crime Reporter Holly Blain

Tokyo Police want to question a man described as an 'Otaku' by witnesses in connection with the death of a teenage Swedish nightclub hostess, the Tōkei Shimbun *can exclusively reveal.*

The man is thought to have been one of the last people to see 17-year-old Elin Granqvist alive. Her body was found yesterday, dumped in the refuse pit at the Shinagawa Incineration Plant.

She had been missing for six weeks. The last previous sighting of the girl had been at a fashion shop popular with teenagers in Takeshita Street, Harajuku.

But exclusive sources have told the Tōkei Shimbun *that after the Harajuku sighting, the girl worked as an underage hostess at a club in the Kabukicho area of Shinjuku.*

She used a passport with a false date of birth in order to secure employment there but left after only two shifts.

On both nights she worked there, a man — described by witnesses as 'looking like an Otaku, not a typical salaryman' — sought her company and bought her drinks.

It's not known if she left with him or saw him outside the work environment.

The teenager failed to turn up for her third shift and did not give the club any warning. Because this is not unusual in hostess clubs, where there is a high turnover of staff, management did not initially alert the police.

The case is being coordinated by Inspector Tetsu Tanaka of the special Gaikoku-jin Unit of the Tokyo Metropolitan Police Department.

Inspector Tanaka told a packed press briefing at the TMPD press club: 'There are some aspects of the case which lead us to conclude that this is an unnatural death, and that we may be dealing with a murder.'

Police are waiting for the outcome of toxicology reports before confirming the cause of death. These are expected later today.

Check the online edition of the Tōkei Shimbun *at www.tokeishimbun.jp for live updates on this and other major news stories.*

The more he read of the story, the angrier he felt. How had Blain got these extra details? Had Izumi leaked them? Tanaka couldn't believe that of him — despite the fact that he had occasional doubts about his deputy. He thought again about that covering on Izumi's arm that the sergeant had been so coy about in the *onsen* bath. They hadn't even told Yoshitake about what they'd discovered at the club. The superintendent would be furious. The only other possibility was that Blain had got the information directly from the Aphrodite-Go-Go. But how would she have singled that club out from the thousands in Tokyo? To do that, she must have been tailing him — that, or getting a private detective to do it for her. It just didn't sit with what he knew of the young woman.

What was done, was done. Now he had to concentrate on damage limitation. He fished into his pocket for his phone, intending to ring Yoshitake. Tanaka could pretend he hadn't seen the newspapers yet and that he was simply updating the superintendent on an important development he and Izumi had discovered. However, before he found the superintendent's name in his contacts, it flashed up on the display. Yoshitake was calling him. That could only mean he'd already seen the newspaper headlines. Tanaka thought about not taking the call. He could claim he was in a metro tunnel without reception — although there was now mobile reception for virtually all networks on the whole of the subway system. But he would have to face up to Yoshitake at some point. It might as well be now.

'Tanaka. I take it you've seen this *Tōkei Shimbun* rag?'

'Yes, boss.'

'How the hell have they got this? How are they ahead of the game? We don't even know this do we?'

'We found out late last night, Superintendent. I was about to ring you...'

'And what exactly did you do? Ring that reporter first? Was she the one at the briefing yesterday — the one who isn't even a full member of the press club, just a stand-in?'

'Yes.'

'Well how did she get this information, Tanaka? Was it from you or Izumi?' It was a rhetorical question. Tanaka could sense it was best to let Yoshitake vent his spleen rather than try to put up any defence. 'You're a pair of idiots so it wouldn't surprise me. Anyway, come in to see me immediately and make sure you have a good explanation. There will be hell to pay over this. The only consolation is those other lazy no-good reporters who spend all their time in *izakayas* — and probably in hostess clubs — have got their bottoms well and truly spanked.'

Tanaka used the metro journey to try to reach Blain. She didn't seem to be answering her calls. Probably because she was expecting him to at least tear her off a strip — if not break off cooperation completely, which was what he was minded to do. Police-press relations only worked if both sides got some-thing from it. In this case, so far, it had all been give from Tanaka — and the result was he was in hot water with his boss.

He tried the Master at Café Muse. He hadn't seen Blain either, but he had seen her story.

'I knew you two would work well together, Tanaka-san. I'm so proud that she's scooped the rest of the newspapers on this. I told you she was good.'

Tanaka didn't feel like joining in the hero-worship.

'Can you pass along a message, Master? Get her to ring me as soon as possible.'

Tanaka knocked on the superintendent's office door.

'Come in,' barked Yoshitake. He didn't initially look up from the paperwork on his desk, as Tanaka stood in front of it like a naughty schoolboy. When he did, and saw it was the inspector, he glowered at his subordinate. This time he didn't even bother to make his usual offer of a cigarette. 'Why are you standing there like a nervous girl? Sit down.'

Tanaka took the seat in front of the desk, as Yoshitake continued to leaf through some paperwork.

'I'm waiting,' said the superintendent.

'Sir?'

'For your excuses and explanations, Tanaka. I've already told you, they'd better be good.'

'I don't really have an explanation, Superintendent. Izumi and I visited the club yesterday evening, as I said. We found out the girl had done two shifts there, and that this slightly nerdy man—'

'The *Otaku* Killer,' said Yoshitake, brandishing the front page of Blain's newspaper in front of Tanaka's face.

'It doesn't actually say that, sir. We still don't know if this was a murder.' Tanaka had faded memories of being told off by his own father for some minor misdemeanour as a child. He felt the same sense of burning anger and injustice now. Of course, Yoshitake *wasn't* his father — and he was no longer a small boy. And there would be no more confrontations with his natural parent. The man was dead, and he wasn't missed. Not after abandoning Tanaka and his mother so many years before. Tanaka tried to cleanse the memories from his brain and concentrate instead on what Yoshitake was actually saying.

'Are you actually taking any of this in, Tanaka? At the rate you're going, this bloody *Tōkei Shimbun* will know whether this was a murder before you do and splash it all over the front page again.' The superintendent eyeballed him, until Tanaka felt forced to drop his gaze first.

'As I was saying, we found out this *Otaku* had spent most of Elin's two shifts with her. I don't know why we're being criticised, sir. We've found out important new information. We've found a new lead.'

'You're being given a rollicking, Tanaka, for a very good reason. This bloody newspaper found out and printed information before your own boss — myself — was even told. It's not good enough. I'm still waiting for this explanation. Have you tackled Izumi about it?'

'I haven't had chance yet, Superintendent.'

'Okay. Well as you seem unable to explain what's happened, I'll tell you what you're going to do about it. You're going to give Izumi a bloody good telling off, just like I'm doing to you. You're going to get hold of this woman reporter — although to me she looked more like a boy — and you're going to read her the riot act. Find out how she got the information and make sure it doesn't happen again. My phone will be going all day with calls from whingeing editors. Either that, or they'll be on the phone to *my* superiors, and then they'll make *my* life hell thanks to a mess-up by you and Izumi. Now get out and don't let me see your face again till you've found out how this happened and have assurances that it won't happen again.'

CHAPTER EIGHTEEN

The start to Blain's day was in complete contrast to that of Tanaka. When she arrived in the newsroom, the other reporters banged their desks in rhythmic fashion, each thwack heightening the blush on her cheeks. Yamamoto pulled her into a hug and then brought out a bottle of sake and three cups from his bottom drawer and ushered her and Hasegawa into his office.

'Fantastic, Holly-san. I knew it was a winner as soon as I saw your copy. We need to have a toast.' He turned to the 24-hour news channel. The red breaking news scrolling headlines were all about 'The "Otaku Killer"'. The TV stations weren't shy in dubbing him that, even though the police hadn't yet confirmed a cause of death. 'Every station is following it up,' said Yamamoto. Just then, the picture cut to Blain's front-page story — highlighted and enlarged.

'Look,' screamed Hasegawa. 'You couldn't buy advertising as good as that. All the crime reporters at our rivals will be getting rockets up their arses. Ha! I wish I could see their faces.'

'So, are you going to tell us who your mysterious source was, Holly-san?' asked Yamamoto. 'I almost wondered whether you made it all up. You didn't, did you?'

Blain shook her head. 'It's all kosher.'

Lining the sake cups on his desk, Yamamoto poured a generous measure into each. 'The owner's already been on the phone congratulating us. He wants to know what sort of contract you're on, and whether it's watertight. If you want to ask for a raise, now's the time.'

'I simply want to do the crime beat, Yamamoto-san. You know that.'

'Well, we'll have to see. You've certainly done your chances no harm. What I can offer you is to stay on this story and see it through to its conclusion — conditional, of course, on you keeping up these high standards.'

Blain joined the others in downing her glass of sake. What she didn't reveal — either to the news editor or his deputy — was that the extra information she'd gleaned had come to her purely by coincidence and synchronicity, not by journalistic excellence or persistence. Her girlfriend's friend worked in the same club where Elin Granqvist had briefly also worked. Even more fortuitously, this friend had been on duty for those exact two shifts. But Blain had obtained everything she was going to get from Haruka. Unless there was another angle linked to the hostess club, then Yamamoto would soon find out that Blain's magic source had dried up. Still, she was going to enjoy her little victory while she could.

Yamamoto, after all the celebrations, had made it clear that any reporter was only as good as his or her next story. Blain had set her standards high — now she would have to keep delivering.

She knew the toxicology results were due later that day. But Tanaka was likely to be annoyed with her and was unlikely to give her a head-start. At best, she'd receive the same briefings from now on as every other reporter. At worst, Tanaka might leave her out of the loop just to spite her. He'd been trying to ring, but she'd avoided him so far. The Master from Café Muse had also left a message asking her to get in touch with the detective.

For any sort of exclusive for the next day, she either had to break her agreement with Tanaka and reveal the details about the neck wound and possible blood-letting — self-inflicted or otherwise — or she had to try to get that same information from another source. She'd also noticed the police — in their briefing — had failed to mention the other missing girl. This was no doubt deliberate. Part of Tanaka's role was to protect the *gaijin* community, not stir up unnecessary fear. Until there was a stronger link between the missing French girl and the dead Swedish girl, the police would probably go out of their way *not* to link the two cases. But with all the publicity surrounding the Granqvist case, the father of the French girl — staying in Tokyo as far as she knew — was likely to be even more worried and perhaps even angry. While he'd be fearful about his daughter's fate after the news about Elin's demise, he'd be annoyed that the extra publicity for the case hadn't been used by the police in a fresh appeal for his daughter. And an angry and upset father of a missing girl was likely to be a good source for a story.

She knew she'd seen a short report about Marie-Louise Durand in one of the papers. Was it in the files? She searched the paper's online archive. It wouldn't be straightforward. It was a case of matching the sounds of Durand's name to Japanese pictograph characters.

Try as hard as she might, and using as many variations as

she could, she couldn't bring up the link to the story, if indeed it had been archived. She racked her memory. The story danced before her eyes, but she couldn't remember the name of the hotel that was mentioned in it. She could try to go through the physical library of newspapers — but that would be laborious and wouldn't necessarily produce a better result.

Blain looked around the office, wondering who she could ask for help with the *kanji*. At that very moment, one of the secretaries walked in front of her desk, and the sunlight made her jewellery sparkle. A diamond ring on her finger. Diamond — *Dai-mon*. It was the key to her mental block. The Shiba Park Hotel in Daimon — that was the hotel mentioned in the report. Where Marie-Louise had disappeared from, where she and her father were staying. Where he might still be staying.

Blain grabbed her jacket and coat and rushed out of the office.

On the short metro journey from the newspaper's head office in Toranamon Hills, she tried to think of a ruse that would ensure the reception staff didn't get suspicious and clam up on her. She couldn't think of anything — she'd just have to play it straight. She checked how she looked in the metro train window, flattening her hair, trying to smarten herself up. A good impression was often half the battle. She didn't want to look like some indie band cast off, but that was what she saw staring back at her.

As she approached the reception desk, she felt her heart hammer in her chest. The receptionist looked up, all smiles.

'Can I help you, Madam?'

'I've come to see Monsieur Pascal Durand. He's expecting me.' It was a lie, but it might just avoid too many awkward questions. If she could only talk to the man on the hotel's internal phone, there was a chance she could persuade him to talk to her.

The female receptionist consulted the hotel's computer system. Blain mentally crossed her fingers that Durand was still staying in the same hotel. She saw a flicker of recognition in the receptionist's eyes. The woman had found his name — and hopefully his room.

'I'll just check if he's in,' said the receptionist. Blain leant over the counter, watching the woman tapping in the room number. She memorised it just in case.

The receptionist was now speaking into the mouthpiece. 'Mr Durand. There's a young woman here at reception. She says you're expecting her.' Blain knew that — with his daughter missing — the man wouldn't be able to resist talking to anyone, hoping beyond hope that this 'mystery girl' would have information to lead him to Marie-Louise. The receptionist passed the phone handset over the counter to Blain.

'Mr Durand?'

'Yes.'

'I want to talk to you about Marie-Louise. My name's Holly Blain. I'm a reporter with the *Tōkei Shimbun* newspaper. We believe we can help you.'

'In what way?'

'I don't want to discuss it over the phone. I'd like to speak to you face-to-face.'

'I saw your report in the paper this morning about the Swedish girl. I got someone to translate it for me from the Japanese. You didn't bother to mention the fact that Marie-Louise was missing. Why should I trust you?'

Blain was conscious of the hotel receptionist frowning at her. She needed to get this over the line quickly. 'I think that's wrong as well, Mr Durand, that the police aren't linking the two cases. We want to make a big splash about it — an appeal to find your daughter. This is your best chance of getting publicity. If you talk to me — and *exclusively* to me — I will ensure the story about your daughter is splashed all over the front page of our paper tomorrow. Everyone is reading the *Tōkei Shimbun* because of our story about Elin Granqvist this morning. All the TV stations, all the radio stations, are watching us like hawks — regurgitating our exclusives. They'll do the same thing tomorrow. After my story is published, everyone in Japan will be searching everywhere for Marie-Louise. That has to be worth it, doesn't it?'

For a desperate father — with no news of his daughter for days, and in the wake of another foreign teenager ending up dead — Blain's argument was irresistible.

The man invited her up to his room.

CHAPTER NINETEEN

Yoshitake's dressing down was still ringing in Tanaka's ears by the time he got to the mortuary for his scheduled meeting with Inspector Nishimura. He felt deflated. He was doing his best, but that never seemed to be good enough for the superintendent. What particularly rankled was that none of it was his fault. Izumi had insisted he hadn't been the one to leak the details from the hostess club. Tanaka still had no idea how Blain had got hold of that. She clearly wasn't the wet-behind-the-ears show business reporter he'd taken her to be.

Winter really did seem to want to make a return. The thin raincoat over his suit failed to keep out the morning chill — but it was at least some protection from the driving rain. Mortuaries weren't his favourite places. The smell was enough to put him off, even before the waxy-looking bodies had been wheeled from the cooler. But as he opened the door from the outside, and tried to tidy his rain-sodden, windswept hair, he was just glad to be anywhere out of the weather.

Megumi Nishimura didn't look as though she had been

braving the elements. Perfectly turned out, she was wearing a similar slim-fitting business suit, but this time with a dark, above-the-knee skirt rather than trousers. He coughed to attract her attention.

'Ah. Tanaka-san,' she said, looking up and smiling at him. 'I was just about to ring you. The toxicology results are through. And I have some other rather interesting findings for you. Let's go through to the office.' Nishimura showed him through to a side-room where the all-pervasive smell of disinfectant was thankfully less apparent. After the shock of seeing Blain's front-page story, and the fall-out with Yoshitake, he still hadn't managed to eat any breakfast. Every few minutes, he was having to swallow back the feelings of nausea. He was grateful for the chance to sit down at her desk.

She showed him a piece of printed paper with lists of figures and percentages on it. 'The important thing here is the metabolites of flunitrazepam, and flunitrazepam itself.'

'Rohypnol?'

'Exactly, Tanaka-san, I'm impressed. Perhaps you should be doing this job, not me. So, these are the levels in the blood, expressed in micrograms per litre. We have a level of flunitrazepam itself of 76 micrograms per millilitre.'

'From what I remember, that seems very high.'

'Correct, Tanaka-san. To give you some comparative indicators, the lowest concentration we can detect in blood is about 4 *nano*grams per millilitre.'

'So, this level was about 20,000 times higher?!'

'Ah, no. Sorry. A nanogram per millilitre is the equivalent amount to a microgram per litre. So perhaps twenty times higher than the minimum concentration we can detect.'

'Aha,' said Tanaka, embarrassed by his schoolboy error. 'That's still significant, though.'

'It is. To put it into context, the lowest concentration we

might expect to find in a fatal overdose would be 100 micro-grams per litre.'

'She didn't overdose on Rohypnol, then?'

Nishimura tilted her head. 'I don't think we can necessarily conclude that from these test results. It depends when a dose was last administered. We also found significant levels of 7-aminoflunitrazepam, desmethylflunitrazepam and 3-hydroxy-desmethylflunitrazepam. These are all metabolites of Rohyp-nol. So, there could have originally been a higher level of Rohypnol in her bloodstream, and that has degraded over time. The level of 7-aminoflunitrazepam was particularly high.'

'Could it have been self-administered?'

'It *could*,' said Nishimura. 'But in my experience, it very rarely is. It has little or no recreational value, if we can call it that. Not for nothing, it is known as the date-rape drug.'

'Did you find evidence of sexual trauma, of sexual assault?'

'No. More than that, I could find no evidence of sexual intercourse at all.'

'Have you managed to establish the cause of death?' asked Tanaka. The toxicology report was interesting. It seemed to rule out suicide, not that Tanaka had ever suspected this was a suicide. But if the girl was half asleep on Rohypnol, accidental death — falling from a bridge, for example, into a refuse lorry — was not beyond the bounds of possibility. It still, however, seemed highly unlikely.

'My best guess is heart failure. That *could* have been a result of the Rohypnol. But we both noticed the neck wound at the incineration plant. I've examined that more closely; it is remarkably neat, as though a special implement was used to extract the blood — some sort of catheter arrangement may have been attached to it. There is evidence, despite the neatness, of the wound having partially healed before being re-opened. In other words, the blood-letting was happening on a regular basis. That is more likely, in my view, to have been the cause of death.'

Tanaka's forehead had been creased into a semi-permanent frown almost from the minute Nishimura had begun talking. He wiped his hand across his forehead, and then rested his head in both hands, elbows on the table. Something that was frowned upon in Japan. But it wasn't a time for social niceties. He sighed. 'Is there any way this blood-letting could have been self-administered?'

'I did do some digging,' said Nishimura. 'There are some articles about it. It does seem to exist — particularly amongst teenagers. But none of the examples quoted mentioned the neck. Normally an arm vein is used.'

'Okay. So where does that leave us?'

'I think your view that this is a suspicious death is inescapable. We have the Rohypnol. We have the blood-letting. We have the apparent restraint used on her leg. What we don't have is enough to say that this was a murder — that she was deliberately *killed*. She may have been deliberately *harmed* but not necessarily killed.'

'But you would support my request for a full autopsy.'

'Without a doubt. I think it is essential. I have already put in the request, but your backing for it would be useful too. There is one other thing I discovered, though.'

'What?'

'Come through into the mortuary room. It's easier to show you.'

Tanaka felt his stomach lurch as he rose to his feet. He took a few deep breaths of air in Nishimura's office — steeling himself for the return to the mortuary. He held his breath as he entered behind the investigator, then followed her to a side table, where the girl's clothing had been laid, like an outfit waiting for someone to take it on a night out. He noticed some strands of vegetable matter attached in some way to the remains of her dress. He peered more closely. Some sort of stalk, or thin branch, was looped through safety pins attached to her dress. Clearly the vegetation had been put there for some reason — it wasn't accidental.

Nishimura had clearly meant him to notice it. 'Interesting, Tanaka-san, isn't it? I've had samples examined at the forensics lab. It is a stem from the Somei Yoshino variety of cherry tree. Or to use its Latin name, *Prunus x yedoensis*. The Japanese flowering cherry. I don't know that this gets us a lot further, because these trees are prevalent all over Japan. The lab was able to tell me that this one had bloomed, however. And if you check the cherry blossom forecast, then, other than the far south of Japan and the Okinawan islands, the only place in bloom so far is the Tokyo area itself.'

Tanaka shrugged. 'Tokyo is a huge city. I dread to think how many cherry trees there are. It would have been more useful if it was something rare.' Tanaka picked up a piece of paper to the side of the clothing. 'What's this?' he asked.

Nishimura looked embarrassed. 'Nothing really, Tanaka-san. Just a doodle of mine. I was just trying to imagine why the parts of the cherry tree had been attached to her dress.'

Tanaka examined the drawing. It looked almost as though the girl was the centre of an elaborate flower arrangement. 'May I take a copy of this?' he asked.

'Of course, Tanaka-san. Be my guest. But it is nothing scientific — it's just an idea I had in my head and may be completely erroneous.'

Tanaka nodded. Then he remembered the flower that had

fallen from Elin Granqvist's body into the rubbish pit in Shinagawa. With all the panic about Blain's newspaper story, he'd forgotten to ask Izumi about it and whether he'd sent it for any tests. He would set about rectifying that immediately.

CHAPTER TWENTY

Tanaka had finally got a response from Blain. She'd suggested a lunchtime meeting at Café Muse. He didn't really have time to waste on fraternising with the reporter, but he did want to spell out some home truths to her. Yoshitake, after all, had insisted he haul her over the coals.

The Master and his girlfriend fussed over them — insisting their lunch should be on the house. 'I'm so proud that someone I introduced to you, Tanaka-san, should have broken the story that is leading all the news bulletins. I told you she was good.' Tanaka watched Blain give the Master a cheeky smile. Tanaka himself said nothing to the man — the café owner was totally oblivious to the detective's disapproval.

'You wanted to see me, I believe, Tanaka-san,' said Blain, studying her steaming bowl as though she didn't want to meet his gaze.

He decided to reply in English. At least then, the Master would be unlikely to understand. It wasn't his fault everything had gone wrong. He was a kind man — Tanaka liked him. 'Your story has caused a lot of problems for me, Blain. That

124

wasn't the point of us having any sort of a relationship. You were supposed to help me — you haven't. As a result, I'm afraid, I won't be able to extend you any further privileges. You will simply get the same press briefings as everyone else. I will treat you fairly, but you will receive no favours.'

'I don't want any favours.' He felt the young woman's dark eyes boring into his own. 'But I kept my side of the bargain. I received the information in that article from an independent source. I didn't break our agreement not to mention the neck wound, the suggestion of blood-letting. If I'd included those details, the story would have been even better. But I didn't want to let you down.'

Tanaka snorted, almost spitting out some of his noodles. 'I'd like to see it when you *do* let me down. Anyway, it's caused problems for me higher up the chain. That's why I won't be able to give you any more information. I still expect you to respect our agreement, however.' He held her eyeline. 'If those other details are reported by you, I could face the sack. It's that serious.'

'I understand. Now you are here, though, can I ask you some questions about the other missing girl?'

Tanaka paused before replying. Why should he trust her, despite her insistence that she hadn't broken their agreement? The answer was simple: he had more chance of controlling her, more chance of ensuring she didn't embarrass or undermine him further, if she felt she was in his debt. And if she felt he was still useful to her. So after a few seconds, he nodded his head. 'As long as my answers are kept strictly off the record, I don't have a problem with that.'

'I understand you have asked the father to come in and see you this afternoon. Is that correct?'

Tanaka banged down his spoon. The Master looked at him quizzically. 'Who told you that?'

'I can't reveal my sources I'm afraid. But is it true?'

Tanaka felt close to exploding. She was throwing things back in his face. He should have known that trying to cooperate with a journalist was a dangerous path. Perhaps in her determination and perseverance he'd seen the woman that — on the day of her birth — he'd envisaged his poor daughter Misaki might one day become. Despite his feelings of anger and betrayal, he tried to keep the emotion out of his voice. 'There are some aspects of the investigation that I am not prepared to talk about,' he said, flatly.

'So it's true?'

'Where do you get your information, Ms Blain? If one of my staff is leaking things to you, then his or her career will be very short-lived. Off the record, yes, it is true. In return, I want you to tell me where you got the information about the hostess club. No member of the press was given that. It can only have come from a leak within the Tokyo Metropolitan Police Department.'

He watched Blain sigh, and then screw up her face in concentration — as though she was debating with herself whether to give him the information or not.

'Look, it wasn't any of your staff, honestly. I've only just started at the press club — how would I have developed close enough contacts to have a mole feeding me information from your team? It's a ridiculous notion.'

Tanaka gave a slight bow of acknowledgement. What she said was true. 'Very well then, tell me how you did find out.'

'I will, but I would prefer you don't repeat it to anyone else. I have a contact whose friend is a hostess at that club, the Aphrodite-Go-Go. It was sheer luck.'

'Out of the thousands of hostess clubs in Tokyo...?'

'I know. I just struck lucky. Sometimes it happens. Perhaps now you can feel more at ease. It was someone who knows someone at the club who fed me the information, although I can't say who. I don't have a mole in your department. So you're unlikely to find yourself embarrassed again. And there is no reason for our relationship to end. I am sure we can still both help each other.'

'Time will be the proof of that, Ms Blain. As far as I'm concerned, you owe me one.'

CHAPTER TWENTY-ONE

Could Pascal Durand somehow be involved in the disappearance of his own daughter? It wasn't something Tanaka liked to contemplate. But it wasn't something he could ignore. Nishimura had highlighted a strange, possibly ritualistic element to Elin Granqvist's death: the use of flowers, possibly arranged around her body — living or dead. If Nishimura's fanciful sketch was anywhere near a true depiction of how Elin's body had been used, then Tanaka would bet his last yen that the culprit was Japanese. Cherry blossom — *sakura* — was such an integral part of Japanese life. But there were nagging details about Durand which made him a suspect too. The fact that he'd admitted visiting adult video booths, although he'd initially tried to hide it, had raised a question in Tanaka's mind. But the revelation that he'd visited the very club where Elin Granqvist worked, albeit briefly, was even more significant. From what Sergeant Izumi had said, the owners of the Aphrodite-Go-Go might be linked to the Yamaguchi-gumi branch of the Yakuza still involved in pornography. It was clear Pascal Durand needed — at the very least — to be given a severe shaking up. That was what Tanaka intended to do.

Tanaka had asked Durand to attend voluntarily. As far as the man knew, it would be to provide him an update on Marie-Louise's disappearance. Tanaka had other ideas.

The detective made sure he said very little to the Frenchman as he led him down to the interview room, followed by Izumi.

'We'll be able to talk in a moment,' was all Tanaka would say in response to the man's questions asking what was going on. He'd already briefed Izumi about his plan.

When they reached the interview room, Tanaka slammed the door behind them, then pointed — unsmiling — to where Durand should sit. The man probably thought that, for some strange reason, he was under arrest. That was exactly the impression Tanaka wished to convey.

'This looks like one of those rooms where you interview suspects,' said the Frenchman, nervously.

Tanaka shrugged. 'We do need to talk to you about certain matters, Mr Durand.'

'And I want to talk to you. You've been making a song and dance in the newspapers about the dead girl. I can understand that. It must be terrible for her parents. But why no mention of Marie-Louise? Surely this is a chance to raise the profile of your search?'

'Why do you think the two matters are connected, Mr Durand?' Tanaka had agreed with Izumi in advance that he would ask all the questions. Izumi's only role was to note down the answers and stare as sternly as possible at the Frenchman. To try to unnerve him. Just in case there was something he wasn't telling them. In any case, Izumi's French was non-existent, and his English barely any better. He was unable to ask any questions the Frenchman would understand. He was also unable to understand any answers — the notes in Japanese he was making were doodles. But Durand didn't know that.

'Well it stands to reason, doesn't it? Two teenage foreign girls, both go missing in the same period, both are interested in *kawaii* culture. Both were last seen in fashion shops.'

'As it happens, we do have our first link between the cases,' said Tanaka, pretending to consult his notes. Then he looked up and stared directly into the Frenchman's eyes. 'It's the Aphrodite-Go-Go hostess club.' Tanaka saw Durand try to disguise his panic. 'In Kabukicho — the red-light area. Are you familiar with that club, Mr Durand?'

'No,' said Durand, his eyes darting to the right, and upwards. Again, the classic sign of an untruth.

'That's odd, because your name is on their list of foreign clients. Out of all the many hostess clubs in Tokyo, it's strange you should find yourself at the only club where Elin Granqvist worked. Quite a coincidence, wouldn't you say, Mr Durand?'

'This is preposterous. Ridiculous. You're treating me as though I'm a criminal.'

'We're not, Mr Durand, I assure you. We're merely having a civilised conversation with you. If we were treating you like a criminal, you'd soon know it. So you don't deny you visited the Aphrodite-Go-Go?'

Durand's head slumped down on the desk, his eyes closed, hands holding the top of his head. Then slowly he met Tanaka's gaze, as he shook his head. 'I can't believe this. It's just a complete coincidence.'

'So you *did* go to the club?'

'Yes.'

'Therefore a moment ago, when you denied you'd been to the club, you were lying. You see our problem, Mr Durand.'

Durand's face turned fierce. He pointed his finger at

Tanaka, shaping it like a gun. 'Your problem is that my daughter is still missing. As far as I can see, you have no leads. Whether I went to a hostess club or not is irrelevant. You should be spending your time trying to find my daughter, not questioning me as though I'm the guilty party.'

The Frenchman's anger simply bounced off an unmoved Tanaka. The detective knew what it was like to lose a daughter. He didn't have to be told — especially by someone he didn't fully trust. He gazed levelly at Durand. 'Where was Marie-Louise when you went to the club? Presumably you didn't take her with you. Or did you?'

'Of course I didn't take her with me.'

'There's no "of course" about it, Mr Durand. It may interest you to know that we're looking into the links the club has to a Yakuza gang involved in the underground production of pornographic films. They've been known to use teenage western girls in them. So it was a very dangerous place to be visiting.'

Durand gave a long sigh. 'As I say, Marie-Louise wasn't with me that evening.'

'Did you want some more "me time", Mr Durand? Like you had at the porn video rental booths in Ikebukuro?' Tanaka knew he was being judgemental.

'Don't be ridiculous. There's nothing illegal about going to a hostess club.'

'I'm sure your wife would agree, Mr Durand. Has she arrived from Paris yet?'

'She's flying in tomorrow.'

'It will be interesting talking to her.' Tanaka couldn't help giving a little smirk. From the word go, he hadn't really warmed to Durand. He wanted to find the man's daughter, of course, that was part of his job. But he had no compunction in making Durand feel uncomfortable along the way. And — of course — there was always an outside chance that his involvement was deeper than he admitted. 'Anyway, you still haven't told us where Marie-Louise was that evening.'

'She wanted to visit a maid café, somewhere in Akihabara. She insisted she was happy going on her own.'

'And so you let a seventeen-year-old girl go there at night, alone, while you visited the hostess club.'

'That's not how it was.'

'It seems that way to me, Mr Durand. Anyway, that's all the questions I have — for now. You're not planning on leaving Tokyo in the next few days, are you?'

Durand got to his feet. For a moment, Tanaka thought the Frenchman was going to punch him. Then he seemed to think better of it.

'Sergeant Izumi will see you out. We'll stay in touch, don't you worry.'

CHAPTER TWENTY-TWO

The next day's splash, Blain hoped, would be equally as effective as today's. In her interview with him, Durand had played into her hands — criticising the police for not doing enough to find Marie-Louise, questioning why they hadn't publicly linked her case to that of the dead Swedish teenager. More to the point, he'd agreed to give Blain first bite of any other leads he became aware of, and not to give interviews to other Japanese newspapers, as long as she made sure his comments got prominent coverage.

There had been more back-slapping and congratulations from Yamamoto and Hasegawa — they were convinced the *Tōkei Shimbun* had another winning lead story. It gave Blain the chance to steal away from the office slightly early, to visit somewhere Durand had mentioned in his interview; somewhere Blain hadn't included in her written story: The Purr-effect Maid Café in Akihabara. Apparently, Marie-Louise had visited there on her second night in Tokyo — on her own, and with her father's blessing.

. . .

If Kabukicho had its sleazy side, parts of Akihabara — certainly at night — were in many ways more sinister to Blain's mind. The Purr-effect Café could only be accessed through what had become known as 'schoolgirl alley' — a narrow street where schoolgirls, or older young women dressed as schoolgirls — tried to sell their services to passing men. It wasn't prostitution — sex was usually not on offer, from what Blain could gather. Some of the girls were simply handing out flyers for various maid cafés, one of the more innocent outlets of anime culture. But some of the girls really were high-school girls — trying to tempt businessmen into 'walking dates', where money would change hands simply for a few minutes walking round and hand-holding or chatting over a cup of coffee.

Blain saw one of the girls start to approach her. She was pretty in a doll-like way, not unlike a slightly younger version of Haruka. She tried to hand Blain a leaflet, advertising some sort of dating service.

'I'm a girl myself,' said Blain. 'And I don't date girls.' The first part of her statement was true. The last, a lie. Blain smiled to herself.

'Oh! *Sumimasen*,' said the girl, giggling and holding her hand over her mouth before moving on to her next potential customer.

After another few yards, she spotted the billboard for the Purr-effect Café: half-a-dozen girls, pictured on a poster in French maid outfits, much like many of the other maid cafés. The difference at the Purr-effect was the maids all looked to be wearing stick-on white whiskers with cat-ear headbands. It seemed to be on the second and third floors of a multi-storey building.

Blain climbed the steps and entered the café. She was immediately shown a table — and decided to pretend she was a customer, rather getting straight to the business of what she wanted. It would give her a chance to assess things.

She ordered a green tea and rice ball cake in the shape of a cat. The maid who served her insisted on being called by her character name before she would agree to do anything. It was tiresome, but if that was what it took, Blain was prepared to play along.

But when the girl came back with her order, Blain beckoned her close to whisper in her ear. 'I'll pay for this, don't worry, but I've not actually come as a customer. I want to see the manager.' She got out her reporter's ID card and showed it to the girl. The waitress feigned disappointment, but asked Blain to wait — she'd see if the manager was available. A few moments later, she returned to the table, and led Blain out to the back, past the kitchen, and down the corridor to an office. The maid knocked on the door.

'Here is the reporter who wanted to see you, Master.' Then she gave a curtsy and showed Blain into the room.

The man indicated a chair in front of his desk, facing him, and Blain sat down.

'Normally,' he said, 'you would require an appointment to get to see me. What is it I can help you with?'

'My name's Holly Blain, I'm a reporter with the *Tōkei Shimbun* newspaper.' Blain gave a slight bow and handed over her business card with two hands. The café owner returned the gesture with his own card. 'Kaneko Kin. I'm the owner of the Purr-effect Café.'

Blain produced a photo of Marie-Louise from her wallet. 'I'm looking into the disappearance of this French girl, Marie-Louise Durand. I believe she visited this café last week, Kin-san.'

'Lots of western girls visit this café.' Then he took the

photo from Blain's outstretched hand. 'Yes, I remember her. She was looking for work.'

'Work? She was only supposed to be in Tokyo for a few days.'

'That surprises me. She had been in contact with us from France even before she arrived. She gave me the impression she was getting a working holiday visa and would be available for up to a year's work.'

'Did you take her on?'

'She was supposed to be coming back next week for an unpaid trial shift. Then I was going to check her paperwork and make a decision. You say she's disappeared? Are the police involved?'

Blain nodded. 'Perhaps you ought to try to talk to them. Otherwise I expect they will be paying you a visit.'

'Why? I have done nothing wrong.'

'I'm not suggesting you have, Kin-san. But as well as Marie-Louise going missing, you may have seen the news.'

'I haven't had chance to read a paper or watch the news. Why?'

'Because a girl of the same age — a Swedish girl — has just been found dead.'

The revelation that Marie-Louise had been seeking work in Tokyo — apparently without the knowledge of her father — was a shock to Blain. Could her disappearance simply be a way of putting distance between herself and her father, in the knowledge that otherwise he would force her to go back to France to continue her schooling? There were too many imponderables. What Blain needed to do was gradually work her way back into the confidence of Tanaka, in the hope of staying ahead of the other reporters covering the investigation. But as she left the café and descended the stairs, she realised that was probably a forlorn hope. Coming up the other way was Tanaka and his deputy — presumably following the same lead as her. She'd got there first. As they passed each other in the stairwell, Tanaka's scowl and failure to greet her told her all she needed to know about the chances of getting back into his good books. Her story the next day — based on her interview with Pascal Durand — was likely to take his mood from sour to apoplectic.

CHAPTER TWENTY-THREE

He followed the procession of tourists as though he was one of them — taking photos of the *sakura* with his smartphone, framing the magnificent white castle with the blossoms, even though he'd already got the specimens he needed safely stored in his rucksack. The *Shirasagijo* — the white heron castle — looked at its most majestic at this time of year. The security official had looked at him quizzically during the bag search, asking if he'd taken the samples from within the castle grounds — they were same varieties, after all: Somei Yoshino, Yamazakura, and Shidarezakura. He insisted that no, they weren't; they were from his private collection. For a moment, he thought the official would summon her superior. But he knew it wasn't what they were supposed to be searching for. Their main target was would-be terrorists — he was hardly going to kill anyone with a few samples of cherry blossom, was he?

As he climbed the floors of the keep, he kept half a look out amongst the tourists — Japanese and European — for someone of the correct complexion, but that wasn't the main reason he was here. It was more a nostalgia trip. He remembered making this exact same climb as a boy, although now the castle looked finer — it had been magnificently restored, both inside and out. Here, he was inside the body of the giant bird. That had been his excitement as a boy, with his parents — when all three of them were happy. Before it all happened.

From the outside, the winged floors of the wooden castle, in their brilliant whiteness, looked like a bird taking flight — a heron or egret. And so, he'd imagined that by climbing up inside the keep, staircase after staircase, floor after floor, he was first in the bird's stomach and then in its brain.

And when he'd looked out of the highest windows all those years ago, lining up his eyes with the wide main avenue which bisected the town, he'd imagined the great bird swooping down and coming in to land. That he was somehow controlling it, like some fantastical computer game.

He reacquainted himself with the view now, his breathing slowing as the memories took over. It was quite as glorious as before. He soaked in the view for minutes on end, until someone nudged him, wanting him out of the way so they could see for themselves. For a second, he was angry and was going to remonstrate about being disturbed. But as he turned, he realised the girl who'd nudged him was perfect. Skin almost as pale as the Swede, red hair in ringlets, eyes made up like his favourite J-pop stars. He wanted to reach out and caress her skin, to inhale her scent more closely. A waft of it entered his nostrils as he brushed past her. He found himself wanting to repeat the contact, but he knew he couldn't. It didn't do to be too obvious. She was on her way up to the top of the big bird too. He would wait in the shadows, then, when she moved to the final floor and the prayer room, he would follow her.

She was like a delicate flower. Her movements were easy,

relaxed. Confident in her own skin even though she was in a foreign land. And she was curious. He liked that. From his vantage point, pretending to read an information board about the castle's history, he watched her head lighthousing round the room. She kept glancing at a Japanese youth about her own age. The man could see the spark of attraction between the two of them and wished that sometimes those sort of looks would be trained on him. They never were.

The girl moved towards the ladder. He shoved a couple of elderly Japanese ladies out of the way to make sure he was next. Close to her. Watching her in the too-tight jeans, as her feet moved up each rung. He could imagine how she looked from the front too. He found himself getting excited. The blood racing round his body, strengthening him. His lungs feeling constricted, tight, as though he couldn't breathe. And yet he so wanted to breathe deeply.

To smell her.

Her fragrance.

He wanted to touch too. But he couldn't. Not yet. Not this one. He had to exercise control. That was what set him apart.

He said his prayer in the prayer room and wrote out his message on the *ema* — the votive tablet. It was a simple wish which he hoped the *kami* or spirits would be able to grant. To be reunited with his mother and father, in happy times, like they'd shared here in Himeji. That's why he'd come here. He would build something as a tribute too — but that would have to wait. He would need to be patient. Until all the tourists had gone. Including the girl. He felt sad about that — but she would have to go too.

He wasn't sure what the sacks were there for. Perhaps the priests or shrine workers collected the votive tablets in them at the end of the day for a mass burning. Or perhaps they had been discarded after new *ema* had been brought to the small shrine. Whatever, they would serve his purpose. He would wait here. And then — at the end of the day — he would hide under the sacking. Until it was time.

As he waited, he kept the image of the girl with the strawberry blonde ringlets in his head. She would inspire him. He was doing it for her — and for his mother and father.

When he was sure everyone had gone and that he'd escaped the closing checks by the officials, he set to work. He'd brought a high-powered torch but didn't really want to use it unless he had to — the light from the top of the castle would have alerted any security guards below. He'd checked earlier in the day that the room he planned to use had no obvious CCTV cameras. He needed to do this in secret.

It was a clear night and would be a lovely day the next day. He could imagine how beautiful the cherry blossoms surrounding the castle would look. But he could not afford to stay and admire them. He used the moonlight streaming through the window to highlight his work, making the best of the materials he'd carefully packed in the rucksack. The stems, the blossoms, the flowers. Removing leaves, even the blossom itself, in places — to get the correct feel, to ensure sufficient *Ma* — sufficient negative space.

When he'd completed his work, he erected it in front of the shrine.

Everything led to the focal point.

The place where, some day, a young woman, or girl, would be. Her beauty augmenting the arrangement. The girl he'd followed to the top of the tower would have made a beautiful centrepiece.

Instead, the focal point was the emptiness.

This time, he'd allowed the girl to go, like a bird released from a cage — free to fly and take her beauty elsewhere.

But he felt he'd made the wrong decision.

It sat uneasily with him.

To be a proper tribute to his mother, she — or one very like her — needed to be there.

CHAPTER TWENTY-FOUR

Tanaka knew as soon as he saw Blain coming out of the maid café in Akihabara that the next day's newspaper headlines were likely to get him into even more trouble. Infuriatingly, she seemed to be ahead of the game. She claimed it was down to luck and fortuitous connections. Tanaka still found this hard to believe. He still suspected a leak somewhere in his department and his mind lingered on that covering he'd seen on Izumi's arm.

His foreboding about the newspapers wasn't misplaced. He was up early again — out of the house before Miho and the boys were even awake, grabbing the papers from the kiosk outside Sendagi station. It was the *Tōkei Shimbun* he turned to first.

MISSING GIRL'S FATHER SLAMS POLICE: 'DOES ANOTHER GIRL HAVE TO DIE?'
EXCLUSIVE

By Crime Reporter Holly Blain

The father of a French teenager missing for several days says Tokyo police have failed to take seriously his fears that her case may be linked to that of the 'Otaku' hostess death.

The search for Mr Pascal Durand's 17-year-old daughter, Marie-Louise, is being handled by the same team investigating the death of Swedish teenager Elin Granqvist, whose body was found dumped at a Shinagawa refuse plant.

In an exclusive interview with the Tōkei Shimbun, *Mr Durand said: 'My fear is that police are waiting for another girl to die before they take my concerns seriously. The latest developments gave the police a chance to give my daughter's disappearance a higher profile. They haven't done that.'*

The story continued for several more paragraphs, but Tanaka had seen enough. He found his hands repeatedly clenching around the pile of papers. This would not go down well with Superintendent Yoshitake, particularly after the furore over the previous day's story.

As Tanaka stomped into the metro station, he felt his mobile phone vibrate in his pocket. It was probably Yoshitake about to give him an earful. He took the phone out and looked at the display. It wasn't his boss — it was Izumi.

'Two things, Tanaka-san.'

'What?' grumbled Tanaka as he held the phone to his ear.

'Presumably you've seen the *Tōkei Shimbun*?'

'Yes, Izumi. But no blame can be attached to us this time. We can't prevent her talking to Durand.'

'Let's hope Superintendent Yoshitake feels the same way, Inspector.'

'What was the other thing, Izumi?'

'The flowers.'

'What about them?'

'Remember you asked me to put out a national alert asking for any reports of suspicious deaths where the body might have been adorned by flowers? Well, something's come back.'

'What?'

'Something from Himeji, in Hyōgo Prefecture.'

'I know where Himeji is, thank you, Izumi. What is it exactly?'

'A photograph emailed through by Himeji police station. It's slightly odd. You need to see it. And I think we need to go there. It would have the advantage of getting us away from Superintendent Yoshitake too.'

'A photograph of what?'

'A flower arrangement, Tanaka-san. But what's odd is it looks almost exactly like the sketch Inspector Nishimura drew for you at the morgue.'

Tanaka felt a lightness in his chest. He tried to swallow. Did that mean another girl had died? Was it Marie-Louise? Tanaka looked around — other commuters were in earshot, he wasn't going to ask the question here. For Izumi to feel they needed to travel all that way, it must be something big. 'Have you checked if a pool car is available, Izumi-kun?'

'It would take too long by car, boss. I've sorted out travel warrants for us on the Shinkansen. Meet me at Tokyo Station. It doesn't leave until 6.50am — so we might have time for a quick breakfast to talk things through. I've printed out the photo and will bring it with me.'

As the Shinkansen sped south, Tanaka studied the photo once more. He'd almost abandoned the trip when he realised a key element that was present in Nishimura's drawing was missing here — there was no centrepiece. No body. Just empty space.

Why were they going all the way to Himeji to study something that was little more than a flower arrangement? He would have a hard time justifying it to Superintendent Yoshitake. He'd already torn Izumi off a strip — but really there was no one to blame but himself.

His sergeant looked shame-faced. 'Sorry, boss. I sort of thought I'd already told you — but clearly I hadn't.'

'No, it's my fault, Izumi-kun. Anyway, we'd better just hope that this somehow does produce a new lead. Otherwise Yoshitake will certainly read us the riot act at the very least.'

Uttering the superintendent's name seemed to magically bring his smartphone to life, ringing and buzzing — with Yoshitake's face and name flashing up. Tanaka could see the other passengers looking round in disapproval. He'd go to the end of the carriage and ring back rather than risk a conversation here in the open. In fact, it was probably best to lock himself in the toilet if one was free.

Once the toilet door was closed, he rang his superior officer.

'You were trying to get hold of me, sir?'

'Where are you, Tanaka?'

'Following a new lead, sir.'

'I didn't ask *what* you were doing, I asked you *where* you are.'

'I see. I'm on a train, Yoshitake-san, about to visit the scene of an incident which may be linked to our inquiry.'

'You're trying my patience, Tanaka. Where!'

'Somewhere west of Tokyo. I'm not sure exactly.' Tanaka knew if he revealed he was with Izumi on what was almost certainly a wild-goose chase to Himeji — nearly six hundred kilometres west of the capital — his boss would blow a fuse.

'Have you seen *Tōkei Shimbun*'s piece *this* morning?'

'I have, Yoshitake-san. But it's certainly not my fault this time. We can't prevent the Frenchman talking to the press.'

'Yes, but we can try to find his daughter to take the sting out of things.'

'I'm sorry, reception is very bad on this train, sir. If you can hear me, I hope to be back in the office this evening. As I say, things are progressing and we're chasing a new lead.'

'Don't use that "bad reception" trick on me, Tanaka. I won't—'

'Sorry, sir. I can't hear you anymore. Sir? Sir?'

'You can hear me perfectly well, Tanaka.'

'Sorry, sir. I'm closing the call now.'

'What sort of mood is he in?' asked Izumi.

'Well, let's put it this way. He's seen Blain's story by now. What sort of a mood do you think that would put him in, Izumi-kun?'

'What did he say?'

'Unfortunately, the line was very bad. I had to close the call down as I couldn't hear him properly.'

'That's strange,' said Izumi. 'Normally mobile reception on Shinkansens is perfect.'

Tanaka didn't bother answering his sergeant and instead opened his newspaper and began to complete its *nanbāpurēsu* — the *sudoku* number puzzle.

They'd phoned ahead and two detectives from Himeji police station were there to greet them when their train arrived. Tanaka looked at the station clock: it had just moved on to 10am. Six hundred kilometres in little more than three hours — no wonder the nation was proud of its bullet trains.

Having made their greetings with bows, the Himeji

policemen took them out to a squad car, and both the Tokyo detectives climbed inside.

Tanaka and Izumi were ushered past the queues at the entrance. A notice had been erected saying that opening to the public had been delayed until 11.30am because of a security incident. Tanaka just hoped that what had been found merited the delay.

'We'll have to climb all the way to the top, I'm afraid,' said the senior Himeji detective, who'd introduced himself as Inspector Honda Shigematsu. He pointed up to the majestic castle keep. 'I hope you're both fit.' Tanaka glanced over at Sergeant Izumi — he wasn't so sure about his deputy, but the exercise would do him good.

'What time did you book for our train back to Tokyo, Izumi?'

'I didn't book anything, Tanaka-san,' said the sergeant, already panting from the gentle incline to the keep. 'But the quickest train is at just after quarter to three this afternoon. It will get us back to Tokyo a little before 6pm. There are usually plenty of unreserved seats, apparently.'

Yoshitake would still be at the office by then. He was early in and late to leave — and expected all his staff to follow his example.

By the time they reached the top floor shrine of the castle keep, Izumi was doubled over and almost hyperventilating, much to the amusement of the local officers.

'You Tokyo policemen need to get out a bit more — get a bit more exercise,' said Shigematsu. 'And not just in the flesh-pots of Kabukicho.'

Tanaka bristled at the suggestion. He knew that was the provincial view of Tokyo detectives — that they were chained to their desks until the end of the day, and then let their frustrations loose in hostess bars and massage parlours. It was a stereotypical image that Tanaka resented. He was a family man, kept himself fit, and the whole point of coming here to Himeji was to see this potential crime scene for himself — although he wasn't sure any crime had actually been committed.

The shrine and its surroundings had been sealed off by police tape. If it stayed like this for the whole day, the visitors patiently queuing at the entrance would feel short-changed. For many, the whole point would be to say a prayer, make an offering at the small shrine, and then ring the prayer bell.

Directly in front of the bell was what they'd come to see.

A strange, giant frame of flowers. A thing of beauty, ringed by very pale, almost white cherry blossom. Tanaka found his eyes being drawn towards the centre of the arrangement, even though there was nothing there. As though the nothingness in itself meant something. Unless something — some living thing — was indeed meant to be there, and this strange flower arranger had, thankfully, been disturbed in the middle of his work.

'When was it discovered, Shigematsu-san?'

'By the night security guard, at about 4am, Tanaka-san. We'd only just seen the bulletin from Tokyo asking all forces to look out for flower arrangements at any possible death scenes or scenes of crime. It was a request that — shall we say — raised a few eyebrows. Although there is no apparent crime here, other than perhaps breaking and entering, or disturbing the sanctity of a shrine, we nevertheless thought it was worth alerting you. We didn't really expect you to come all this way to look for yourselves.'

Tanaka glanced round the rest of the room. 'And there is no CCTV up here?'

'Up here, no. I've suggested to the castle authorities they might like to rethink that. However, we do have some blurry CCTV images of who we think may be the culprit.'

Feeling the tendons in his neck tighten in anticipation, Tanaka watched the Himeji inspector pull his smartphone from his pocket. It was one of the newer, large-screen versions — unlike Tanaka's own basic, outdated model.

Shigematsu found the video then turned the phone towards Tanaka and pressed the play icon.

'We think he deliberately waited for the guard to make his rounds, then as the guard opens the keep door, he slips out.'

As Tanaka viewed the grainy image, his excitement mounted. He had to bite his lip to avoid shouting in glee. Although the video was far from clear — it was clear enough. A thin, awkward-looking man, dressed all in black. And — despite the fact it was the middle of the night, and the only light was from the moon — he was wearing sunglasses. This was his man.

'I want everywhere that he may have left fingerprints dusted and checked, please, Shigematsu-san. Izumi and I will take away samples of the flowers and blossoms. Do you recognise them? Are they from the castle grounds?'

'I have checked that already, Tanaka-san. I can tell you quite categorically this cherry blossom is not from Himeji. The trees here are not quite as far advanced in bloom as yours in Tokyo — they have only just blossomed. These flowers were more open. I would hazard a guess they are from Tokyo itself, which tends to bloom earlier than here, or from further south.'

What did that mean? thought Tanaka. The man must have come all the way to Himeji for a reason. Yet it didn't seem as though — if he was indeed holding her captive — he'd brought Marie-Louise Durand with him. Perhaps that was a good thing. For now, it appeared she may have escaped the same fate as Elin Granqvist — being the lifeless centre of one of this strange man in black's flower arrangements.

CHAPTER TWENTY-FIVE

When she had started out on local newspapers in the UK, Blain had been shown the art of literal 'ambulance chasing' by her alcoholic news editor. The phrase had come to be associated with lawyers chasing accidents and disasters, trying to sign up clients to fight for compensation — out of which the lawyers themselves would take a hefty cut. But in its purest form, when there was a dearth of other news, ambulance-chasing *Scarborough Gazette*-style involved, quite literally, chasing ambulances, fire engines, and police cars. One particularly quiet afternoon, the news editor had shown her the ropes. They waited in his car by the fire station, drinking coffee after coffee, reading books and newspapers, on the off-chance there might be a call out. They struck lucky — a single fire-engine hared off from the station amid a blare of sirens, and the news editor sped after it, keeping in the tender's slipstream as it dodged the traffic. The resulting story — a frightened kitten stuck up a tree — was never going to be a world-beater. But it did give them a very cute front-page photo-story, and Blain got her first by-line.

Her plan for ambulance-chasing Tokyo-style involved staking out Tanaka's home and following him at a distance. She'd planned to get there for 5.30am in case he was an early riser, but an early-hours visit from Haruka had left her exhausted. She slept in. It was pure chance that, as she was rushing up, Yanaka Ginza to get in position outside Tanaka's house, she spotted him — head down — walking quickly towards her. Blain ducked into a side-alley before he could see her, waited until he'd gone past, and then followed him to Sendagi metro station. She had to hang around again, carefully hidden, as he made a phone call. Then eventually she followed him down to the Chiyoda line trains. The likelihood was, of course, that Tanaka would simply lead her seven stops down the line to Kasumigaseki station. If he did, it was less than a kilometre for Blain to walk on to the *Tōkei Shimbun*'s head office. Nothing would have been lost.

At first, that's what seemed to be happening. Blain kept watch on him from the other end of his carriage, carefully hiding herself behind other standing passengers — plentiful even at this early hour thanks to Japan's long-hours culture. But after four stops, Tanaka surprised her by getting up and going to stand by the exit door. He was getting off at the next stop — Nijubashi-Mae.

Blain continued to follow. Tanaka seemed preoccupied, so she thought there was little chance of him spotting her. She realised from the direction he was walking, he was heading for Tokyo's mainline rail station. The question was where next? Could she find out — and was she prepared to follow?

She wasn't quite sure how she'd done it, but she was proud of herself nonetheless. She'd followed Tanaka to a café by the entrance to the Shinkansen platforms, where he was met by another, fatter man — the same one she'd seen the previous night with the inspector on the steps of the maid café in Akihabara. She could only assume they were planning to get a bullet train. The question was, where to? And how the hell could she find out without giving herself away?

Blain racked her brain for the answer. She spotted a hand-some-looking male backpacker checking a map and realised he might be her 'in'.

She approached him, first making sure she was out of the eyeline of the two detectives.

'Hi. Do you need any help finding where you are?'

'That sure is kind of you,' the young man replied in an American accent. 'But I'm fine. Are you some kind of tour guide or something?' He eyed Blain suspiciously.

She lowered her voice and handed him her *Tōkei Shimbun* business card. 'No, I'm a reporter, and I need a little help. You see those two guys in the café there?'

'What, the chubby one and the one who looks a bit like a university professor?'

Blain nodded. 'They're detectives, working on the same story as me. Now, how would you like to earn a bit of beer money by helping me for just a couple of minutes?' She got her wallet out and flashed a couple of thousand-yen notes.

'Well, listen,' he said, glancing at his watch. 'I got a bullet train to catch myself in twenty minutes. I don't want to miss it.'

'It will only take a minute.' She put on her best pleading look. 'Pretty please?'

'Go on, then. Sounds quite exciting, as long as I won't get in trouble with the police.'

At that moment, Blain could have kissed him. She was going through a girl-phase with Haruka at present — but with his long hair and southern drawl, the man was definitely her type. 'You won't, honestly.'

Blain explained what she wanted him to do: play the confused foreigner and ask them for information about his own bullet train. And then, in the same breath, find out where they were going. But he shouldn't make it obvious that he was pumping them for information, and, above all, he mustn't mention that Blain had put him up to it.

'Okay, Miss Holly Blain. That seems straightforward enough. How many of those thousand-yen bills does that earn me?'

'One,' she said.

'No deal, miss.'

'Okay, two.'

He shrugged. 'Okay. You're on.'

'Once you've found out, meet me over there.' She pointed to a ticket machine, well out of sight of Tanaka and his deputy. 'Make sure you don't act suspiciously, and don't approach me if they move and can see us.'

The man nodded and winked at her. 'Okay, miss.'

Blain watched him walk up to the two detectives and then engage them in conversation. She could see Tanaka looking at his watch, as though he couldn't be bothered with the interruption. His deputy, though, was more enthusiastic. She moved towards the ticket machine meeting point.

After a couple of minutes, the American was back.

'Well, that was easy,' he said.

'Where is it they're going?'

'Well, now. It would be remiss of me to tell you without getting my payment first.'

Blain peeled off two one-thousand-yen notes and handed them over. 'So?'

'They're off to Himeji.'

'Himeji! Are you sure that's what they said?'

'Yup. Because I said, "That's got a mighty fine white castle, hasn't it?" I'm planning on going there myself in a few days once the cherry blossom is fully out. It's supposed to make for some fantastic photos. So yes, I'm absolutely sure they're off to Himeji. Unless they were spinning me a line.'

'Why would they?'

'Why indeed? And one more bit of info for free. They're not planning on staying. There and back in a day, they said. So, I said, you won't get chance to visit that castle, then. Then one of them said, oh yes, that's exactly where they're going. I think that was the junior one. His boss seemed annoyed he was blabbing too much and shut him down after that. So what are you going to do yourself? Are you off to Himeji now too, to follow them?'

Blain nodded.

'Hmm. Well, it was lovely to meet you. I'm almost tempted to come there myself, but I'm heading to see the snow monkeys before all the snow goes, so I'm off to Nagano.' He got her business card out again that he'd stuffed in his pocket and peered at it. 'But I might give you a call, Miss Holly Blain, when I'm back in Tokyo if you're up for a drink one evening?'

Blain laughed. It might be fun. 'Okay, you do that. Sorry, I didn't catch your name?'

'That's because I didn't give it. But it's Brett.'

'Well, thank you, Brett. Enjoy the snow monkeys.'

Blain toyed with the idea of getting Yamamoto's permission to follow Tanaka and his deputy to Himeji. But her news editor might have raised objections: if Blain was discovered trailing them, the *Tōkei Shimbun*'s membership to the TMPD press club might be revoked. There was also the danger that Yamamoto could get another reporter to contact Himeji police and try to find out any relevant information directly — which in itself had the danger of alerting Tanaka that Blain and her newspaper knew about this fresh Himeji angle.

It was better to watch and learn. She bought her ticket for the next service that stopped at the city — then surreptitiously followed Tanaka and his deputy to the platform, keeping herself hidden until they boarded the train. Then she made sure she sat several carriages away from them. For the next three hours or so, she could relax. If the American's information was correct, and there was no reason why it shouldn't be, there was nothing for her to do until all three of them arrived. Then, it might get more difficult. But the fact that they were going to the castle, and the fact that the castle itself was a shortish walk from Himeji station, would simplify matters.

It did become much more complicated at Himeji. Tanaka and his deputy were collected in a squad car by the local police — there was no way Blain could follow them. Instead, she waited in the — thankfully short — taxi queue for her own chauffeur-driven ride. But her 'ambulance chase', such as it was, was at an end. She'd lost them — she just hoped the American's information about their destination here was accurate.

Once she'd got out of the taxi, she joined the procession of tourists snaking over the bridge crossing the moat and then through the outer walls of the castle grounds. She didn't really know where she was heading, but at least at the main entrance to the castle proper she would be able to ask questions. And perhaps even find out what had brought the two Tokyo detectives here.

. . .

At the main entrance, it was clear something was wrong. Various nationalities of tourists were queuing up and complaining that the castle keep — the highlight of any visit here — hadn't opened on time. Blain checked the time on her smartphone. 10.20am. The noticeboard said normal opening hours were 9am — yet according to another hastily printed notice pinned over it, the keep wasn't allowing anyone in until 11.30am. The answer as to why was surely what had brought Tanaka all the way from Tokyo. Had there been another death, another killing?

Blain tried to find out what was going on from the taciturn security guard. He wasn't playing ball. She flashed her reporter's ID and asked to see his superior.

Another official came out, and Blain could see the suspicious look on her face as she examined the ID. Blain needed a reason to persuade her to talk. 'We've had complaints to the office that the castle is not opening when it should. My editor wants me to do a story. But I think that might unfairly sully the reputation of the administration here. I'm sure it's nothing to do with you. I'd heard it was a police matter.'

'*Okyaku-sama*,' the woman said with a pained smile. 'This way if you please.' She clearly didn't want Blain causing any trouble. But, at the same time, she moved the rope barrier to the side and gestured her through to the administration offices. Inside the building, she showed her into a smaller office.

'I'm sorry for that,' said the woman, 'but I didn't want you talking about "police matters" in public. We're having enough trouble with the crowd as it is. Even though it's not yet full *sakura* season here, we're still very busy today. But it's only a temporary delay. Why would your readers be interested in that? There is no story here.'

'I believe you,' said Blain. 'But I have to have a good reason to tell my editor so that we can kill the story, and make sure that a critical report doesn't go in the paper. I'd heard that a couple of detectives have come down from Tokyo to investigate.'

The woman sighed slowly and cocked her head. 'I cannot confirm anything.'

'I appreciate the need for discretion,' said Blain. 'But if I'm not told what's actually going on, there's a danger my editor will want me to speculate. And the two detectives who've arrived are involved in a murder hunt in Tokyo.' It was a small lie — there had as yet been no confirmation of cause of death for Elin Granqvist. And the police still hadn't released the toxicology results — if they ever intended to. 'If we don't know what's actually happened, we're likely to speculate that there may have been a murder here.'

There was a sharp intake of breath from the woman. 'It's nothing like that. Alright, I will tell you. But you didn't get it from me.'

Blain listened with growing incredulity as the woman explained that all it was was some sort of flower arrangement which had been constructed illegally overnight in front of the shrine at the top of the castle keep.

'And there was no indication of any body having been found?'

The woman shook her head. 'No. We assume there was a break-in. Though we can't understand how. The culprit let himself out as the security guard opened the main door to start his early morning rounds.'

'At what time?'

'Soon after 4am.'

'Did the guard see the culprit leave?'

'No.'

'So how do you know he did — and at that time?'

'Because the main gate is the only area with CCTV. We saw him on the CCTV footage — we've passed that to the police.'

'Can I have a look at it?' asked Blain.

'What?'

'Can I see this clip?'

The woman frowned. 'Why should I let you do that?'

'Because it will be the final thing which will clear up this matter. To make sure no negative story about the castle is printed in the newspaper.' Blain was making an offer she didn't intend to keep.

The woman gave another long sigh, as though Blain was testing her patience. 'Alright then, but never tell anyone that it was me who showed you it.' She moved to her desktop computer and then drew up a stool next to her own chair.

She called up a video clip, but Blain asked her to pause just before she hit the play icon. The reporter got out her phone to make her own copy of the video.

'You can't do that,' said the official. 'It will be obvious where you've seen it.'

'I'm going to zoom right in,' said Blain. She showed the woman the framing on her phone. 'Look, you can't see it's your office, or that it's your computer. I could have got this from the local police.'

The woman shrugged and finally pressed play.

As Blain watched, she felt as if her blood had turned to ice.

A thin, ungainly, thirty-something man dressed all in black. An old-fashioned look like a fifties or sixties pop star. And dark glasses. The middle of the night, but he was wearing dark glasses.

She immediately recognised both his dress and the distinctively awkward gait of his walk.

She'd seen him before.

When this all started.

At the Hello Happy Princess meet and greet.

The man with the candy-coloured clown.

He was also the *Otaku* who'd been at Aphrodite-Go-Go — the one smitten with Elin Granqvist. Of that she was sure.

CHAPTER TWENTY-SIX

As they sped on the Shinkansen back to Tokyo, Blain's mobile number flashed up as a missed call on Tanaka's phone. He regretted giving her his personal number. The young woman was never going to give him any peace unless he resumed cooperating with her. Then a text arrived from her, and he felt a flush of heat and anger.

We need to talk. I know about Himeji. I'll be at Café Muse at 8pm. I'll buy you dinner. HB

How? How in God's name does she know about that? His anger was building into a fury.

'What's wrong, Inspector?' asked Izumi.

Tanaka was annoyed with himself for letting his feelings show on his face. 'Nothing, Izumi.'

'It wasn't a message from Superintendent Yoshitake, was it?'

Tanaka slammed his phone down on the bullet train table. 'I said it was nothing, Izumi-kun.'

. . .

When they arrived back at TMPD headquarters, the guard on the door checking IDs handed Tanaka a message.

Tanaka, see me immediately you get back.
Just you, not Izumi.
Yoshitake.

It wasn't anything Tanaka hadn't been expecting. He wanted to see his superior too, wanted to try to clear the air. He never worked very well when there was a cloud of disapproval hanging over him. It just made him nervous.

'Tanaka,' thundered Yoshitake, angry spit flying out of his face at the same time as his words, 'why on earth have you and Izumi been on a day trip to Himeji, costing the department I don't know how much money and all to see some ridiculous flower arrangement. Have you finally lost what's left of your mind?'

Tanaka wiped his face. 'I felt we needed to see it first-hand.' He hadn't told Yoshitake where they were going or why. But the superintendent had obviously found out. The travel warrants obtained by Izumi would have given away their destination to anyone who'd bothered to check, and Yoshitake obviously had. The information about the flowers he must have got from Himeji police.

'Why? Why wasn't a photograph good enough? Why wasn't a phone call good enough? In this day and age, it would be easy enough to do a FaceTime or Skype call — you could have had a virtual look round it, without actually going there. Who's been looking after the investigation at this end? And

I've had the top brass moaning away in my ear about that reporter's latest bit of made-up nonsense.'

Tanaka sighed. If he didn't do something, it would get worse before it got better. Perhaps he ought to go to that meeting with Blain and pull her over the coals once more. 'I'm doing my best, Yoshitake-san.'

'Well, no more day trips unless you clear them with me first. In fact, no more swanning off at all. I want you here at headquarters during all normal office hours. If you have to go out to chase something up, you ask first. Understood?'

Tanaka rose to his feet and bowed. 'Of course, Yoshitake-san.'

Café Muse used to be his sanctuary — his Friday night, end of the week bit of 'me time'. Inadvertently, the Master — lovely man though he was — had changed all that by introducing him to Blain. Now, for Tanaka, it was almost a place to fear.

Arriving just after 8pm, he felt he'd been summoned by the reporter. There she was, sitting at her favourite corner table, studying her phone. She'd probably already filed her next day's report and, in it, included the Himeji lead and countless other things Tanaka would rather be kept quiet to avoid alerting the man they were hunting.

When she finally saw him, she gave a broad grin. He didn't return it.

'I'm glad you accepted my invitation,' she said. 'I'm buying.'

'I assure you I am not accepting your invitation, and I am not staying to eat with you. I've just come with a warning. If you print anything revealing where I've been today — or indeed anything about what's happened in Himeji — I will ensure your newspaper's press club membership is revoked. Do I make myself clear?'

'You might want to wait until you see what I have on my phone before you do anything hasty.'

She was scrolling through the photos on her phone. She found the one she was looking for and rotated the device to show him.

'What!' Tanaka found himself looking at the flower arrangement in the castle, in situ in front of the tiny shrine at the top of the keep. He was tempted to dunk the device in the girl's green tea — render it useless. But she was clever enough. She would have emailed herself a back-up copy, or already downloaded it back at her office. 'Where on earth did you get this?'

'From the authorities at Himeji castle. They showed me what they passed to the police there.'

'You cannot print this,' warned Tanaka. 'I've told you what will happen if you do.'

'And there's also this,' said Blain.

Tanaka watched in horror as the CCTV images rolled across Blain's screen. 'If you print or circulate either of those things, or — as I've said — include anything about the Himeji find, I will go even further than revoking your press club membership. I will bring charges against you — for inter-fering with a police investigation.'

'I don't think you really mean that — and I doubt very much whether the law allows you to do it, Inspector. But I *will* agree not to publish, with one important proviso.'

Tanaka gave a long sigh. His bluster had indeed been half bluff — and the young woman had called him out on it. 'What proviso?'

'I want us to go back to how we were when we were first introduced — with you keen to get information from me and me happy to help you. A kind of symbiotic relationship. We don't have to like each other. I get it that I'm not exactly your favourite person. But that doesn't stop us working together. And I've got a theory I wanted to thrash through with you.'

Holding his hands above his head, Tanaka leant back in his chair. It wasn't true that he didn't like her. In some ways, he admired her ability to be ahead of the game. He admired her headstrong nature and persistence. If baby Misaki had ever been lucky enough to reach adulthood, then he'd have been very proud if she'd turned out like Blain. Holding her head up in a male-dominated world and putting the other reporters to shame. It was just it was also causing difficulties for him, day after day, front-page splash after front-page splash. It was exhausting. Now she was almost blackmailing him. Still, maybe it was worth hearing what she had to say. He felt his stomach rumbling — he hadn't had a proper meal all day, just snacks on the run and on the train.

'I will let you buy me dinner. And I will listen to what you have to say. But I'm making no promises about any special favours.'

CHAPTER TWENTY-SEVEN

I t was one of his favourite games. He knew that — from his mother's point of view — it was simply to persuade him to pose in traditional clothes, so that she could take photographs of him. But he didn't mind. For him, it was an opportunity to spend intimate time with her. To admire her openly without it seeming peculiar. He loved his mother's costume. She looked so perfect, so elegant.

She let him watch her get ready at her dressing table, but she pretended he wasn't there. He wasn't allowed to talk to her — this was part of the ritual. Even before the point was reached, he too had to dress up.

That meant the formal *hakami* trousers, the *zori* sandals and white *tabi* socks, then the grey *haori* jacket. Finally, the *himo* — or ties. This was the only part his mother helped him with. He found the system of loops too complicated to follow.

'You'll have to learn to do it yourself, one day, Kelton-chan.'

He wished she wouldn't add the '-chan' — it sounded so girl-like and feminine. But he knew it was just his mother's way of being affectionate. And when she drew close to tie the *himo*, and he breathed in her perfume and womanly scent, he almost felt like he was in a dream that he never wanted to end. His mother was so beautiful, so perfect. One day, he would marry a woman exactly like her. He knew, too, that one day his mother would grow old and wizened. He could hardly believe it and didn't want it to happen. Somehow, he told himself, she would always be there for him, and always be as beautiful as she was now.

When he was ready, he sat obediently on the *tatami* floor, and watched his mother prepare in the mirror. From now on, she ignored him. She was in her own world. Transforming herself. Shedding the skin of her pupa, and becoming a magnificent, radiant butterfly.

First, she put her long hair up in a bun. He knew his father preferred it down, but he loved to see his mother's neck, her smooth pale skin — almost too pale for a Japanese woman. Then she began to apply wax to her face, neck, and chest. He especially liked the little thrill he got as she brushed her collarbones, just above the swell of her breasts. He wanted to offer to do it for her but knew that would break the spell.

Then it was time to stir the face powder into a glass of water till it became a stiff white paste.

She started to apply it with the brush, over all the areas she'd waxed. The only exceptions, the centimetre-wide strip of bare skin adjoining the hairline and — on the nape of the neck — two prongs of bare skin, pointing downwards, to the mysteries below. Her neck was so beautiful — the tingles were back, in his stomach, and below. He almost felt light-headed. As though he was in love. He supposed he was, although he knew it was wrong to love your mother that way.

Then she dabbed all the white areas with a sponge to pick up any excess moisture, before using *kona oshiroi* — the traditional white powder — on a fluffy make-up brush, applying it to the exact same areas.

She'd already covered up her eyebrows. Now — miraculously — they reappeared, drawn in, in heavy black, with a gentle arch.

Closing her eyes, she used a red make-up pencil on the outer corner of each eyelid. Red for danger, he thought. Red for excitement. Red for secrets — and this was a secret they shared, this little ceremony.

And it was red again for her lips. First just an outline and then filled in. Luscious, delicious red this time — but still dangerous to him.

Finally, her hair. And at last, he was allowed to help. For this part only.

He pulled her hair into four sections as she'd taught him, sectioning it off, caressing each section as he did. It had a silky, sensuous quality he loved. The sections at the back and top of the head were held up with hair clips, leaving hair hanging down on each side of his mother's head. His mother created loops with each of these, circular rings with spaces inside. Empty space — so important in flower arrangements too.

Under the top hair, she inserted a hair sponge to give more volume. An illusion. Like magic. The sponge completely covered so no one would know. Then there was more looping and shaping, so quick he lost track.

Then, as finishing touches, she added the flowers, the pins, the ornaments, and combs.

The end product was so beautiful he wanted to kiss her all over. But he knew he couldn't, and he knew he shouldn't even think those thoughts. Instead, he was required to go into the living room and wait at the table.

In the *tokonoma*, before the ceremony, his mother would

have prepared a new flower arrangement. Fresh flowers before each ceremony.

The waiting at the table was perhaps the most exciting time for him. There was an exquisiteness to the anticipation that gave him the same tingles he felt below when admiring her neck or watching her powder her chest. He remembered earlier times when they'd bathed together, and he'd asked about the berries on the end of her breasts. Could he taste one? She'd laughed an embarrassed laugh and said that he'd used to, as a baby, and that had been an enjoyable time for her. But they couldn't do that anymore, now he was a big boy — she wouldn't mind, but father would be angry.

When she was ready, she would call to him. He would leave the room. He'd see her shape through the rice paper screens — just a silhouette, like something from an old cartoon.

And then she would call him in.

At that first glimpse of her, in all her beauty, surrounded by the traditional equipment, it was like the air had been knocked from his lungs. Each time it was the same.

Then he would make himself comfortable, and he would drink. He didn't like the taste, he never had. He didn't like the smell. But he would drink her offering because it pleased her.

Because it was their special time together.

Because he wanted it never to end.

CHAPTER TWENTY-EIGHT

As soon as Tanaka said he would accept her offer to buy him dinner after all, she knew she had him in the palm of her hand. She didn't want to cheat him, she didn't want to ruin his investigation or get him into trouble with his superiors. But she did want to be at the heart of the investigation. She was ahead of the game so far, mainly through luck. It wouldn't last. She couldn't even pull her 'ambulance chasing' — or rather *policeman* chasing — trick again for fear of being discovered. This time she would have to play by his rules: that meant she had to prove her value to him.

'What is the common thread through all of this?' she asked him, as the Master and his girlfriend prepared their meal. Blain always had the same thing — tempura prawns to start, then chicken katsu. She needed to stay thin and wiry for the band. She had to have the right 'indie' look, otherwise they would get another guitarist, no matter her abilities. Her visits to the café, and the calorie-stuffed meals she opted for there, were her one culinary luxury.

'The man in black?' asked Tanaka.

'Yes. Maybe. Obviously, a key to it is identifying him and catching him.'

Tanaka laughed. 'If you're just going to tell me the obvious requirements of my job, I don't think this is going to go very far. You'll need to do better than that.'

Blain nodded. 'I wasn't thinking of him in particular. As you say, that's obvious. The common thread — in my view — is the flowers, the blossoms. They must have a significance for him.'

The detective sighed and twiddled with his spoon. 'Again, that is obvious.'

'The question is what is the significance? And why did he suddenly go to Himeji?'

'He was grandstanding?'

Blain turned up the corners of her mouth. Then she delved into her bag. 'I was looking at the *sakura* forecast for this year, and the pattern of blossoms.'

'Why?'

'Because I think there's a reason he went to Himeji, and I think there's a reason nothing really happened there. But we may not be so lucky next time.'

'And what is that reason?'

Blain turned the piece of paper she'd pulled out of her bag so that the detective could see it. 'This is the *sakura zensen* — the cherry blossom forecast. Everything's gone a little haywire this year. The late season cold snap has slowed everything down. Himeji, for example, was almost two weeks late coming into bloom.'

'I can't see what the relevance of all this is,' said Tanaka, a bored expression on his face. Blain looked over towards the Master — she hoped the food would arrive soon. It might help get Tanaka in a better mood, help to win him round.

'What if our mysterious man in black has a fairly lowly

job? He can take holiday, yes, but he has to request it in advance, and can't easily change it.'

'That's the case for most people, lowly job or not. I'm no different.'

'Okay, no. Neither am I. That aspect doesn't really matter. The point is, perhaps he's already booked his vacation time. And Himeji Castle is well known as a beautiful *sakura* site. So perhaps he was planning to be at Himeji for full bloom — for his flower arrangements — but then something wasn't quite right. Perhaps the flowers were only just opening.'

'Pah!' snorted Tanaka, shrugging his shoulders. She liked observing him. He had all these western mannerisms and was clearly only part-Japanese. Yet he sometimes — with his bows, and in the home life she'd seen — tried to be more Japanese than anyone else. 'But he still made his flower arrangement,' said Tanaka. 'If the Himeji blossom wasn't ready, it didn't stop him.'

Blain knew the detective was right. She also knew her theory didn't necessarily hold water. But she just needed him to cling on to a little part of it, see some merit somewhere. Enough to invite her back into his confidence. That was her sole aim. 'Okay, I might be wrong. But say I'm not.' She pointed to the *sakura zensen* forecast chart again. 'Where is there a famous place for *sakura* that is due to come into bloom next?' She gave him a big clue by hovering her finger next to the name of the city.

'Kyoto?' He shrugged again, but this time it appeared to Blain there was more interest. Maybe she was slowly winning him over. 'Perhaps. The Philosopher's Path is well known — the cherry trees run down each side. The Heian Shrine and the Okazaki canal running alongside. Marayuma Park is well known too, especially for *hanami* parties.'

'You're sounding like an expert now,' laughed Blain.

'Miho and I did a tour in the early days of our marriage, before we had children. Aha. Here's our food.'

It seemed like Tanaka was pleased about the interruption, as the Master brought them a large plate of tempura prawns to share. 'I hope she is helping you with information to solve your case, Tanaka-san.'

'I hope so, Master. I hope so.'

They ate in silence for a while. Blain allowed Tanaka to pick up the thread of the conversation — she didn't want to appear to be pushing things.

'Alright, Holly-san.' It was the first time he'd used her Christian name for a while — Blain took it as a good sign. 'Just for the sake of argument, let's assume you're correct. What do you suggest we do?'

Not just using her Christian name but talking in terms of 'we'. She was winning this battle. 'I think one or both of us needs to go to Kyoto, to see what we can pick up there — if anything. And I have one more idea.'

'What?' asked Tanaka, crunching on a prawn.

Blain finished her mouthful, savouring the firmness and the briny taste of the ocean that seemed to come with every bite. 'We know what this guy looks like.'

'If indeed he is the person involved in Elin Granqvist's death,' said Tanaka.

'And I understand why you haven't put out an image yet.'

'We may try to get something from the CCTV, although it is very grainy. We're just assuming it is the same man from his clothes and sunglasses. It is a big leap. With his eyes covered, it's very hard to identify him. I'm reluctant to put out any public appeal that makes him change his appearance. So far, we've limited our notifications to other police stations — all around the country.'

'Anyway,' said Blain. 'I have a friend who's a data scientist.'

'How's that relevant?'

'She's working on a programme that can identify people whose photos turn up in Facebook posts, Instagram, etcetera.'

'Okay. What about Line? That's the biggest site in Japan still, although I accept the others are growing.'

'It may include Line, too. I'm not sure — I think all the data on there may be private. The point is our man is very identifiable, isn't he? Some newspapers have dubbed him the "Otaku Killer", and he *is* an *Ot*—'

'How do you know?' said Tanaka, rapping his chopsticks on the table, suddenly more animated.

Blain immediately realised her error. She'd identified him in the Hello Happy Princess line-up all those days ago but hadn't let Tanaka know.

'I saw him. At a meet and greet for an idol group.'

'When was this, Ms Blain?' Tanaka was almost shouting now, an angry expression on his face. And he lapsed back into English. He was treating her more formally again — the window she'd prised open had been slammed shut again. 'And why didn't you tell me before?'

'I only realised when I saw the video from Himeji. The meet and greet was several days ago now — last Friday, the day we first met here.'

Tanaka immediately stood up, dragging his chair back with a screech. He pointed his finger into her face. 'You should have told me this. Here we are talking fanciful theories about cherry blossom forecasts and photographic recognition programmes. All the time you are withholding information of a much more important nature.' He pulled out his notebook and pen. 'Write down the name of this group, where the meet and greet was, who your contact for the press was. Now.'

She felt her face, neck, and ears burning. As though she was being told off by her father, rather than one adult to another. This had all gone horribly wrong. She tried to remember the name of her contact in Hello Happy Princess' management.

As she wrote, she half-saw Tanaka roll his eyes. 'You realise why this is so important, Ms Blain? He would almost certainly have had to register for this so-called "meet and greet". If you told me this straightaway, we could have saved ourselves a lot of trouble.'

'As I say, I only realised this afternoon when I saw the Himeji CCTV video. I haven't deliberately withheld information in any shape or form.'

Some of Tanaka's anger seemed to have dissipated. 'Perhaps. Anyway, I need a formal statement from you. Please come to see me at headquarters at 10am tomorrow morning.' With that, he turned to leave.

'Don't you want your meal?' she shouted after him, as the Master arrived with two *katsu*. But Tanaka had already slammed the door behind him.

The next day, Blain's mood went from bad to worse. As soon as she arrived at work, Yamamoto called her into his office then threw that morning's copy of the *Asahi Shimbun* at her.

'Well?' he asked.

She read their front-page headline.

'OTAKU KILLER' USED DATE-RAPE DRUG

'Oh God! They've gone and got the toxicology reports, while I was chasing up another lead.'

'I can see that,' Yamamoto said. 'The question is, why? Why've you missed it, and where the hell were you yesterday? I tried to ring you several times.'

It was true. Blain had simply ignored his calls. 'Sorry, I saw I got some missed calls but only got the alerts in the evening. I thought it would be too late to ring you back then.'

'Don't try to deceive me, Blain. Otherwise you'll be back on show business before you know what's hit you.'

Blain looked at her news editor's face. She'd never seen him so furious. She decided she had to come clean. 'I decided to follow Tanaka.'

'What! Are you crazy? That sort of thing could lose us our hard-earned place at the TMPD press club. Did he spot you?'

'No. Definitely not. He knows I came by certain information, and he's annoyed I found out, but he doesn't realise how I got it. He just thinks I strike lucky all the time.'

Yamamoto pointed in agitation at the newspaper Blain was still holding. 'Well, your luck's run out now, hasn't it? And if you *were* following him, what did you find out? And why didn't *we* have a story about it in today's paper?'

Blain closed her eyes and wiped her hand across her face. All of a sudden, she felt incredibly tired. The adrenaline rush had carried her so far... now things were going horribly wrong. With Yamamoto *and* with Tanaka. But she'd only get anywhere if she had space to think — if she managed to get Yamamoto off her back.

'Look, there are several developments that I am party to exclusively. Once they all come together, they will knock stories like this...' she paused and pointed to the *Asahi*'s front page, '...into a cocked hat. But it needs time. I was talking to Inspector Tanaka last night. We think we've identified the killer. We think we've got a photo of him. We even think we've got video of him.'

'We, we? If you've got a photo and a video, why the hell isn't the picture in our paper, with a link to the video on our online edition?'

'Because he's taken me into his confidence. I saw this guy — the "Otaku Killer", if you like — at a show business meet and greet last week. I've got to go to the police headquarters now to give a statement about it. You will have your story for tomorrow. It may not have everything I've mentioned just now, but it will be better than anything our rivals have, I promise you, Yamamoto-san.'

It was a rash promise, Blain knew it. But it was her only way out. The trouble was, she would have to let *someone* down. Either Yamamoto. Or Tanaka. They both wanted different things from her, and the pressure was starting to make her head explode.

She tried to get an early night, but found herself tossing and turning, unable to sleep, the images constantly appearing in her head the way they always did when she was on the brink of a depressive episode. She felt that way now. On the way back from Café Muse, there were at least a couple of occasions when she'd turned in panic, thinking she was being followed. No one was there of course. She had to hold it together. This job — this story — was important to her. She couldn't afford to lose her grip on either of them.

CHAPTER TWENTY-NINE

A night's reflection and rest — and an evening spent chewing things over with Miho — found Tanaka softening his attitude to Blain by the next morning. It helped her cause that this time it wasn't the *Tōkei Shimbun* causing the police embarrassment, but a much bigger concern — Japan's biggest-selling newspaper, the *Asahi Shimbun*. On top of that, if Yoshitake wanted to have a go at someone, it had to be Inspector Nishimura rather than Tanaka himself. Someone in the forensics department — if not Nishimura herself — must have leaked the toxicology information to the *Asahi* reporter. Also, his hopes that the man they were hunting was on the Hello Happy Princess fan list had been dashed for the time being — people in the idol group's management knew of him from the description, but they didn't know his name, and didn't take the names of those involved in the meet and greets as a matter of course.

His conversation with Miho had been important in his mood change too.

'She seemed like an honest woman to me, Tanuki-san.'

Tanuki — a play on Tanaka's surname — was a Japanese raccoon dog, often depicted in a cutesy way in stories and fables. Half raccoon, half dog was what it looked like — just like Tanaka looked half-Japanese, half-American. 'Yes, maybe bringing the *sakura* ice cream was a bit of a trick, but I liked her, the boys liked her. And remember, she's a foreigner in a big city, just like you.'

'I am not a foreigner.'

'Oh, Tanuki-san, don't be angry. I'm only teasing. Anyway, she seemed honest to me. The sort of daughter anyone would be proud of.'

Miho had lapsed into silence for a moment. Each had known what the other was thinking.

She had sighed before continuing. 'And perhaps her *sakura zensen* idea does have some merit. Maybe you should go to Kyoto for a while — you could take me with you. It would be like the old days, before we had the children.'

A knock on his office door cut short Tanaka's memory. He looked at his watch. 10am. If she'd obeyed his instruction to come in and give her statement, it would be Blain.

It was indeed. She looked less confident. Less like an angry indie-rocker. More like someone's vulnerable daughter. *Whose* daughter, he didn't know. She never talked about her family back in the UK — never talked about her past, almost as though she didn't have one, or that there was something there she couldn't confront. For a moment, he felt sorry for her.

'Ah, Holly-san, please come in.' Although she didn't know it, she had Miho to thank for his more cordial greeting. He got up to greet her, almost wondering about giving her a hug but then thinking better of it — that would be going too far. 'There's no need for that formal statement. I think I was overreacting yesterday evening. I was tired. Let's go for a coffee and see if we can work something out.'

Tanaka proverbially laid all his cards on the table as soon as they'd got their drinks in a café near TMPD, with him picking up the tab.

'I followed up your sighting at the idol group meet and greet last week. Thank you for that.' He could see Blain looked slightly startled by his mood change. But he wanted to explore her ideas. Even if they came to nothing, he'd decided it was better to have her on board, to cooperate with her, than not. As long as she was prepared — for the most part — to abide by his rules. 'Unfortunately, they don't keep a list of fans' names. They recognised him from the description but couldn't give me any more information. So, we're back to square one on that. However, I have thought about your data scientist idea. I am all for trying to harness new technology where possible. I would like to explore that option with you.'

There was still a look of surprise plastered all over Blain's face. 'Fantastic. I'll get on to her right away.'

'Obviously do it discreetly,' said Tanaka. 'I don't want your data scientist friend to know *why* we're looking for this man.'

'What about my *sakura* forecast idea?'

'It has merit, I agree. I think it's a long shot, though. I don't see how I can justify going to Kyoto to follow it up. I'm not even sure *what* I would be following up. If you wish to go there, Holly-san, that is your concern. What I can do is brief the Kyoto police as fully as possible. Make sure they are looking out for anyone of his description. I've also asked Himeji police to check all CCTV recordings they have access to, to see if our man appears on any of them. Particularly ones at the station. So far, nothing positive has been reported back.'

Blain had her notebook and pen out and now glanced down at it. 'There is one other thing, Tanaka-san. The *Asahi Shimbun*'s exclusive on the toxicology results — it's placed me in a rather embarrassing position.'

'Your newspaper surely cannot expect you to get the best exclusives every day, Holly-san.'

'Unfortunately, that's exactly what they do expect.'

'I don't see how I can help you there. The leak didn't come from me or my department. We are as angry about it as you are.'

He watched Blain frown. 'Is there any way you can help me? I need a story for tomorrow. A good one. I don't want to break our agreement.'

Tanaka stroked his chin. He wanted to help. But he didn't see how he could.

Blain was doodling on her notebook. 'How about this?' she said. 'You give me an exclusive interview. You don't have to release key things you want to keep from the public — and from this so-called "Otaku Killer".'

'We still don't know he's a killer. I need to remind you of that.'

Blain nodded. 'Of course. But you need to give me something. We need some sort of hook. How about we say you've identified the killer?'

'But we haven't. And as I've just said, he may not be a *killer* as you put it. Tiresome as that may be for journalists. It's not up to the police to parcel everything up nice and neatly so that it fits your stories.'

'Okay. How about we say you have information that the culprit has widened his area of operations. That there is evidence he was planning something at Himeji Castle and that the police foiled it. Then that makes the police look good.'

'I don't want Himeji mentioned. You could just say a

provincial castle, or a castle in a city hundreds of kilometres from Tokyo. Leave it vague.'

'The flower arrangement. Can we mention that?'

Tanaka shook his head. 'No, absolutely not. But we could say police are considering using new facial recognition techniques and data science to try to track down the k—' Tanaka stopped abruptly and laughed. She had won him round, just like a favourite daughter would. 'You see, you've nearly got me saying it too. Anyway, I'm happy to talk about your data science angle. You could say that the castle incident has provided vital new evidence. Let's work through it now. I'm sure we can come up with something that keeps us both satisfied.'

CHAPTER THIRTY

After working through with the detective what she was — and wasn't — allowed to say, Blain returned to the office to start writing up her story for the next day. She wanted to get it in early — then try to catch up with her data scientist friend, Emily. Tanaka had reluctantly agreed to allow Blain to show the CCTV images of the *Otaku* to her contact — but only if Emily undertook in writing not to show them to anyone else. In any case, the detective had expressed doubts as to whether the video would be good enough quality to be of any use in Blain's plan.

When she arrived, her plans — and her head — were thrown into turmoil. The newsroom assistant said a package had been hand-delivered to the front desk, addressed to her. Eventually, it would make its way to Blain via the internal mail. She decided instead to return to the lobby and collect it from the despatch area.

Initially, she wasn't particularly suspicious. All reporters were familiar with the occasional crackpot communication from readers — although it might not even be that. She signed for the package and then picked it up and examined it. Nothing unusual about the exterior: a plastic padded bag, with a printed address label and a warning: 'Fragile — do not crush'. Yet from its relatively light weight, it felt as though there was almost nothing inside.

She waited until she was in the lift before opening it. But even then, held off until the other occupant had exited at a lower floor. There was a prickling sensation on the back of her neck — somehow, she already knew this was important.

Finally, she tried to prise the self-adhesive plastic flap apart, hoping not to destroy the packaging. Just in case. In case it was something to do with the Otaku Killer story. The plastic stretched but wouldn't unstick.

Losing patience, she tore it open, fingers stretching and tearing until it broke.

The first thing she saw was a photograph on glossy paper. A *geisha*. Or a woman dressed as a *geisha*.

The only way she could tell it was a woman was from the body and the traditional dress. The hair in the *shimada* style, a black bun piled on top of the head, with two smaller buns sectioned off on each side.

From the face, she couldn't tell.

It had been scratched from the photograph. Completely obliterated.

And Blain could imagine — from the sharp, repetitive lines — the fury, the anger, the hate, behind the scratching.

There was something intrinsically evil about the faceless image.

Further down in the packaging, something else. A small paper box, like a giant, numberless dice.

The bell in the lift rang, signalling she'd reached her floor.

Just before she left the lift, she opened the lid of the box, and felt her heartbeat hammer in her head.

The elegance of what was in the box contrasted with the apparent evil of the faceless image.

It was a single white flower.

Pristine in its beauty, as though to pluck it had itself been a crime.

At first, she thought a petal had fallen off.

Then she realised, it was intact.

The asymmetry was nature's design.

The Japanese were obsessed by *Ma*. In the gap between the first and fifth pure-white petal, it was as though nature had given the Japanese flower arrangers a nudge.

She felt her hand trembling as she gently replaced the bloom.

The sender didn't need to add a name or signature.

Blain didn't understand what the message meant. But she was in no doubt at all who it was from.

Instead of going straight into the newsroom, Blain went via the ladies' toilets. She put the package on the side of the sink, and then felt the need to wash her hands. As she did, she looked at her face in the mirror. The face looking back at her was no different to usual. But inside, she *felt* different. As though somehow, the Otaku Killer, The Flower Arranger, call him what you will, had managed to invade her very soul. She kept the cold tap running, and cupped her hands under it, then splashed it over her face. She only ever wore minimal make-up, a touch of eyeliner. She dabbed away where it had run with a paper towel then breathed in. Nothing had changed. She still had a story to write. *You've faced worse than this in your life*, she told herself. The question was, should she tell Tanaka? Perhaps, but in her own time. When it was to her own advantage.

Blain finished off the story — making no mention of the strange package she'd received — and marked it as ready for editing in the pending news folder. Immediately, Yamamoto's login had locked the file as he started to edit it. After a few minutes, he called Blain over to his side office.

'This is good, as far as it goes, Holly-san. But what about the photograph of the flower arrangement, the video of the man said to be this "Otaku Killer"? Why can't we actually mention Himeji Castle?' He waved a printed sheet of Blain's story as he questioned her, slapping it against the desk to emphasise each point.

Blain shook her head and widened her arms, the palms of her hands outwards like a supplicant. 'I've done all I can without seriously pissing my detective contact off. How many times are you going to have a reporter who's like this with her police contact?' She wrapped her middle finger over her index finger — trying to demonstrate the closeness of her relationship with Tanaka, even though in reality she knew he blew hot and cold.

Yamamoto leant back against the wall, his arms folded across his stomach. Blain's story had been abandoned on the table. 'Okay. Read it to me. Maybe it will feel better read aloud than it does being read on a computer.'

This was more a radio journalism technique. Blain knew because back in the UK she'd done a few radio news shifts — she'd hated the superficiality of it. The inability to treat a story with any depth. But she humoured Yamamoto, and began to read it aloud:

POLICE FOIL NEW 'OTAKU KILLER' INCIDENT

By Crime Reporter Holly Blain

Yamamoto interrupted. 'You know it's not up to you to write the headlines, Blain?'

'I know. It's only a suggested one. I'm sure the subs will come up with something better.'

'And don't assume we'll give you a by-line, either. They have to be earned. Anyway, carry on.'

Blain began to read her story out loud again. It almost felt like she was back at school, giving a presentation to the teacher.

Tokyo Police — in an exclusive interview with the Tōkei Shimbun *— say they have thwarted a new potential attack by the man who's become known as the 'Otaku Killer'.*

The man is being hunted in connection with the death of teenage Swedish nightclub hostess, Elin Granqvist.

But in a worrying development, the police also have evidence that the man they're hunting has widened his area of operations.

The officer leading the inquiry, Inspector Tetsu Tanaka of the Tokyo Metropolitan Police Department's Gaikoku-jin Unit, said the fresh incident — at an historic castle hundreds of kilometres from the capital — has given the police important new evidence.

'The suspect got away this time, but the net is closing around him,' said Inspector Tanaka. 'Thankfully, in the latest incident, the man was disturbed before he could do anyone any harm.'

Inspector Tanaka said the police were considering new data science facial recognition techniques to track down their suspect.

And — for the first time — Inspector Tanaka said police are now linking the disappearance of another foreign teenager to the death of 17-year-old Miss Granqvist.

*The missing girl is Marie-Louise Durand from Paris, France —
also aged 17 — who disappeared from her hotel in the Daimon
district a week ago.*

*Inspector Tanaka rejected criticisms from the French girl's father
that police weren't doing enough to try to find his daughter.*

*'We have a team of detectives and plain-clothes officers working
round the clock on these cases. We will not rest until Marie-Louise
has been found safe and well, and the man responsible for Elin's
death has been caught.'*

Blain stopped reading and looked up expectantly at her
news editor.

'Hmm,' he said. 'Well, it does seem better when you read it
out, I admit. But where does the *police thwarting a potential new
attack* bit come from? That isn't backed up by quotes from
your inspector friend.'

'He was happy for us to say that — I made sure I ran it by
him.'

'I'm sure he's happy for us to *say* it. It paints the police in a
good light even though — to my mind — they seem to be
screwing this up without any help from us. The question,
Holly-san, is *is it true?*'

Blain shrugged. 'It's true enough, Yamamoto-san.'

'Pah!' The news editor gave a long sigh. 'Okay, let's run
with this, then, for tomorrow morning. What's your next
plan?'

'I'm helping the police with the facial recognition angle.'

'How?'

'With a data scientist friend of mine.'

Yamamoto whistled through his teeth. 'Impressive, Holly-
san. Maybe you should do a background feature on that too.
Anything else?'

'I want to go to Kyoto.'

'*Kyoto*? Why? We're mainly a Tokyo newspaper. But we do have a stringer in Kyoto. He's going to think you're trampling on his patch. Why can't you just get him to do what you want?'

'Because I need to firm it all up first. But I think Kyoto is where he's likely to strike next.'

'Okay. A city of more than 1.5 million people. Even if you're correct, why do you think you'll be able to find what's going on? It will be like searching for a needle in a haystack.'

'Have I been delivering you regular lead stories, Yamamoto-san?'

'Yes, but—'

'Then trust me on this one. Just trust me.'

CHAPTER THIRTY-ONE

Catching the Shinkansen to Kyoto seemed almost like a re-run of the trip to Himeji, although a shorter journey by some forty or so minutes. It was a clear day this time, so Blain made sure she sat on the right-hand side of the train as it glided along the tracks — at bullet-like speed as per its nick-name, the towns and countryside flashing by. The reason for her seat choice: after about an hour there was a beautiful view of Mount Fuji, at this time of year at its most beautiful, topped with a sugar-coated icing of snow. Fuji-san to the Japanese. It had always made her smile, thinking they were giving the mountain an honorific, like 'sir'. Only later when her Japanese had improved did she realise her mistake. The *kanji* for 'mountain' — almost like Neptune's trident, but without the handle — also had the 'san' sound.

Her meeting with her data scientist friend, Emily, hadn't gone as well as she'd hoped. Emily would try to use a still from the video feed but didn't have much hope that it was good enough quality. Only when Blain said the man looked like the famous — and dead — American singer Roy Orbison did Emily start to get more enthusiastic.

They searched through photographs of Orbison on the internet — all the time, Emily wanting to know which looked most like the man Blain had seen in the Hello Happy Princess meet and greet line-up. They finally decided on one particular photo from the early 1960s: black suit, narrow tie, dark glasses, and his jet-black hair at its fullest pompadour style — almost like that of the faceless *geisha* whose photograph had been sent to her. Swept back from his unsmiling face and piled high over his forehead. In it, he could almost pass for a Japanese salaryman. That was a problem — said Emily — it might be too like millions of other Japanese men. But if the *Otaku* really did — for some unknown reason — style himself after Orbison, this was the look he would end up with.

They cropped the photo to leave head, shoulders, and upper body, taking out the cherry red guitar Orbison was cradling. As a guitarist, this was almost sacrilege to Blain. But this wasn't Orbison's most interesting 'axe' — that was a special black number with a Gretsch body and Gibson neck. How Blain would have loved a chance to play it.

'So how is this going to work?' asked Blain.

'It might not at all — or it might come up with too many matches,' said Emily. 'The idea is that if a photograph similar to this pops up on Facebook, Instagram, Twitter, or Line, then I get an alert, and I'll text you immediately. But it's slightly experimental — I've still got to perfect the algorithm. And if a photo is on someone's feed but they have strong privacy settings, then it won't flag up. I'm giving no guarantees. And our biggest problem, of course, is that he's not Roy Orbison himself. It will be a question of how good a likeness he has. I have to be honest with you now and say I very much doubt it will work.'

She'd booked herself into a renovated historic *ryokan* in Higashiyama — not far from Gion, the most famous *geisha* district in Kyoto. If the so-called 'Otaku Killer' *was* deliberately targeting western girls, this was the tourist area where they would most likely congregate. The area had the advantage, too, of being nearest to some of Kyoto's best cherry blossom viewing sites.

Blain stretched out on the futon in her traditional tatami-mat room, with her arms stretched out in front of her, her hands cradling her smartphone. She simply stared at the home screen — willing an alert to pop up from Emily, even though she knew it was unlikely to happen.

Before she knew it, she'd fallen into a deep sleep.

A beep from her phone woke her, and she scrambled to find it. Then she realised it had simply fallen on her chest and rolled off when she jumped up. She picked it up, hoping beyond hope that it was Emily with some news. It wasn't. The message was simple:

Ring me. Urgent. TT

She looked at the last character in confusion, still half asleep. TT. Her written Japanese was good — but she didn't recognise the *kanji*. It looked a little like the Greek letter 'pi'.

Then she realised. It was simply the font. It was two capital Ts together. TT. Tetsu Tanaka. He must be on a different mobile number to the one he'd given her, that was why her phone hadn't recognised it as him. Or he'd deliberately put his phone in private mode.

She rang back immediately on the number she did have.

'Inspector. It's me, Holly Blain.'

'Holly-san, good. Thank you for ringing back so quickly. You said you were going to Kyoto to try to follow up your cherry blossom theory.'

'That's right. I'm here. I've just checked in to my *ryokan*.'

'How quickly can you get to the *Miyako Odori*?'

'What *is* the *Miyako Odori*?'

'It's one of the spring shows of dancing, singing, and theatre performed by *geishas* and trainee *geishas* — the *maiko* — in Kyoto.'

'Hang on — let me check how far away I am.'

She tapped the information into her maps app.

'It's saying I'm only about 400 metres away — so four minutes' walk.'

'Okay — I'm in a taxi from Kyoto station at the moment. We should arrive at about the same time. I'll meet you outside.'

Tanaka ended the call, before Blain had the chance to ask him the relevance of the meeting place.

She hurried through the streets, trying to dodge all the tourists. While they had time to marvel at the beautiful traditional wooden buildings, with the lanterns casting a white-orange glow, Blain had one thing on her mind. If Tanaka had bothered to come all the way to Kyoto, something must have happened. Her theory — really it was little more than a hunch — must have been right.

The Otaku Killer was here, somewhere on these streets, she felt sure.

. . .

When she arrived at the Gion Kōbu Kaburen-jo theatre, the traditional home of the *Miyako Odori*, her heart sank. It was closed. Not just for the day, but for renovation. A notice said all performances were being held at the Kyoto Art Theatre Shunjuza, part of the city's University of Art and Design.

She checked her maps app again. Thirty minutes by bus, and she'd have to change. Or a 15-minute taxi ride, but she was in a pedestrianised street. She checked the nearest way to a main road and then started to run.

By the time Blain reached the theatre, Tanaka was nowhere to be seen, and the performance had already started. She didn't know what to do, and he wasn't answering her phone calls. If he was already inside the auditorium, he'd probably been forced to turn his phone off. Even if he'd shown his police ID.

'Can I still buy a ticket and enter the performance?' she asked.

'You can,' replied the vendor, 'but you will have to be very quiet as you go inside. The ushers have absolute discretion about when they can let you in — it cannot be during a quiet or dramatic part of the performance. So, you may miss an important part. It's up to you.'

Blain accepted the conditions, bought her ticket, and made her way to the auditorium. Thankfully, the usher let her in almost immediately.

Once she was seated, she scanned both the circle — where she was — and the stalls, trying to locate Tanaka — if indeed he was here.

After a couple of minutes of frustration, her eyes zeroed in on him on the opposite side wing of the circle seats to her own. She tried without success to attract his attention. He — like her — was scanning the auditorium. His deputy, by his side doing exactly the same thing. The only faces in the theatre not trained on the stage. Presumably trying to spot their target: a nerdy Roy Orbison lookalike. Meanwhile, on the stage, various *maikos* and *geishas* were performing their traditional dances and songs — waving fronds of fake cherry blossom in one hand, fans in the other amidst a riot of pinks, blues, and yellows. A second attempt to catch Tanaka's eye merely succeeded in angering those in the adjoining seats: Blain realised she would have to leave and try to work her way round to Tanaka's side.

She again attracted disapproving looks as she stood up, both from her neighbours and then from the usher. Blain didn't care. The story was more important than the sensibilities of the *Miyako Odori* audience and staff. She walked round to Tanaka's side, but the usher there refused to let her in — trying to make her go back to her original seat.

'You don't understand,' said Blain. 'I'm a reporter from a national newspaper.' She pointed through the half-open curtain down to Tanaka's head. 'And that man is a homicide detective from Tokyo. We are working on something together.'

The woman usher looked at her as though she was half-crazed.

Blain performed the same pleading motion she'd used on Yamamoto a few days earlier, when originally securing her foothold on the crime beat — bringing hands together in front of her face. *'Onegai.'*

The usher relented, but only partially. 'I cannot let you in here on that ticket. But at a break in the performance I will let him know you are here.'

A few seconds later, the audience broke out in a round of applause, and the usher went to alert Tanaka. The detective immediately got to his feet and climbed up towards Blain.

'What took you so long, Holly-san?' he whispered.

'I went to the traditional theatre where the performances are usually held, Tanaka-san. I didn't realise it was closed for renovation. Anyway, what's happened? Why are you here?'

'It may be nothing, but the staff here reported someone acting oddly at the tea ceremony. They alerted Kyoto police. The man's description matched that of the man we are looking for.'

'Why was he at a tea ceremony?'

'Before each performance, audience members can pay extra to take part in a special tea ceremony performed by one of the trainee *geishas*, a *maiko*. This man came to two ceremonies in a row — and was the first in line both times so got to the centre of the front row. In those seats, you are served by the *maiko* herself, rather than one of her assistants. The *maiko* felt uncomfortable with him — she believed he was staring at her all the time and that he was almost sniffing the air around her. Anyway, that — combined with the fact that he oddly attended two ceremonies in succession — was enough to provoke the staff here to contact the police. And when the local police heard his description, they contacted us. I'd hoped he might still be hanging round here — but we cannot see him anywhere.'

Blain felt guilt course through her. Had the package and photograph that she suspected the Otaku Killer had sent been a warning — that a *geisha* was next? If she'd told Tanaka, could it have prevented another attack? She kept these thoughts to herself, although she felt her face redden. 'Have you checked the CCTV cameras?' she asked.

'There are none here on the campus. The only place the university has them is around the halls of residence, for students' personal safety. Here on campus, the students themselves voted against CCTV — claiming it was an infringement of their personal liberties. Anyway, we have asked the local police to check any feeds in the surrounding area — so far nothing has turned up. What about your data scientist, Holly-san? Any luck with her?'

Blain shrugged. 'I don't know. She's going to try but wasn't very hopeful. And she still has to complete the writing of the algorithm to make the photo recognition system work, whatever that means.'

Tanaka nodded. 'Let's go back in, although I don't think we are going to get anywhere this evening. The next tea ceremony is tomorrow. We can stake that out.' The detective moved to go back into the auditorium.

'The usher isn't letting me in here,' explained Blain.

Tanaka got out his TMPD identification badge and showed it to the woman. 'She's with me and needs to come in here.'

CHAPTER THIRTY-TWO

Tanaka wasn't sure whether he and Izumi were wasting their time. Yoshitake had been angry enough when Tanaka insisted he and his deputy needed to go to Kyoto in person to chase this new sighting. If the two detectives failed to progress the inquiry while they were here, then the superintendent wouldn't hesitate to hand the case to another team. He'd already been muttering about bringing in homicide specialists because of Tanaka's slow progress.

Both detectives had got the permission of the *Miyako Odori* staff to hide themselves in the tea ceremony room in case their target appeared again. Blain had offered to wait in the queue. The *maiko* performing the ceremony was the same one who'd done it the previous day — so if it was she that the Otaku Killer was fixated on, then the bait had been set. The director of the theatre had counselled against the same girl performing the ritual once more: but the girl herself had, the previous evening, seemed quite excited about the possibility of helping to catch a criminal and insisted that was what she wanted to do.

As members of the public were shown into the room where the ceremony would take place, Tanaka realised that the man wasn't here. At least, if he was, this time he hadn't managed to get in the front of the queue. But Tanaka had arranged with the local police to have lookouts on every entrance to the theatre. If he arrived, the local police should be able to warn them. So far, nothing.

Everyone was seated now, waiting for the ceremony to begin. People began to get restless as nothing happened. Tanaka, in a crouching position behind a curtain, had to stretch as his calf muscle started to cramp. Still nothing. Then raised voices from behind the curtains at the front from where the *maiko* and her assistants were due to emerge. Suddenly one of the assistants ran out towards Tanaka, opening the curtain which concealed him.

'Oh, Inspector,' she shrieked. 'The *maiko* has disappeared. She's vanished from her room.'

Tanaka followed her to the back, while instructing Izumi to ensure all members of the public left the tea ceremony room. The inspector was dimly aware of Blain following him without permission — but he didn't have time for niceties.

When they reached the *maiko's* room, various assistants were gathered round, fretting and crying. Tanaka chose the calmest of them, bowed to her, and asked her to give him an explanation.

'The *maiko* was here, putting the final touches to her hair. I checked on her just ten minutes ago. Then, when she didn't come out on time, I assumed she must have needed the toilet at the last minute or something like that.'

'Wouldn't you have seen her going to the toilet?' asked Tanaka.

'No, there is another entrance.' She pointed towards a side door.

Izumi had now joined Blain and Tanaka in the *maiko's* room. 'Izumi-kun. Stay here and take some statements.' Without stopping to think whether he really should be descending a staircase to a *geisha's* private toilet, Tanaka pulled open the door and ran down the stairs, two at a time. Behind him, he could hear the clatter of feet. He had no doubt it was Blain chasing on his heels.

In the toilet area, there was no one. Both he and Blain searched high and low.

'I can hear voices,' said Blain.

Tanaka stopped and listened. It was everyday conversation, punctuated by the sounds of toilets flushing. The public toilets seemed to be the other side of a thin wall. But no way through.

Blain had disappeared round the corner. Then she yelled at him to come.

'Tanaka-san. Here!'

Rounding the corner, Tanaka saw daylight streaming in through an open fire exit doorway. He rushed through following Blain into a back area of the theatre, a small yard that in turn led on to an open street. He searched round for the Kyoto police officers who were supposed to be on guard at every entrance and exit.

No sign of them.

Not at the fire exit itself, and not at the open gateway that led to the backstreet outside. He felt anger course through him, virtually every one of the muscles in his body quivering in his rage. *Idiots!* He'd asked the local police to do one simple thing, and they hadn't managed it properly.

The man the press had dubbed the 'Otaku Killer' had given them the slip again.

CHAPTER THIRTY-THREE

At first, she didn't want to cooperate. All he wanted was his own private ceremony.

He'd dressed in all his traditional clothing, got all his mother's old tea equipment ready, and showed her where she could do her make-up.

Still she refused.

He didn't want to hurt her. He never wanted to hurt them, but sometimes they didn't make it easy for him.

He wasn't sure whether to keep her with the other girl. He knew that would be kinder for them, but they might talk. They might plan. They might try to leave him. He didn't want that. Not until he was ready.

When he pulled the knife out, both girls started to scream. High-pitched, terrified wailing. But even in their panic, you could distinguish between the nature of their screaming voices. Even when they weren't using words. One Japanese. One European.

Of course, their screams were in vain. The room was soundproofed, as well as completely hidden behind the bookcase. Even if the police searched here, he was confident they wouldn't find it. Even if they suspected something was behind the old bookcase, they wouldn't be able to move it. Only pushing a particular sequence of what looked like light switches on the wall would enable the bookcase to be moved on its hidden wheels across the polished floor. Get the sequence wrong, and you had to wait thirty seconds for the system to reset itself. He'd designed it himself. They might call him an *Otaku*, they might laugh at him at the idol concerts, but some things he had a talent for.

He brought the knife to her pretty throat.

'I don't want to have to harm you. I just want you to serve me tea. I like the way you do it. If you serve me tea in exactly the way I want, dress in the exact style of the photo I've left on the dressing table, then you will not be harmed, and I will let you go.'

The French girl started whimpering at this. He didn't want to upset her either. She was too pretty. Too young.

'I will let you go too,' he said. 'When the time is right.' He pressed the tip of the knife into the *maiko's* delicate throat, watching the white powdered skin start to yield. He wasn't going to break it. Wasn't going to hurt her.

As long as she did exactly what he required.

The *maiko's* head gave the slightest of nods, as though the girl was afraid that if she moved more, the knife would puncture her soft, snow white skin. He didn't like puncturing skin. Except when it was necessary, to try to match the colour of the petals. He tried to do that with the Swedish girl. He was so sad it had gone wrong.

'Good,' he said. 'Let's go upstairs, then.'

'What about me?' whined the French girl. It was a good thing she could speak English, as she clearly spoke no Japanese — and he no French.

'You wait here,' he said and then heard her start to cry again. He wanted to go over and comfort her, like his mother used to comfort him when he'd had a bad dream. But he couldn't really do that. It would be improper. She was too young. He never should have taken her.

He showed her the photographs — the front of the face and hair, and the back of the head and neck, with the arrows of white pointing lower, to the mysteries below.

'Like this,' he said. 'Exactly like this, please.' He framed it as a request, but he still held the knife in his hand, just in case she disagreed.

She set to work, using similar methods to his mother. Her face, neck, and chest were already powdered white, but the pattern his mother used was different — particularly the two prongs of bare skin on the back of the neck. So, in areas, the *maiko* had to remove the powder, re-wax, and apply again.

He watched particularly carefully as she waxed her upper chest. It was the part that got him the most excited. He could hear his own breathing coming in short rasps, and he was sure she was aware of it too. If he had been brave, he would have asked her if she'd allow him to do it. But that would be impolite. That would be overstepping the mark. Taking advantage of the situation. It was better that it was like this. Everything done properly.

The tingling was back as soon as she started to apply the red. To her eyelids. To her lips. So like his mother when she was younger.

That was why he'd chosen her.

. . .

She looked surprised as he moved forward when she started to arrange her hair.

'I want to help you with this part,' he said.

'You cannot. It is not allowed. You should not even be here watching me.'

He felt the tears then, pricking his eyes. He knew he could force her. He knew he could use the knife, and she knew that too. Yet still she was prepared to disappoint him. Because of the rules, the conventions.

She looked up at him in the mirror. He felt ashamed and knew she could see the tears running down his face from under the wide, dark sunglasses.

'Please,' he asked.

He heard a sigh. Then he saw her give a slight nod of her head.

And then he was behind her, his hands parting her rich black hair into sections, just as he did with his mother.

He was so thankful to her. Letting him touch her like this.

And then he knew he would have to break his promise.

He could never let her go.

CHAPTER THIRTY-FOUR

Tanaka felt things were spiralling out of control. He knew Yoshitake would have to act. He and Izumi had been ordered back to Tokyo by the superintendent when he heard — from Kyoto police, not Tanaka — that the man had escaped their clutches once more.

Standing side by side with Izumi in front of Yoshitake's desk, Tanaka waited for his superior to deliver the news he expected: that they were being taken off the case. But it was almost worse than that.

'We can't have this continuing, Tanaka. You have had plenty of chances to catch him. You've messed up each time, so you've left me no option. Chief Inspector Sano Heizo will be taking over this inquiry now — you're to report to him.'

'I thought Heizo-san was working on that serial rapist case in Hokkaido, Yoshitake-san.'

'He is. But I've ordered him back here to take charge of you two. He'll be here in two days' time once he's wrapped things up there. So, I suppose, technically, you've still got two days to redeem yourselves. Although, quite honestly Tanaka, I could give you all year to crack this one, and I don't think you'd get anywhere, the rate you're going.'

'That's not as bad as it could have been, Boss,' said Izumi as they left the meeting.

'How do you work that one out, Izumi? I've no desire to work under Chief Inspector Heizo, have you? He might get results, but he doesn't exactly play by the book. We're just as likely to end up on a corruption charge if we do things his way.' As he said the words, Tanaka tried not to stare at Izumi's suit-sleeve covered arm. Was that why Izumi didn't have any compunction about working under Heizo? Were Izumi's Yakuza links, if that was what the tattoo signified, still active — and would he make them available to the Chief Inspector? Tanaka tried to banish the thought as soon as it jumped into his head. He either had to trust his deputy or get him replaced. For the moment, he needed all the allies he could muster.

For his part, Izumi seemed oblivious to his boss' suspicions. 'Look on the bright side, Tanaka-san,' he said. 'We could make a lot of progress in two days. Don't give up yet. I still have faith in you.'

It was the sort of faith an old flea-riddled dog that a vet was about to put down might still have in his master, thought Tanaka. But perhaps that was unkind to his sergeant. He needed all the help he could get. He knew he wouldn't be getting much from Holly Blain. She'd witnessed everything in Kyoto first hand and had insisted she'd have to put it in her next day's newspaper report. At least now Yoshitake had made his move. Nothing Blain wrote could make things any worse.

Tanaka and Izumi sat in the inspector's office drinking green tea. It had a calming effect on Tanaka and helped him to think. He wandered over to the window and gazed out on the cherry blossoms of the Imperial Palace gardens. They were in full bloom now and had been for nearly a week. Soon the petals would be falling. It would mark an end but was a beautiful sight in itself: the *sakurafubuki* — the cherry blossom snow storm. If Tanaka and Izumi were to avoid becoming Chief Inspector Heizo's lapdogs, then before *sakurafubuki* commenced, they would need to have cracked this case or at least made significant progress.

The inspector suddenly turned and eyeballed his sergeant. 'We can still do this Izumi-kun. We just need a break.' He got the papers on his desk, shuffled them, and then banged each side of the sheaf until they made a neat pile. 'Let's go through everything, in a logical way, and work out what we haven't done, and where we could still make progress.'

They ploughed through all their files, made new flow charts, lists of the pieces of information that were missing, and rearranged the photos of missing girls and their suspect on the magnetic board. By the end of the process, Tanaka had at least identified three areas to look at.

The obvious thing would be to release an image — or the actual video — from the CCTV captured in Himeji. Or at least make it clear they were looking for a Roy Orbison-lookalike, not that the American singer would mean a lot to 21st-century Japanese people. He was probably not that famous in Japan even at his peak. Tanaka had steadfastly resisted this, and, on that, Yoshitake had at least agreed with him. The best way of finding this man, unless they could find his name, was via his appearance. But, as soon as they released his appearance to the general public, you could be certain that he would change it. Holly Blain was the only reporter who knew this aspect of the case, and thankfully she had agreed to keep it out of her reports.

Nevertheless, there were still two things Tanaka felt they could usefully do before the Chief Inspector arrived to piss on their party. One, they should have already looked at and dealt with. But better late than never. The other was more of a flyer — a bit like Blain's theory about Kyoto that somehow, in a continuation of her lucky streak, had come good. But Tanaka knew you made your own luck, found your own coincidences — all through hard work. He vaguely remembered the maxim of some once-famous golfer his father had been a fan of. The man wore black most, if not all, the time — just like the man they were hunting. But it was his words that had stuck with Tanaka: 'the harder I work, the luckier I get'.

The first action point did involve hard work. Lots of it. But they could delegate it to civilian staff in the records department. He wanted a thorough search of all crimes and incidents going back forty years — which should more than cover the full lifespan of their chief suspect. What the records staff would be looking for would be two things: crimes or incidents involving strange flower arrangements and crimes or incidents where any of those involved had an unhealthy obsession with fifties and sixties American music, particularly Roy Orbison.

The second action point involved going back to Holly Blain's list of favourite cherry blossom viewing points across Japan and her detailed print out of the *sakura zensen* forecast. Tanaka compared the two lists, and one place immediately leapt out at him. One of the next places to come into bloom was the grounds of another castle. While Himeji's predominantly white keep had seen it compared to a heron in flight, the castle Tanaka had in mind had a much more forbidding presence.

It was black.

The black crow castle of Matsumoto.

Tanaka delegated the task of overseeing the records check to Izumi. He decided to take on Matsumoto. Because it was more of a hunch, and had less chance of paying off, if things went wrong, he could be fully held responsible, rather than any blame resting with his sergeant.

The inspector toyed with the idea of letting Blain know about his plans. She was helping him with her social media photo recognition idea, so perhaps it was only fair. And it had been her theory about the *sakura* weather front. In the end, though, he decided his plan was too tenuous, too open to embarrassment to share.

The first day of full bloom at Matsumoto was, according to the forecast, due to be the next day. Would the 'Otaku Killer' — even Tanaka had started to think of him by that name — secret himself in the black crow castle, looking to build some set piece arrangement as he had at Himeji? The trouble was, Tanaka didn't really know *why* Himeji had been chosen, let alone why, on that occasion, the arrangement had been left with an empty space at its centre.

When he phoned the detective chief inspector at Matsumoto police station, from the pregnant silence at the other end of the line he could tell how well his idea had been received. You could tell when people were interested in, rather than dismissive of, something. They would ask questions, make suggestions, sound enthusiastic. The head of the Matsumoto Criminal Investigation Department sounded bored and morose. When Tanaka said he was planning to come to the city in person, he thought he could hear the chief inspector trying to suppress a laugh. That angered Tanaka. Perhaps the idea was a little off-the-wall. But it was certainly no laughing matter.

By the time he got to the city, via a Shinkansen to Nagano and then a limited express train, dusk was already closing in. The effect on the castle itself was even more forbidding. In the half-light, its black exterior did have an evil, hooded, crow-like appearance, as did the surrounding darkness of the mountains — save for the whiteness of their snow-capped peaks. It almost had Tanaka believing he had to be right — this had to be the setting for the Otaku Killer's next set piece.

But when he questioned the 'team' sent by the chief inspector to help him, he realised that the police here felt it was just a wild goose chase.

'How many men are being deployed?' he asked the sergeant who met him at the station.

'Myself, Tanaka-san. I am Sergeant Kinnosuke Junsa, and police officer Subaru here.'

'*Two* uniformed officers. A sergeant and a police constable. Myself and two uniformed officers to stake out a whole castle?'

'That's correct, Tanaka-san. And I'm afraid Officer Subaru and myself can only help you until 10pm.'

Tanaka's heart sank. Perhaps it had been a last, desperate, stupid idea. A vain attempt to find something before handing over the inquiry to Chief Inspector Heizo and being forced to do his bidding and bend the rules in the way he liked them to be bent. Whatever, with just three officers involved it had very little chance of success.

One thing in Tanaka's favour was that Matsumoto castle seemed better served by CCTV than its white sister castle at Himeji, and Sergeant Junsa — to his credit — had already enlisted the security team there to help. They'd been monitoring the feeds virtually ever since Tanaka's midday call asking the Matsumoto police for assistance. So far, the mysterious man in black either wasn't here or had evaded the security cameras.

With Junsa and Subaru's guidance, Tanaka began a search inside the castle itself, room by room. They used torches rather than turn all the lights on — although Tanaka wanted to find the man, if he was here, he didn't want to alert him that anything was wrong.

Tanaka swore under his breath when his mobile suddenly beeped. He should have switched it to silent. But as soon as he read the message, he realised the search and stakeout here was as good as over. It was from Blain.

Ring me as soon as you get this. Emily's algorithm seems to have worked. She's got a sighting. HB

Fantastic. Well done. Where?

In Osaka. I'm on my way there now. Ring me.

I just need to finish up here then I will.
I'll make my way there too. Where shall we meet?

In front of the Glico Man. You'll understand why when you ring me. I can also give you details of the people who took the photo.

Tanaka had already come to the conclusion that he was wasting his time here in Matsumoto. Blain's message was the confirmation. He broke the news to his two helpers. They didn't seem too disappointed, or indeed surprised.

CHAPTER THIRTY-FIVE

W hy was he trying to relive his life? He just felt some basic urge to retrace, relive, the happiest parts of his childhood. Perhaps it was a need to right the wrongs that had been done to him.

The tea ceremony with his mother, helping her with his hair. He wanted to be able to do that again. He'd been robbed of it, and it wasn't fair.

The flower-arranging that his mother had taught him. Passing on what she learnt in her *Ikebana* classes.

The excitement he'd felt when visiting his first historic castle outside Tokyo, at Himeji.

And the visit to the Glico Man.

Everyone knew the Glico Man. He'd been so proud posing in front of it with his parents, then showing the photograph to his classmates. They were a small family but a happy family. Until it all went wrong.

He remembered the buzz of excitement when he'd first seen the neon signs blazing alongside the Dōtonbori canal. Running ahead of his parents, despite his mother's worried shouts, wanting to be the first to stand in front of the sign he really wanted to see.

The Glico Man sign. A victorious athlete, arms aloft and outstretched, one leg bent at the knee, against the blue running track. Like so many before him, he'd copied the pose, trying to balance at first, then his mother and father holding each side of him as a stranger kindly took a photograph of all three of them.

It still felt just as special now.

He simply stood in front of the sign for a few minutes, letting the memories flood his brain. They brought a tear to his eye. But no one would see. He had his glasses on.

'Hoi, Roy! Get out of the way. Give someone else a go.'

He turned round. Three American tourists. They looked like they'd had too much to drink.

'Oh my gawd. It really is you, Roy.'

He was becoming embarrassed. Sweating in his dark suit. Something made him say it, in halting English. He should have kept quiet. 'My name not Loy.' He knew he hadn't pronounced it correctly — he never could. 'I am Kelton.'

'Aww, don't give us that, Roy. I'm one of your biggest fans.' He wasn't sure if the American was teasing him — surely, he knew Roy Orbison was dead? He'd died of a heart attack in 1988, a few years before everything had gone wrong. 'I sure as hell know Kelton's just your middle name. How about a picture Roy, in front of the Glico Man, is that okay?'

He was embarrassed. He didn't know what to say or do. Should he run? Should he say 'no'? In the end, he just looked at the camera without smiling.

'Mean and moody, Roy. That's how I'll always remember you, fella.' The man was patting him on the back now. 'Is it okay if I take a selfie too? You can smile this time, Roy, only if you want to, buddy.' The man put his arm round him as he took the photo with his phone, the camera flash causing him to blink even behind the dark glasses.

'Well, you've sure been a good sport, Roy. Is it okay by you if we put these on our Facebook pages?'

He didn't know what to say. They'd trapped him. He gave a small bow. 'Yes. Please,' he said. Saying it, but not meaning it. What he meant to say was 'please delete those photographs now' and 'please leave me alone to remember'. But he didn't. He didn't know sufficient English.

The American was holding out his hand to shake. He didn't want to. He gave another bow and hurried off.

Over his shoulder he heard the American's friend remonstrate with him.

'Chuck, you're such an idiot. You know the Japanese don't like to shake hands. You've frightened him off.'

'That was no Japanese man. That was Mr Roy Kelton Orbison himself come back from the dead to have his photograph taken with me in front of the Glico Man sign.'

CHAPTER THIRTY-SIX

B lain knew this was her best lead yet. Her best story yet. She texted Tanaka as soon as she got the alert from Emily. At last, she felt she was contributing. Then she rang her friend.

'This is fantastic. Tell me more, Em.'

'An American man, Charles Zglobis.' Emily spelt out the name. 'Z-G-L-O-B-I-S, Zglobis — maybe he's originally from a Russian or Polish family or something, I don't know — anyway, now he seems to live in Myrtle Beach, South Carolina. He's been posting loads of cherry blossom photos from Japan, obviously he's on holiday here. Then suddenly he posts a selfie, with the text *"Roy Orbison and me in front of the Glico Man. How cool is that! The Big O is back. Attaboy, Roy!"*'

'He sounds like a complete idiot. Still, your photo-identification alert worked. Amazing! Well done, Em.'

'Sadly, it didn't really work, Holly. I also set up another algorithm, to detect mentions of Orbison's name. That's what triggered the alert, not the photo. Anyway, maybe you can try to contact this Zglobis guy. And I can use the photo he took to set up a new photo identification alert. It's so much clearer than the CCTV image, and it's really him this time — if we're sure it *is* him.'

'Hang on Em. I'll just look up this Zglobis guy's Facebook page... there he is... and yes, that's certainly our man. Before you go, I was wondering if it's worth setting up another text alert too. I told you the guy we're looking for seems to have an obsession with flower arrangements featuring *sakura* or cherry blossom. Could you put those text terms into an alert too: flower arrangement, *sakura*, and cherry blossom.'

'I will, but that's going to be a nightmare. We'll pick up far too many references — I suppose if I just had all three together, so that all three have to come up in the same post or mention? Would that work?'

'Sure, whatever you can do. Fabulous. Well done. I owe you several drinks, Em.'

As soon as she was off the phone call, Blain started to message Charles Zglobis on Facebook. They weren't Facebook friends, so there was a chance the message wouldn't pop up instantly, but she said she was a British reporter on a Japanese newspaper, intrigued by his Roy Orbison lookalike photo, and left her mobile number for him to ring back. What he said would determine whether it was worth trying to get to Osaka tonight.

Within half an hour, the return call came.

It soon became apparent that Charles Zglobis — even in that half-hour — had been hitting the beers, or sake, or both. His speech was slurring. But despite his inebriation, Blain managed to get permission to use the photo without payment, and also establish that he hadn't taken the man's phone number or email address. Blain had been holding out the hope that Zglobis might have done, in order to give the Otaku Killer a copy of the photo. He had no idea where the man lived, what he was doing in Osaka.

'It was just a chance meeting, lady. I was pulling his leg, really, but he was a good sport to play along.'

'Was there anything else he said that might be useful?'

'Useful to what, lady?'

Blain suddenly realised she was probably making the man suspicious. She had to think up a good reason. 'Because of Japan's strict privacy laws, I really need to get his permission as well before I can use the photo. It would be useful to know his real name, for instance.'

'Well, I didn't get that, I'm afraid, lady. I mean he did say his name was Kelton, but I think he was just joshing with me.'

'Why do you say that — did he look like he was joking?'

'Nah, not a bit of it. To be honest, he looked dead embarrassed. Wouldn't surprise me if Kelton was his real name, but that would be a bit odd, wouldn't it?'

'Why?'

'Well, it doesn't sound too Japanese, does it. More to the point, Roy Orbison's middle name was Kelton. Roy Kelton Orbison. And he looked so like him. By God, he did look like him.'

Blain could see there was little point heading to Osaka based on that conversation. She'd found out everything she was going to get from Zglobis: the man sounded like a complete buffoon. But if the Kelton name *was* true, it was a huge breakthrough. Should she keep it to herself and try to track him down alone? That was what a good journalist should do. But already she'd encouraged Tanaka into thinking he should be making the trip to Osaka himself — he might already be on his way. She needed to ring him to warn him off.

Tanaka's mobile started vibrating. He'd put it on silent because he knew how other passengers hated mobile phones ringing — or people having conversations on them. He saw it was Blain and toyed with the idea of not answering. After a few seconds, he accepted the call.

'Tanaka-san?'

'Yes.' He tried to keep his voice as low as possible, but already people were looking round in disapproval.

'You sound like you're on a train or something. I hope you're not heading to Osaka. It really isn't worth it.'

'No. I'm on a bus, Holly-san, heading back to Tokyo. Why wouldn't Osaka be worth it? I checked, and I couldn't have got there tonight anyway. But wasn't it him after all?'

'No, it *was*. Definitely. It's quite exciting. He was definitely in front of the Glico Man. An American put a selfie with him on Facebook because he thought he looked so like Roy Orbison. So, we have a new photograph of him. I've sent it to Emily. She'll be able to use it and says we've got a much better chance of success now we've got a high-resolution photo that's actually of him.'

'Good,' said Tanaka. He was deliberately trying to be as unforthcoming as possible. He'd received some information of his own from Izumi, as a result of the past cases search. He hadn't expected it to come up with a result so quickly, but it had.

'There was one more thing.' The young woman didn't seem to have picked up on his desire not to talk. 'I think I have a name for him. Well, a first name, at least.'

A couple of hours ago this would indeed have seemed like

a big breakthrough to Tanaka. But now he already knew what she was going to say, thanks to Izumi's information. He decided not to steal her moment of triumph, however. And he was interested that she'd decided to tell him — rather than trying to find the *Otaku* herself.

'It's Kelton,' she said breathlessly. 'Bizarrely that was Roy Orbison's middle name. Not only does he look a bit like him, he's named after him too.'

Tanaka knew all this already. Izumi had told him about an hour earlier, which was why he'd got the Matsumoto police sergeant to turn on his blue lights and race to the bus station to enable him to get the last bus back to Tokyo. Izumi's team had uncovered a double suicide of a couple in 1992 after they lost their house and all their savings in the Tokyo bubble crash. The father had bizarrely been dressed as a Roy Orbison lookalike, the mother as a *geisha*. The father had shot himself — the mother bled to death in the middle of an elaborate flower arrangement. The date: April 15th, 1992. The 25th anniversary of their death would be in a week's time. The couple had one surviving son, Kelton Sakamoto. He'd been taken into care. Nothing had been heard of him since — until now.

When he'd heard the news, Tanaka had momentarily felt an empathy with the man they were hunting. The detective knew the devastation the sudden loss of a father could wreak on a young boy. He'd faced that himself when his mother had admitted his Papa was never coming back. Had Blain ever suffered a similar loss? He didn't know — he'd never asked her. He didn't want to lower his own guard in front of the journalist, in case she used it to her advantage.

Nevertheless, even though he'd already obtained the information through police work, Tanaka knew Blain had done well getting hold of Sakamoto's first name. She'd been loyal to him by passing it to him first. It was time to pay her back, and he knew she would give them good coverage.

'Tanaka-san, are you still there?'

'Sorry, Holly-san. It's difficult to speak.' He mouthed another *sumimasen* to his fellow passengers, as they continued to glare at him each time he spoke. 'I'll send a text. Get some sleep after receiving it — you'll be getting up early in the morning.'

CHAPTER THIRTY-SEVEN

Tanaka had only managed to get a couple of hours' sleep on the bus then about three more in his office, with the emergency futon from the cupboard. But the adrenaline had kicked in now. He didn't feel tired.

He and Izumi were in an unmarked pool car about to set off behind a minibus — full of armed riot police. Behind them, the police's own press office team with a video cameraman. The only journalists travelling with them: Holly Blain and a photographer from her paper. It had been Tanaka's little reward for Blain to allow her to tag along. But the deal was the news would be carefully managed. The press office video wouldn't be given to broadcasters until at least the next day, allowing Blain's newspaper to have a free run at the print story.

Just before they set off, to Tanaka's surprise, Superintendent Yoshitake jumped into the back of his and Izumi's car.

'I can't let you youngsters have all the fun, Tanaka.'

'I think Sergeant Izumi is older even than you, sir.' He glanced across and smiled at Izumi, but his sergeant was concentrating on not losing the minibus ahead of him as it started to set off. 'And I thought we were in your bad books, and you were bringing in Chief Inspector Heizo to babysit us?'

'Don't get cheeky, Tanaka. Wait till we see if the bugger's actually at home and has the girls there before you start your victory dances.'

First, they sealed off the street with tape, traffic cones, and diversion signs. Then the armed police got into position, with Tanaka giving them orders via radio mikes and headsets.

Once all the officers were in position, they gave the 'ready' cue to Tanaka. He counted all the answers, made sure Blain and the press office team were safely out of the way, then gave the command.

'Go, go, go!'

The rhythm of his command was almost instantaneously answered by the bang, bang, bang of the battering ram breaking down the door.

Room by room, he heard the 'Clear' shout over the radio from the lead armed officer. Each one was somehow deflating. He wanted to find the girls, the Japanese *maiko* from Kyoto and the French teenager. He wanted to find this strange man who'd been leading them in a merry dance, before he had the chance to strike again.

But he could see which way this one was going and wasn't surprised to finally hear the words: 'All clear, Tanaka-san. It's empty.'

Tanaka, Izumi, and Yoshitake climbed slowly out of the car. Tanaka almost didn't want to look at the superintendent, but he seemed in a perfectly cheerful mood, considering the time of day and the fact they'd failed to find the girls — or Kelton Sakamoto.

'Don't worry, Tanaka-san.' For his boss to use an honorific was noteworthy in itself. 'Whatever happens — getting his name, where he lives — it's a big breakthrough. Once you've interviewed all the neighbours, combed this shitty little house from top to bottom, you will have more evidence. Just because we haven't got him today, doesn't mean he's going to give us the slip.'

Tanaka caught Blain's eye as he went in. The deal was that she and her photographer had to stay outside the house until Tanaka had checked it. Then they and the press office video team would be allowed inside for some shots. He knew she'd be able to tell from his expression, even if she hadn't over-heard Yoshitake's comments, that they'd failed to locate the man they were hunting.

Tanaka and Izumi slipped on protective footwear, overalls, and gloves, then got the evidence bags from the back of the car. The armed police, meanwhile, had all trooped back to the minibus, ready to go back to base. Tanaka was surprised when Yoshitake got lightweight protective clothing from his brief-case, too, and began to suit up into it.

'You're joining us, Yoshitake-san?'

'Of course, Tanaka. Delighted to get the chance to do it, really. When you get to my level — or in your case, perhaps I should say *if* you ever get to my level — you'll realise how much you miss real policing like this. I love the chance to get my hands dirty, even if it's only getting my hands round the neck of some Yakuza scum in an interview room.'

They divided up the rooms of the run-down house among them, filling the evidence bags as they went. The most inter-esting things were in the bathroom — strange-looking medical implements and tubes. Still with old blood on them.

Was this the equipment that had been used to drain Elin Granqvist's blood? Forensics should be able to provide a match — it could be the evidence that would see him convicted for causing her death, if not for actual murder.

Other things of interest included a large collection of Roy Orbison records and CDs and a badly maintained electro-acoustic guitar, missing two of its strings — the bottom and top E strings, thought Tanaka from his rudimentary knowledge.

In the lounge, Tanaka emptied the bookcase, bagging everything up. He was half-hoping that by taking all the books out he might uncover some sort of secret panel, leading him to where the girls were being held. Unfortunately, things like that only seemed to happen in Agatha Christie novels.

Suddenly, there was a shout from the kitchen.

It was Izumi. 'Boss, come and look at this.'

Izumi had pulled a kitchen unit away from the wall. Behind it was a boarded up and locked door.

'Careful, Tanaka,' said Yoshitake once he'd arrived to see what Izumi's shout was all about. 'The armed officers clearly didn't see that — so it hasn't been checked. Have you both got your guns?'

'We've got to get it open first, sir,' said Tanaka.

Izumi opened the back door. 'Hell! We'll be here all day. I've never seen so much shit in such a small space.'

Tanaka looked over his sergeant's shoulder. The tiny yard was full of debris. It would all need bagging up, yet most of it would probably prove useless.

'Are forensics on their way to check for prints and every-thing?' asked Yoshitake.

'I told them the time and address, Yoshitake-san,' said Tanaka. 'I'm surprised they're not here yet.'

Yoshitake pulled out his mobile. 'I'll chase them up.'

Izumi had meanwhile returned to the kitchen armed with a rusting iron bar, presumably to lever open the locked door. 'Are you going to keep me covered as I do it, Inspector?'

'Of course, Izumi. But it doesn't look as though anybody has been in there for years. I don't think anyone is going to burst out and attack you.'

Tanaka watched the blood vessels bulge on his sergeant's face as he wrenched the lock off the door, then watched him stagger backwards as it finally splintered and gave way. Then Izumi stood aside. 'After you, sir.' Then he pulled his handgun from its holster. 'And yes, I've got you covered.'

All Tanaka could see was steps leading down into a pit of blackness. Some sort of cellar. He searched for a light switch, found it, and tried to switch on the light. Nothing happened.

'Have you got a torch?' asked Izumi. Almost before he'd finished the question, Tanaka had got out his pocket torch and switched it on. It felt as though he had a pair of birds or butterflies trapped in his stomach, it was fluttering so much. Were the girls in here? If so, he feared for their state of health. It was deathly quiet.

He began to climb down the steps into the dank space, ducking his head down to avoid hitting it on the low, sloping ceiling. In seconds, he'd reached the bottom. He swung the torch round the small, damp room. There were piles and piles of things, most covered in black plastic bags. But no sign of life. It just seemed to be another dumping ground like the back yard. Tanaka, his hands still protected by gloves, ripped open one of the bags. It was full of photo albums, from the days when everyone used film and printed everything out. What a shame, thought Tanaka, as he leafed through them, that these days so many photographs just stayed in computers, eventually — in all probability — being lost to subsequent generations. Here there was a family's story.

He spent a few moments flicking through the album. The cover had the year's date and month on it — April 1991 — and some subject headings. Himeji, Kyoto, and Osaka. They must have gone on some sort of holiday, and from the photos it appeared to have been during *sakura* season — which would tie in with the April date too.

Izumi disturbed his reverie, shouting down the stairs. 'Are you alright, Tanaka-san?'

He'd been holding his pocket torch in his teeth to free his hands to look at the album. 'Yes, Izumi-kun,' he mumbled through the end of the torch. Then he freed his mouth to be able to speak more clearly. 'There's nothing much here. I'm just looking through a few bits — I'll be up in a moment.'

Tanaka placed the small torch between his teeth again and re-opened the photo album. There seemed to be a family of three — an older man, who seemed to favour wearing black and big hair, but nothing like the slavish look of his adult son. His wife looked considerably younger and was — Tanaka confessed to himself — stunningly beautiful, though fragile. And then the boy. Aged... what? Seven? Maybe eight? Nothing particularly special about him, and he looked to have inherited his father's sharper looks than the doll-face beauty of his mother.

Some of the photographs were of them individually, some of all three together. More of the mother and the boy than the father, who'd probably been doing most of the photography.

The first section was Himeji. The grounds and cherry trees. In a boat, going round the castle moat, wearing traditional Asian *sugegasa* hats. And then various shots at the different levels of the castle keep. The final shot in that sequence — the mother, holding some sort of cherry blossom flower arrangement, pictured in front of the castle shrine, her arms hugging her son.

Tanaka knew he ought to stop this — Izumi and Yoshitake would be getting impatient. They could get the local uniformed police to bag all this up, and then go through it back at headquarters. But it was slightly addictive.

He allowed himself a quick flick through to the end, like one of those old flicker books he used to have as a kid — the torchlight accentuating the almost filmic effect. Shot after shot of the *Miyako Odori* — but the traditional theatre, not the new one at the university. The tea ceremony too. Photography wasn't allowed in either — the father must have done it all surreptitiously.

The album ended with the pose of a triumphant athlete. The Glico Man sign, advertising some local Osaka confectionery company's offerings. The athlete himself: white vest and shorts with red lettering on it, arms aloft against the background of a vivid blue athletics track, one running leg raised. And in front of it, the son — Kelton Sakamoto — copying the pose.

A pose that — as an adult, a very disturbed adult — he'd apparently repeated in Osaka just a few hours earlier.

CHAPTER THIRTY-EIGHT

The moonlit night was perfect and boded well for the next day. He'd checked the weather forecast too — there should be the synchronicity he wanted. The bright sun shining on Fuji-san to give the best possible light. The winter snows still not fully melted — so the iced peak of the mountain would be looking its best. And the blossom caught just before full bloom, the petals yet to show any degradation. Perfect white petals, with a hint of pink to match her skin.

It was a view known throughout Japan, throughout the world. The Chureito Pagoda in the foreground, snow-capped Fuji-san in the background, and, in between, a sea of pink and white cherry blossom.

The crimson red walls of the five-storey pagoda were a perfect match of her lips, and the red highlights on her eyelids. In the correct light, each of the roofs of the pagoda's five storeys appeared jet black — matching her hair.

He hadn't been able to decide which of the two views to choose. This one, or the lake. Lakes had always excited him. He associated them with boat trips, ice creams, being spoilt by his mother and father. Pointing to things in souvenir shops and being bought exactly what he wanted. Sometimes he missed not having a brother or sister. But then he would have had to share. And he was never alone. His mother made sure he was never alone. Even at night, if he had one of his terrible dreams, she would climb into his bed and comfort him until he went back to sleep.

That didn't happen now, because she was gone.

Now his dreams tortured him.

The advantage of the lake was that — on a clear, still, perfect day — Fuji-san appeared twice. Once, in its natural state, pointing to the heavens. The second image — its mirror reflection in the black waters of Lake Kawaguchi — pointing down to the depths. The yin and yang. Heaven and hell.

He'd started to try to capture that. To build his construction there... but something wasn't quite right.

He still had time. But not much. He had to work quickly. Before the photographers arrived, trying to capture the perfect image.

The next morning they would see something perfect.

A tribute to the beauty of his perfect mother.

Perfect, that is, until she decided to abandon him.

How could she have done that? It wasn't fair.

He would say that to the *maiko* if she started to whine and complain. If the effects of the Rohypnol began to wear off.

It was a quotation from somewhere, that his father often said to him, when he was whinging about something or other, or on the rare occasions his parents didn't give him what he wanted.

'Life isn't fair. It's just fairer than death. That's all.'

And then he'd put on one of his favourite Roy Orbison tracks.

'Life Fades Away'.

CHAPTER THIRTY-NINE

The second package Blain received arrived in the same way: hand-delivered to her office block's despatch area, in a similar plastic-covered padded bag. This time she took it straight to the office toilets and hid herself away in a cubicle before opening it. She still hadn't told Tanaka about the first delivery, and she knew that was wrong. Both packages could be examined for fingerprints — possibly even DNA evidence —unless The Flower Arranger wanted to be caught, Blain expected him to have made sure he hadn't left anything traceable.

This was all starting to feel personal. What did the man actually want her to do with the material? Put it in the newspaper? There was nothing really to hang a story on. And even if there was, she didn't really want to *become* the story.

Her eagerness to see what was inside was counterbalanced by a shiver of fear. She could feel the goose bumps on her arms, as, once again, the stuck-down plastic refused to be prised apart. Even from the outside, though, she could tell the contents were similar. Same weight, same shape — giving away that there was presumably another small cardboard box at the bottom.

And there was. She thrust her hand in and brought it out, before examining what looked like a similar photograph.

Another single bloom.

Exactly the same slightly asymmetrical shape. Or at least, it had no rotational symmetry — though the left side was the mirror image of the right, it looked almost as if a petal had already been plucked.

But this time, there was a difference. The flower was a deep red colour. The colour of a *geisha's* lipstick.

An almost unnatural red.

Blain rubbed the smoothness of the petal, between fore-finger and thumb.

Silky smooth, almost like skin.

Then she realised why the colour had seemed unnatural. It was, and much of it had rubbed off in her fingers. It had simply been painted on.

Full of foreboding now, she finally pulled out the photo-graph. As soon as she saw it clearly, Blain knew that, this time, she couldn't keep things from Tanaka.

It was the same woman dressed as a *geisha* — and once again the face was obliterated.

But her face hadn't been scratched off.

It had been covered over with the face of a teenage Lolita. Made-up, eyes staring.

The face of Marie-Louise Durand.

When the next alert came through from Emily, Blain was unsure what to do. Professionally, she needed to get on and write up the story of the raid for the next morning's paper. Ethically, she really ought to inform Tanaka about the two strange packages she'd received. But somehow, in holding back information about the first, she'd constructed a lie. It was a lie she didn't want to admit to — not yet. And she didn't want to face the detective's anger and likely withdrawal of cooperation, when he realised she'd withheld information from him.

As a favour to her, Tanaka had given the *Tōkei Shimbun* unprecedented access — they would wipe the floor with all their print rivals. And he had kindly agreed to make the embargo for the police press office video and news release a mid-morning one the next day. That way, the police could appear to be cooperating — but all the morning outlets would have to refer to the exclusive *Tōkei Shimbun* coverage for their stories. She didn't want to undo all the good that had been done thanks to their relationship — for now, she convinced herself that keeping silent about the packages was in everyone's interest. The photo of Marie-Louise was, at least, the one that had been released to news organisations. It wasn't as though it was a photograph of her in captivity. And — she told herself — there was no guarantee the packages actually were from Sakamoto. They could just have easily been sent by a crank.

So, for now, Emily's use of social media still seemed the best way forward. While she'd been waiting outside the Sakamotos' house for Tanaka to give her and the photographer permission to enter, she'd narrowed down some of the search terms with Emily in a phone call.

'The trouble is,' said Emily, 'it's sending alerts to me all the time. And it's only 7am. Imagine what it's going to be like later in the day.'

Blain racked her brain. How could they narrow it down? 'What about if we combine certain locations with the search terms so it only flags up if those locations are mentioned — *and* the other three terms we outlined?'

'That might work, yes. We could try. Certainly there would be less stuff to check.'

Blain looked through the latest *sakura zensen* forecast. Where was coming into full bloom next? There were five or six options, covering a wide area of Japan. Most of it further north now — but mountainous areas in the centre, west, and south too. She gave a list to Emily and crossed her fingers.

About three hours later, once she was back in the office, starting to write up the next morning's story, the alert from Emily flashed on her mobile screen.

A photo had been posted on an English woman's Instagram account. Normally, the account in question focused on interior design — the author seemed to be a leading home interiors feature writer for British magazines. But she appeared to be on holiday in Japan, and this photograph was of Mount Fuji. Framed by *sakura*, with an inverted mirror image of the mountain top reflected in the glassy stillness of Lake Kawaguchi, in the Fuji Five Lakes area — a sort of Japanese version of England's Lake District.

It was a scene that would appear on many tourists' photo streams at this time of year. The difference, though, was explained in the caption.

Strange giant flower arrangement of cherry blossom by Mount Fuji, latest stop on our sakura tour.

Blain picked up the jacket from the back of her chair. 'I need to borrow the pool car,' she said to Yamamoto.

'I'd rather you finished the story first, Blain-san.'

'It's something I need to check to do with the story.'

'Can't you get the metro? The car is normally reserved for awkward-to-get-to places and breaking news.'

'Look, Yamamoto-san.' She knew she could afford to put her foot down now. Without her, there would be no story for tomorrow's paper. She had the upper hand. 'You will get your story. Without fail. I just need to make it as good as I possibly can. And for that, I need to check something else out. With the pool car.'

Yamamoto sighed, opened his desk drawer, and — in a motion like a baseball pitcher — threw Blain the keys.

'Don't be gone long. And don't let me down.'

Before she left the office, Blain placed the two packages she'd received in her bag. Perhaps an opportunity might arise to tell Tanaka — and rid herself of her feeling of guilt.

Blain ignored as many of the speed limits as she could while not attracting the attention of the police. It was a good enough story — the *Tōkei Shimbun* could afford the speeding fines. With her phone in the dashboard cradle, she used the maps app as her satnav rather than the built-in system which she'd never been able to fathom. Little more than a hundred kilometres, but, with the daytime traffic, the journey time was coming up as two-and-a-half hours. And would she really find anything when she was there? Her hope was that Emily's application — having alerted her to a new flower arrangement — might come up trumps again with an actual sighting of Kelton Sakamoto, if he was still in the area.

Should she ring Tanaka? If she wanted more exclusive access like this morning's, then, really, she had to play ball. Keeping her eye on the traffic in front, she flicked from the maps app to recent calls and found and selected his number. The phone rang and rang without him picking up. Really, she should have texted before she set off. It would have to wait now until she arrived — she wasn't confident enough about her driving in Japan to risk texting while she was at the wheel.

Blain wasn't exactly sure where the Instagram photo had been taken from, but, from the view of Fuji-san, it had to be somewhere on the lake's northern shore. As she filtered off the highway and onto the local lakeside road, she saw a collection of tents and marquees by a group of cherry trees. Some sort of *sakura* festival. As likely a place as any for an English tourist to have been.

She parked the car and then half-ran towards the lakeside, her phone in her hand with the photo saved and displayed. All she had to do was try to match up the view of Mount Fuji with her own eyes with the one in the photograph. She reached the shore — too many people were milling about. She couldn't see any sort of flower arrangement — but then, perhaps she was too late. Or perhaps the Instagram user hadn't actually posted the photograph at the time she took it. It could have been days earlier. Next, Blain tried to line up the view in the photo with the view before her own eyes. The angles weren't quite right. Triangulating with landmark buildings on the opposite shore, she realised she was too far to the east. She needed to be further along. But there was some sort of river or canal bisecting the shoreline here — she couldn't go on foot.

She ran as fast as she could, back towards the car, ignoring the confused looks of the festival goers. Then she drove along the road in a westerly direction, all the time leaning down to check the view from the passenger window. A lorry blared its horn at her as she veered into the centre of the road. She quickly yanked the steering wheel back.

After a few hundred metres more, she saw a sign on the

left for a lakeside viewing area and car park. She took a quick glance from the window. This looked more promising. She turned down the short lane, and then parked, and rushed from the vehicle down towards the shoreline.

There it was. Right in front of her, surrounded by a handful of gawpers. A strange framework of flowers and branches. Beautiful in itself, with its use of the blossoms. Yet feeling as though something was missing. Its centrepiece. Blain could only give thanks that the centre was empty. Elin Granqvist hadn't been so lucky.

She started to take some of her own photos from different angles and a few close ups of the flowers and blossoms — intending to show them to Tanaka. She knew she ought to ring him straight away.

'Beautiful, isn't it?' said a nearby tourist, obviously recognising her as English — or at least European — despite the fact that many Japanese these days treated her more like a native. 'What do you think it is?'

Blain knew very well what it was. And that its beauty was of an entirely sinister nature. But she didn't want to get into a conversation. She didn't have time.

'I've no idea,' she said, unsmiling, determined to close down the exchange. She moved a few paces away and then rang Tanaka. Hopefully, he would be pleased with her. Hopefully he would have seen her earlier missed call so he wouldn't tear her off a strip for not alerting him sooner.

But what he said had her fighting for breath.

'There's been another one. At Fuji Five Lakes.'

'I know,' she said. 'I'm right by it. On the northern shore of Lake Kawaguchi. I'm looking at it now.'

'I don't know what you're talking about, Blain-san. But if you're in the area, come now. To the Chureito Pagoda. If

you're on public transport you need Shimoyoshida station —
then it's a twenty-minute walk up the hill.'

'I'm not. I'm in the pool car.'

'Ring me when you get here, and I'll get you through the
cordon. But I warn you, it's not a pretty sight.'

CHAPTER FORTY

The call to Tanaka had come through soon after they'd left the Sakamotos' house. A body had been found. And as it had been ritualistically placed in the centre of a giant flower arrangement, the local police had made the connection and alerted Tanaka's team in accordance with the national police bulletin he'd issued soon after the Swedish girl's death.

As he and Izumi wound their way up towards the pagoda, Tanaka was thankful they didn't have to climb the hundreds of flights of steps: the usual access for visitors. The Chureito Pagoda was a thing of great beauty — Tanaka knew of it from calendar photographs and magazines, although he'd never visited before. One day, when all this was over, he should bring Miho and the boys.

Through the canopy of cherry trees, they caught their first glimpse of its magnificence. It wasn't an ancient monument — although it looked like it. On the way, chauffeured by Izumi in the squad car, Tanaka had carried out a little mid-drive internet research. It had been built as recently as the 1960s. But, with its five-winged storeys, each painted in brilliant crimson red with white highlighted panels, it was a perfect complement to the sea of cherry blossom and, in the distance, snow-capped Fuji-san.

The local police had already taped off the pagoda and the bankside leading to the forest behind it. That was where most of the police activity seemed to be. Already a small tent had been erected in what seemed a particularly awkward spot above the pagoda, and a number of officers were milling about in protective suits.

Tanaka and Izumi parked the car and introduced themselves to the senior local officer.

'Thank you for coming so swiftly, Tanaka-san. I'm Inspector Masuda Michihiro of Fuji Five Lakes Police Station.'

Tanaka returned Michihiro's bow. 'I'm sorry we're not meeting in more pleasant circumstances, Michihiro-san. This is Sergeant Izumi, my deputy at the Gaikoku-jin Unit.'

Izumi and Michihiro also exchanged bows, and then Michihiro led them to the stairs which climbed higher, towards the back of the pagoda itself.

'The body is in quite an awkward spot, I'm afraid. The ground was already quite muddy from all the photographers — amateur and professional — who gather there each day trying to get the best shot. It's ironic that it's considered a stereotypical view of ancient Japan — yet the pagoda itself wasn't built until the 1960s, as you're no doubt aware.'

Tanaka nodded somewhat sheepishly. He was aware of that now — but hadn't been until about thirty minutes ago when he swotted up on it in the car.

'It was one of the photographers who discovered it, at about 5am this morning. They get up very early to try to bag the best position. It gets very crowded on sunny days in *sakura* season.'

Tanaka could already hear Izumi panting behind him from the exertion of the climb.

Once they'd ascended around fifty steps, Michihiro turned off and made his way at a right angle towards the tent, with the Tokyo detectives following behind. When they reached the hastily erected canvas structure, Michihiro pulled the back flap aside to let them in.

Since they'd first seen the tent from below the pagoda, one of the officers had folded back the front wall flaps, presumably to allow more light for the police photographers who were busily snapping away.

It meant that Tanaka's first view of the body — and the flower arrangement — was presumably exactly how Sakamoto intended.

Tanaka's eye was initially drawn to the pristine beauty of Fuji-san, shining brightly on the horizon, the sun glittering on its snow-capped conical peak, like a giant pointed meringue. Only then did he pull his view backwards and observe what almost looked like floating clouds of white-pink *sakura* on the mountainside. Then finally, he focused on what he'd really come to see, although he didn't really want to.

The *maiko* was exquisitely made-up, her powdered white face a perfect match with the pristine snow of Fuji-san. The red of her lips and lids of her now closed eyes were exactly the same tone as the crimson-walled pagoda behind her. The few areas of bare skin — around her hairline, and no doubt the back of her neck if he walked round her — they too were an exact colour-match: for the sea of pink-white *sakura*. It was almost a thing of beauty, a work of art, especially combined with the frame of the flower arrangement itself. The different varieties of cherry blossoms. Orchids too, Tanaka believed he could see.

But one thing disturbed the scene. The wound on her neck,

and the darkened trail of blood leading from it, sullying the pure-white of the powdered skin.

That and the fact that — suspended as she was on some sort of strange wire frame — she was very much dead. And this time, Tanaka believed, not even Inspector Nishimura could claim it had been an accidental death.

CHAPTER FORTY-ONE

B lain was grateful to Tanaka for letting her in to see the crime scene, but it was strictly on the understanding that any photographs or other detailed coverage had to be run past him first. Normally, she would resist all attempts by sources to vet her copy. But this was slightly different. It was the lead story across the whole of Japan — what everyone was talking about. And she was at the centre of it.

'Two minutes, Holly-san,' warned Tanaka. 'That's all. But that will give you time to view the body and take some photographs. That is something almost unprecedented in Japanese police-press relations. Don't abuse it. And don't tell anyone else you're with the newspapers. If anyone asks you anything, refer them to me.'

When she finally got to the tent and saw the body for the first time, it was like someone had placed an ice pack next to her heart. She felt unable to even breathe. She wanted to tear her eyes away from the sight of death but found she couldn't. Quickly she took photographs, though she knew some of them would never be used. They were just too shocking. And the dead *maiko* reminded her of the woman dressed with traditional *geisha*-like clothes, and with a *geisha's* hairstyle, in the photographs *she'd* been sent. This, though, was definitely not the time to tell Tanaka.

When her phone bleeped in the middle of the tent, she felt horribly self-conscious. The eyes of the various police officers suddenly turned on her, as though they were wondering for the first time who she actually was. But given what was happening, she couldn't be a blushing violet. She took out her phone from the protective overall and saw it was another alert from Emily.

Quickly, she turned and searched for Tanaka in the sea of faces. He was deep in conversation, but she wasn't about to stand on ceremony.

'Tanaka-san. I've got a visual alert from Emily. Fuji Q Highland amusement park. Just now. He's still in the area.'

'Where's that?' Tanaka shouted back.

Blain pointed down the mountainside, to the other valley. 'Over there. You can just see the top of the giant roller coaster.'

Tanaka barked various instructions to the local officers as he and Izumi raced off to the steps to take them back to the squad car. Blain ran after them.

When they reached the car, Blain climbed in the rear seat without waiting for permission. 'Remember,' she said to Tanaka, 'you've got this information thanks to me. I need you to drop me at my car. It's halfway down this road.'

Tanaka glowered over his shoulder but gave a silent nod in answer to Izumi's questioning look. 'We're not waiting for you though,' he said.

'Did I ask you to? Just drop me off — I'll catch you up there. I'll send you the photo now.'

She'd deliberately parked facing downhill in case she needed to make a quick getaway, so, almost as soon as she'd climbed in, she was underway, first having to remove the parking ticket stuck to the windscreen. Yamamoto could pay that.

At the bottom of the hill, she took another risk, jumping the lights in order to try to catch up with the detectives. They'd turned the blue lights and sirens on. It was another 'ambulance chase' for Blain — of a police car. At least she'd been well-trained.

It was the roller coaster where the photograph had been taken. Again, it was the name — rather than the actual photograph — that had triggered Emily's alert system. Another tourist — this time an Australian man — had taken a photo of a 'realistic Roy Orbison lookalike' in the roller coaster car behind him as it climbed up to the top of the structure, with its heart-stopping views towards Mount Fuji and the lakes.

By the time Blain arrived, Tanaka and Izumi were already questioning the staff at the entrance to the roller coaster, and other park-goers, showing them the photo she'd texted them.

There were animated conversations and pointing. They'd seen him — but they'd also seen him leaving. Someone had even talked to him. He'd left a large rucksack in their left-luggage lockers and was apparently heading back to Tokyo.

'What are the options for getting back to Tokyo from here?'

'There's a direct bus from Fuji Q Highland — or the train from Kawaguchiko. You can get the local train from here to there and a few services stop at this station. Or, of course, by car.'

'He doesn't have a car,' said Tanaka aloud. 'I've already checked that. What's the name of the bus company?'

The official handed over a leaflet. 'Izumi. Ring this lot — demand that they check their passenger lists and see if he's booked on.'

Blain and Tanaka looked at each other, both wondering what more they could do. Suddenly, Tanaka was on the phone again. 'It's Inspector Tetsu Tanaka here from the Tokyo Metropolitan Police Department. Put me through to your controller, please. It's urgent.' She watched him roll his eyes as he waited. Then he was speaking again. Blain struggled to make out what he was saying, with Izumi shouting in her other ear. 'I want you to stop all trains from Kawa—'

Tanaka stopped mid-sentence, as Izumi frantically waved his arms in front of his face.

'I've got him, Tanaka-san. He's on the bus, not the train. The 2.23pm from Fuji Q Highland.'

Blain looked at her watch. It was just coming up to 2.45pm. She still had to get the next day's story written and had been ignoring Yamamoto's calls. But she felt she had to stay at the centre of the action.

'It's too dangerous to take you, Blain-san. I'm sorry. We'll catch up later.' Tanaka and Izumi started running back to their car, with Tanaka making more frantic calls on his phone, presumably asking for roadblocks and back-up. Blain ran after them. She wasn't going to give up the chase, even if she had to use the newspaper pool car to do it. As she ran back to the car park, she checked the bus' route. It didn't go the most direct way. It looked like it followed the expressway to Gotenba then made a right-angle turn towards Tokyo. By using a different route, it might be possible to overtake them. But Tanaka would — presumably — be already on to the bus company, getting them to alert the driver.

All Blain could do was follow the training her local news editor had given her when she'd started out as a reporter. Put her foot down hard on the accelerator and make sure she didn't lose the flashing blue light of Tanaka and Izumi's squad car.

CHAPTER FORTY-TWO

Tanaka phoned police headquarters, leaving an urgent message requesting Yoshitake to instruct the bus company to get their driver to stop. But when the superintendent got back to him, it wasn't good news.

'There's a protocol for these things, Tanaka. I can't just go round breaking it. We don't know if he's armed or not. We do know that he's dangerous. So it's madness to alert him. The best way is simply to send a unit to the bus station at Shibuya Mark City and head him off there. He won't be able to go anywhere.'

Tanaka slammed his hand down on the squad car dashboard, attracting an angry glare from Izumi. 'Come on, Yoshitake-san. You know that's not good enough. Why can't the driver simply pull over and pretend he's got a puncture? That way Sakamoto won't be alerted to anything.'

'I can't go against protocol, Tanaka, and I won't. If you're haring after this bus, turn your blue light and siren off too. We don't want him to pull some sort of stunt on the bus. At the moment, we have two deaths on our hands. We don't want a whole bloody bus full. And you can bet there will be foreign tourists on it. We'd be in deep shit if any of them get hurt — especially with the French girl missing, and the Swedish girl dead.'

Tanaka cut the call in anger and slumped back in the passenger seat. 'He won't do it.'

'Why not?' said Izumi.

'He says it's too risky. Sakamoto might get all jumpy and start taking hostages.'

'He's got a point I suppose, Tanaka-san.'

'And he wants us to turn off the siren and blue lights.'

'If we do that, we'll never get through this traffic. It's our only chance of catching them up.'

'And what if we do speed up and catch them, Izumi? Given what Yoshitake's just said, he doesn't want us heading them off. He's happy to simply wait till Mark City and arrest him there.'

Tanaka's sergeant just stared straight ahead, grim-faced. 'I don't care what he says. After all this, I'm keeping the blue light and siren on, at least until we see them or until we near Shibuya. I don't want to miss seeing the handcuffs go round his wrists, and I shouldn't think you do either.'

The minutes passed without any sign of the bus. They'd now been driving for more than an hour, weaving their way through the traffic. Tanaka had stuck Post-it notes with the name of the bus company, the make of vehicle, and the vehicle registration number to the dashboard in front of Izumi to help him know what they were looking for.

'How much longer till we get there, according to your satnav, Tanaka-san?'

'About twenty minutes.'

'Well, it's already gone 4.05pm. The bus arrives at 4.25pm. We're not going to beat them, but we might arrive at just about the same time.'

They finally caught the coach just as it was turning right to go up the ramp into the Mark City bus station, on an upper floor of the Shibuya shopping complex which bore its name. By then, Tanaka had ordered Izumi to shut down the light and siren. If Sakamoto turned round and looked through the rear window, though, he would no doubt be suspicious that a police squad car was heading into the terminal directly after the bus.

As the coach came to a halt and a squad of armed officers surrounded it, Tanaka and Izumi leapt out of the car. With a screech of brakes, they heard another car stop behind them. Tanaka turned. Blain. She was determined, he'd give her that.

Ignoring the reporter, Tanaka and Izumi rushed to the bus as the door opened, showing their warrant cards and ordering the armed officers to step aside. Tanaka wasn't going to be denied the moment of arresting the man he'd been chasing for so many days.

The driver and passengers looked completely bemused.

Tanaka scanned the seats. People were starting to stand, and to get up, obscuring his view.

He drew his gun. 'Armed police. Sit down everyone. Now. And no one move.'

They hurried to obey. Tanaka, followed by Izumi, checked each seat in turn. The bus was only half full, if that. By the time they were three-quarters of the way down the aisle, Tanaka realised it was a lost cause. He carried on right to the back of the vehicle to double check, but it was obvious

Sakamoto wasn't there. Perhaps he'd made the booking just to throw them off the scent.

Tanaka moved back to the front of the bus where the driver was — as requested — sitting tight and not moving. He got the wanted poster which had been distributed to all police stations across the country and showed it to the man.

'This guy. Kelton Sakamoto. He was booked in all the way from Fuji Q Highland to Mark City, yet he's not here. Did he even get on?'

'Yes. He had a heavy rucksack. I had to help him load it on and off the luggage bay.'

'He got off? Where?'

'At Gotenba. I queried it as he'd paid right through to Shibuya, but he just said he'd changed his mind.'

Tanaka drew in a slow, long breath. Then he turned back to the passengers. 'Okay. Many thanks for your assistance, and sorry if I startled you. There's no need to be alarmed. And please feel free to now get off the bus. However, if during the journey any of you spoke to this man...' he waved the wanted poster in the air, '...then please give a statement to my sergeant here. Otherwise, you're free to go and thank you for your time.'

Tanaka stepped down from the bus and walked over to a waiting Yoshitake. He was aware of Blain hovering, trying to overhear. He didn't really care at this stage.

'Well?' the superintendent asked.

'Given us the slip, I'm afraid. He got off at Gotenba.'

'Okay. I think that means we're going to have to change tactics. I've supported your plan to keep his identity from the public so far, but since this morning's murder — and I'm going to call it a murder even though we're not certain yet — the situation has changed. He's a killer. Two women are already dead, and we believe he's holding the other somewhere. He's got to be stopped. By any means.'

When he got home, he could tell Miho knew he was in a foul mood. She didn't try to ask him how his day was and didn't ask why he hadn't got home in time to kiss the boys goodnight. She simply made him his own pot of green tea and then started preparing a meal for him.

'You don't have to do that,' he said. 'I can do it myself.'

'I want to. You look exhausted.'

Tanaka laughed, and drew her into a hug. 'I am exhausted. We were so close to catching him today. A hair's breadth away.'

'Go and sit down. Change into something more comfortable and just relax. At least for a couple of hours. Then let's go to bed early.'

Tanaka raised his eyebrows.

Miho gave a tinkling giggle, like a girl. 'To sleep, husband. I can tell you need some sleep. That's all.'

But Tanaka couldn't sleep. He went over everything again and again in his head, trying to find the piece of the puzzle that might finally trap Sakamoto. He knew tomorrow's newspaper and press stories would be a game changer. They'd finally released his image — with an embargo of 6am the next morning, allowing the overnight newspapers and the breakfast television news to break it at the same time. Only one reporter had the full story, though, and that was Blain. She deserved it for all her help via her data scientist friend. It had so nearly paid off — after all, that was how they ended up at the amusement park, how they nearly caught him on the bus. But after her story hit the news-stands tomorrow morning, everything would change. He hoped Yoshitake had decided not to replace him with Chief Inspector Sano Heizo after all. There had been no further mention of it, and, as far as he knew, Heizo was still up in Hokkaido on the multiple rape case. But once everything was splashed over the newspapers, including the second death, Yoshitake would be breathing down his neck every five minutes expecting results. The death of a foreign teenager — was one thing. The killing of an innocent *maiko* from the *Miyako Odori* was quite another.

It was an attack on Japanese culture itself.

A sacrilege.

Still sleep wouldn't come. Too much racing round his brain. He tried daydreaming. Taking himself back to his childhood in the Okinawan islands, when his mother, father, and himself had been a happy family. Just the three of them, in many ways mirroring Sakamoto's family. Sakamoto — judging by the photos he'd seen — looked like he'd been a spoiled brat in his youth. Tanaka had been an only child too, but he'd had to grow up quickly when the Americans finally pulled out of Japan, and his American father had pulled out of the marriage to his mother. Tanaka had had to assume the role of man of the family, the responsible one. Perhaps it explained his boring, sober nature that Miho and the boys always teased him about.

He rolled over. Miho was fast asleep. He didn't want to disturb her.

He went downstairs and made himself another green tea. But still the thoughts raced. The answer had to lie somewhere. Perhaps it was in the photo albums. Sakamoto seemed to be on a tour of nostalgia — nostalgia and death. The clue to where he was going next might be in one of the picture collections. Tanaka resolved to check them all thoroughly in the morning.

The thought of the albums got him wondering about Sakamoto's house again on the north-western outskirts of Tokyo, in the Oizumigakuen-cho district of Nerima. The house was run-down — worth at most ten million yen if you were to buy it, possibly less, small beer by Tokyo property standards, even in spite of the crash. But if Sakamoto was a single salaryman, it was still unusual to own a house at all. A house with a cellar, too. Even Tanaka and Miho didn't have a cellar.

He was half-dozing on the lounge futon now. But the thought of the cellar suddenly concentrated his mind. It was a narrow cellar, filled virtually to the brim with bags and rubbish. Tanaka pictured it in his mind again. It must have taken up only about a third of the floor width of the house. He pictured the walls in his head. On one side, the torch had shown the house's old concrete foundations, fractured and repaired in several places, no doubt due to earthquakes. But the other side! *It was a new breeze-block wall. No fractures, no cracking, no repairs.*

Tanaka was up on his feet in an instant. He crept upstairs and grabbed his clothes without waking Miho. Then he quietly stole downstairs again and wrote her a note and left it in the kitchen. She would be angry with him, but she would understand he needed to do this now.

He finished his tea, then looked in the cupboard for the caffeine tablets. He took two, then put the packet back. Then picked it up again and put it in his pocket. He was going to need them.

Tanaka opened the car door as quietly as possible. They had off-street parking, but such a narrow space took real skill to avoid scratching the paintwork each time he parked or set off. He was especially careful now and tried to rev the engine as little as possible.

The drive to Oizumigakuen-cho would take forever in the daytime traffic. But now, just after midnight, his maps app was showing just 38 minutes to Sakamoto's house, including traffic. Even so, halfway there he took another caffeine pill.

He showed his ID to the uniformed officer who was taking his turn as part of the 24-hour guard outside the house, just in case Sakamoto tried to come back. The officer lifted the tape so that Tanaka could park his car in the parking space.

Tanaka hurried the guard along, telling him to let him into the house immediately. He didn't bother suiting up — forensics had already done their sweep. And there may be no time to lose. He knew Sakamoto wasn't here — the question was, had he taken Marie-Louise with him?

First, he raced to the door in the kitchen which led down to the cellar, just to check his memory wasn't playing tricks. He got out his pocket torch again, swung it left and right, over each side wall. *He was right.* On the right-hand side, old and repaired concrete foundations. On the left-hand side, a new breeze-block wall — not a crack in sight. He tapped it with the end of the torch, to try to gauge its thickness. The sound it made didn't really tell him anything.

But then, almost inaudible, he thought he heard an answering thud.

He did it again, adrenaline coursing through his body. Banishing his tiredness better than any caffeine pills could.

Again, the same answering thud.

He shouted out. 'Hello, is anyone there?' No reply. He

scanned the new wall again with the torch beam — but there was no entrance, no way in.

Tanaka ran as fast as he could back up the stairs, and out into the yard. He fell over some of the rubbish, making a terrible clattering sound and cutting his trousers and leg on some old rusting dustbin lid. Pain shot through his leg, as neighbours started turning their lights on, wondering what was happening. He struggled on, playing the torch beam over the exterior wall and what little he could see of the yard floor, trying to find an entrance. Again, there wasn't one.

He limped back into the house and searched in the bathroom cupboards for a bandage and some antiseptic. The leg was bleeding badly now. He couldn't find anything. He looked in his pockets. His face mask. Tanaka rarely wore one, but they were so ubiquitous in Japan he felt he had to carry one. He fashioned it into a makeshift dressing, tying it as tightly as he dared around his shin. The trousers, though, were ruined. He'd have to buy a new pair.

Sitting down in the lounge on the dirty *tatami* matting, he tried to think. If there was a part of the cellar which was accessible, if he wasn't imagining the banging just now — and he was sure he wasn't — then there must be a way in. If necessary, come daylight, he'd get a demolition gang round to knock the breeze-block partition down. In fact, if he could locate a sledgehammer at this time of night, he might have a go himself.

Then his eyes were drawn to the bookcase. The bookcase where before he'd wondered, if the books were removed, would it reveal a secret passageway or panel or door? There was nothing there. But there *was* something strange about the bookcase itself. He saw it now — he hadn't before. It was much deeper than a bookcase needed to be. Deep enough, wide enough, to conceal a very narrow flight of stairs. But a flight of stairs only needed to be as wide as the person descending or ascending. If they went sideways, it could be even narrower.

Tanaka frantically tried to dislodge the furniture. It wouldn't move. He went to the front and called the police officer there inside.

'I want to try to move this,' he said.

They both set to it, pushing and pulling. Still no movement.

'I don't think it's going to budge,' said the policemen. 'Why do you think it will?'

'I think there's a staircase below.'

The officer scrunched his face in doubt. 'Okay. Well, if there is, and if it's deliberately concealed, perhaps it operates electrically.'

'Good thinking,' said Tanaka.

They looked around for some sort of control panel. They couldn't see anything. Nothing but a row of light switches next to the bookcase.

Tanaka got his torch out. The bookcase was jammed in a corner. If it slid to the side, it could only move one way — to the left where the bank of switches were. Or did it pivot? Or was he just imagining the whole thing? Had tiredness finally sent him crazy?

He knelt down on the floor and peered at it with his torch. He couldn't see anything — no marks to indicate movement, no scratches, nothing. Then he got out his phone and turned it to its brightest, most battery-draining setting, and then turned the torch app on. It gave out a beam even brighter than his actual torch. He got his eyes right down to floor level and looked again.

'There!' he shouted, pulling the police officer's face down

next to his. 'Look, see those faint lines.' The officer nodded. 'It moves. It definitely moves this way.'

His eyes were drawn to the bank of light switches. Yet there were other light switches by the door. He went over to them, switched them off. The entire room was plunged into darkness. Reversing his finger movements, he switched them on again. So if they controlled the lights, what did the other switches do?

A bank of four. It triggered a memory in his brain somewhere. A bank robbery case from when he'd just started out as a detective. No one could understand how the safe had been opened, and the money stolen, yet the combination lock appeared untouched. They'd finally realised that the safe had an override mechanism operated by the switches. You keyed in a memorable date to the four switches, using the Japanese numerical date system: year, month, then day. But even if he got the order of entry right, what would the key date for Sakamoto be?

His brain answered that question straightaway. The key date would surely be the one at the heart of this whole case. The day of the double suicide. When Sakamoto — as a young boy — had discovered the bodies of both his parents. His father shot dead. His mother bled to death. Both at their own hands. No wonder the man was utterly messed up. It would be enough to send anyone off the rails.

Tanaka frantically searched his smartphone. Somewhere he had the email Izumi had sent him with the details. *There it is!* The 15th of April 1992: so 1992-4-15. He tried to remember from that old case the method of entering the numbers. He thought you started from the left. So one flick of the left-hand switch, nine flicks centre-left, nine flicks centre-right, two flicks for the right-hand. Then a pause. Then four flicks of the left-hand switch. Then a pause. Then one of the left-hand, five of the centre-left.

That's it, he thought.

But nothing happened.

In the bank robbery case, any time a wrong code was entered, they had to wait thirty seconds for the system to reset itself. Tanaka started the stop-watch on his smartphone — he allowed a minute, just to be on the safe side. He entered the same numbers again, using the same sequence again for the year. But for the month and day he did everything from the right-hand side instead. So four flicks of the right-hand switch for the month. Then a pause. Then one flick of the centre-right switch and five of the right-hand switch.

Surely that had to be it?

But again nothing.

Tanaka slumped to the floor, his back against the bookcase, his head in his hands.

'Are you alright, Inspector?' asked the other officer.

'Yes, yes. Don't worry about me.'

The trouble was, if Tanaka was honest with himself, there were any number of dates that Sakamoto could have chosen as his unlock sequence, if Tanaka was even correct and that was what the strange switches were. His own birthday. That of his mother, his father. Anything. Even Roy Orbison's. *Even Roy Orbison's!*

That was it. That had to be it. But which — birthday, or date of death? Somehow, in the circumstances, the fact that it had happened in Sakamoto's lifetime, Tanaka suspected the latter. He quickly checked on his smartphone. December 6th, 1988. Aged just 52. Far too young, thought Tanaka. It wouldn't be so very long until he himself hit his 50th.

He keyed in the numbers corresponding to 1988-12-6, trying the left-aligned version of his system.

On the last of six flicks, he heard an electric clunk.

An unlocking.

'That's it!' shouted the officer. 'Well done.'

They both pushed their weight against the side of the bookcase but found themselves stumbling as it glided easily on some hidden roller system. Underneath, a trap door was revealed in the floor, with a leather pull handle.

Tanaka pulled it, and immediately heard a girl's frantic screams.

It was the first time in his life that screaming had provoked tears of joy.

He ran down the steps, trying to remember some rudimentary French.

'Je suis un officier de police!' he shouted. *'Vous n'êtes plus en danger. Parlez vous anglais?'*

He rushed towards the girl, as she in turn cowered away from him.

He stroked her back, comforted her as far as he could, as she sobbed uncontrollably.

'Do you speak English?'

She nodded, her face still curled into her chest. 'I want my mother. I want my father.'

'Don't worry. They are here in Tokyo waiting for you. We will take you to them. You are safe now.'

The girl finally looked up at him, and he could at last confirm it was indeed Marie-Louise Durand. Her face was made up in Lolita style, and she was still wearing her flouncy Little Bo Peep-style Victorian dresses. Tanaka pulled her into a hug.

He had a quick glance around the room. Sakamoto might be completely crazed, but down here he'd provided a flush toilet, which, despite the fact the girl was on a long shackle attached to her leg, was still in easy reach. A fridge, presumably containing food. A washbasin. Even a make-up stand with a mirror. It wasn't the dark, dingy, damp cellar prison he'd been expecting. It still was a prison, though.

The girl, clinging on to him as though her life depended on it, might have been the lucky one. It didn't appear as though she had been physically harmed, although only careful questioning would establish that.

But even if she hadn't been physically hurt, she would almost certainly bear the mental scars, carry the terrible memories, for the rest of her life.

CHAPTER FORTY-THREE

B lain didn't expect to get much sleep either, for very
different reasons, but a few kilometres across Tokyo she
was totally in the dark about Tanaka's night-time activities,
and the rescue of Marie-Louise Durand.

The bus chase at Shibuya Mark City may have ended in anti-
climax, but Blain knew she had the makings of a story that
would blow the *Tōkei Shimbun*'s rivals out of the water. She'd
overheard the superintendent say to Tanaka as he got off the
bus that Sakamoto's name and identity could now be revealed.
She had the *maiko's* death which still hadn't been released to
the press. Not only that, but they had been the only newspaper
with exclusive access to the early morning raid on Sakamoto's
house.

Yamamoto was beside himself. He and Hasegawa sat on
Blain's shoulder as she wrote the material, editing it on the fly.
The whole of the front page was given over to the story of
Tokyo's most-wanted. As well as the news story, they wanted a

background feature on Sakamoto's house, interviews with neighbours, and interviews with *Ikebana* experts about the meaning of the flower arrangements. Blain was given another two reporters just to do her bidding — working under her, pursuing the angles she didn't have time for.

When it was all done, Yamamoto and Hasegawa wanted her to hit the *izakayas* with them in Akasaka. She knew what that would mean: getting home in the early hours, roaring drunk, and then a crushing hangover the next day. She couldn't face that.

In any case, during all the mayhem, she'd had a text from someone she very much wanted to meet. Brett, the long-haired American from the deep South. The one who'd helped her establish Tanaka and Izumi's intended destination when they were in the café by the Shinkansen platforms at Tokyo Station. He wanted to hook up for a drink, now he was back from his snow monkey adventure. Blain remembered his pretty face, his cheeky smile. She liked his confidence, his sense of adventure. The fact that he went out on a limb to help a stranger — and a journalist at that, a profession many despised. But journalists held people to account. It was often those people who had been held to account who said the most poisonous things about the profession.

She turned Yamamoto and Hasegawa down. They didn't look too pleased about it. But Blain was the flavour of the month: she could do whatever she wanted, as long as she continued to produce front-page scoops.

Instead, she'd arranged to meet Brett at a seventies-themed live bar in Ueno. And Haruka had managed to get the evening off and was coming too. It promised to be a fun evening. Thankfully, Haruka wasn't the jealous type.

. . .

Blain had brought her guitar, and the three of them put their names down to do some songs. The bar operated a little like an open mic night where anyone could turn up and sing or play, with an emphasis on the 1970s. A succession of Japanese businessmen — and women — trotted out classics like Simon and Garfunkel's 'Scarborough Fair'. The guitar playing was often excellent, the singing tuneful — but the lyrics were mangled in a kind of Japanglish, with the words only bearing a passing resemblance to their English originals, and the singers apparently not always understanding what they were singing.

The three of them — Blain, Haruka, and Brett — sat at a table, drinking beer after beer, and discussing what they would play and sing. The Master and his girlfriend from Café Muse were there too. Blain knew he was a Neil Young nut — and had even travelled all the way to London especially to see him play in Hyde Park one year.

That seemed to decide it.

'Neil's cool,' drawled Brett. 'But we southerners don't like any of the 'Southern Man' shit. I'm not singing that one.'

'I think it maybe depends what I can play. I only know a few of his,' said Blain.

'I don't know any, Holly,' complained Haruka. 'Can't we do something Japanese? Some J-pop maybe?'

'It's supposed to be a '70s theme, Hari. I don't think that would work.'

Eventually, they decided to do the only song that — in her beer befuddled state — Blain could remember. 'Cortez the Killer', one of the first tunes she'd learnt. It had three easy chords — Em7, D, and Am7 — repeated ad nauseam, with just a few hammer-ons and pull-off twiddles for effect.

As they waited, Blain started to recount her incredible day. Brett took particular interest in the way the police had located Sakamoto on the bus by checking the passenger lists with the company, even though, eventually, they'd been foiled.

'I wonder what he'll do after seeing your story tomorrow? Unless he's already done a runner — or a flier. Have you or the police checked with the airlines?'

'The police may have, I don't know,' said Blain. 'But they'll have alerted all ports and airports and exit points from the country.'

'What about internal flights, though? You know, I might be able to help you there. Up in snow monkey land I met a very sweet Japanese girl.'

'Oh yes.' Blain winked at Haruka, but she still felt a small stab of jealousy at the same time.

'Yes. She was *very* sweet. And she took a shine to me.'

'Ah, Brett,' said Haruka. 'Did you fall in love?'

'I'm not sure about that,' he laughed. 'But here's the interesting thing, Holly. She worked in administration at Japan Airlines. Don't they do most of the internal flights over here?'

Blain felt a flutter in her stomach. She couldn't help thinking about work — even on a night out. 'Many. Not all. There are budget airlines too, just like in the States or Europe.'

'Okay. But say he wanted to make himself scarce for a while. Japan has plenty of far-flung places, doesn't it? Even though some of the time it just feels like it's one big giant city. Remember that Sarin gas killer back in the nineties.'

'I'm not sure I was born,' said Blain. 'Or if I was, I would have been a baby. But yes, I know about it.'

'Well yeah, I mean, I'm a youngster like you too.' Brett winked at her. 'We learnt about it at school. All I'm saying is, didn't he disappear to some far-flung part of Japan before he was caught?'

The Master — who'd previously only joined in the conversation when they'd been discussing which Neil Young song to play — suddenly spoke up. 'Ishigaki. It was Ishigaki, Blain-san.'

Brett nodded. 'See. That's my point. Anyway, if you like, I could try to text this girl. See if I can get her to help.'

'Help how?'

'By checking the passenger lists. Seeing if he's booked on any internal flights.'

Blain turned her mouth down. She didn't see how the girl — however much she was sweet on Brett — would get that sort of information, not without some sort of court order. The Japanese defended their privacy to the death. 'By all means, give it a try. I don't think it will succeed, but yes, if you're willing to have a go, please do.'

Haruka started nudging her. 'It's our turn next. I don't know this song — I might not come up on the stage, Holly.'

'Oh come on, Haruka. You've got a great voice. Just do backing hums if you don't know the words. Hum some harmonies. And you, Master.' Blain started dragging him to his feet. 'We're doing it for you. We need you up there.'

'I'll be with you in a sec,' said Brett. 'I'll just text my Japan Airlines girl.'

They stayed so late drinking and chatting that Brett missed the last metro train back to his rented apartment in the western suburbs.

'You can crash at mine,' said Blain. 'As long as you don't snore.'

Blain and Brett had to prop up Haruka on the way to the metro — she wasn't used to drinking so much.

'It's my lucky night,' laughed Brett. 'Going home with two hot girls.'

'Holly's a boy really,' slurred Haruka. 'Aren't you, Holly? You're my best boy.' She lurched towards Blain trying to kiss her, but missed, and Brett had to hold her to prevent her falling.

When they arrived at Blain's share-house in Itabashi, Brett tried to insist he'd sleep on the sofa in the common lounge.

'Don't be daft,' said Blain. 'I've got a spare roll-up mattress. There's enough space on the floor in my room.'

The two of them half-undressed the by now sleeping Haruka and tucked her in on one side of the bed. Then Blain pulled Brett's face towards her and kissed him hungrily, her tongue forcing its way into his mouth until he began to reciprocate, her pelvis grinding against the hardness in his jeans.

'Whoa girl,' he said, pulling back slightly, grinning from ear to ear. 'Where did that come from?'

'You've helped me twice. And you're hot. That means you get a reward.'

She woke in what she thought was the middle of the night. Then she saw the beginnings of weak daylight creeping under her blind. Her mouth was dry, her tongue stuck to the top of her mouth, and her lips felt bruised.

She tried to turn over, then realised she was squashed between the tiny, waif-like body of Haruka and someone larger on her other flank. It was Brett, looking at his phone.

'Sorry, did that wake you?' he whispered, trying not to disturb Haruka. 'It was my Japan Airlines girl — she's on the early shift. She'll see what she can do. She's got some important meeting, then she'll have a look. If anything comes of it, I'll text you later.'

Blain made some sort of grunt in assent then turned over and tried to get back to sleep. It was likely to be another hectic day ahead. She could hear Brett getting ready, feel his weight leaving the bed. She didn't want to acknowledge it — she didn't like tender goodbyes.

CHAPTER FORTY-FOUR

He read the newspaper front page with a mixture of sadness and pride. He hadn't meant everything to end the way it had at the pagoda, but he knew they were closing in. When the Englishwoman had taken a photograph of the unfinished arrangement by the lakeside, he knew it would end soon. But he didn't want it to end yet.

She had a picture by-line this time. Her face was almost Japanese, even though he knew she wasn't. It was beautiful. So like his mother. The same jet-black hair and almost pixie looks — like something from an anime film. He knew then that he had been right to send her the presents, his little gifts. Feeding her bits the other reporters wouldn't have. He didn't want it to end — not yet — but he did want to help her, especially now he'd seen her face. How she was perfect for the part he wanted her to play.

There was one last, very special, place he wanted to go. Somewhere that meant so much to him.

And now it all made sense.

Seeing the newspaper was useful for another reason. They

knew his name now. He thought they did. That's why he'd deliberately made the bus reservation in his real name all the way through to Shibuya, although he was always intending to get off at Gotenba, where the car was. It wasn't registered in his name, so they wouldn't trace that. But the airline seat was. He would keep that booking — let it show up as a 'did not show' on the passenger lists. He had a passport with a false identity and similar credit card. There was plenty of room left on the plane. He would just book again under his assumed name — after all, money didn't really matter anymore. That way, the routine police checks which he was sure were in place wouldn't flag him up.

But if she'd done her research properly, she would recognise that assumed name. She wouldn't be fooled. He was proud of her.

You could tell from her report how much of herself she'd put into this — how much she cared. She would do anything to make sure she got the story.

She would come after him.

He was broken, like a favourite toy — but she would put him back together.

She was his. And she would make him complete again.

CHAPTER FORTY-FIVE

The one name Blain wasn't expecting to flash up on her mobile was Pascal Durand's. But that was what happened the minute she stepped through the door of the *Tōkei Shimbun*'s Toranomon Hills high-rise office. As she answered the call, she gazed out of the window over the vista of Tokyo. The view here from the 33rd floor was almost as good as from the Tokyo Tower or Skytree — and it was free. Traffic buzzing round the sprawling metropolis like miniature model cars and buses. So high, you could feel the tower waving from side to side when earthquakes struck. She hoped that was still the case if there was ever a really big one — that it swayed, rather than collapsed.

She answered the call.

'She's free,' the man said, breathlessly.

'Fantastic,' shouted Blain, but at the same moment cursed Tanaka for not letting her know. That wasn't really keeping his side of their unspoken agreement. Then she remembered the packages. The fact that *she* hadn't told him about those. This news about Marie-Louise at least lifted the guilt about that second photograph. If it had been a message that Sakamoto was holding her, then it no longer mattered — at least in terms of the French girl's welfare. 'Where was she found?' she asked.

'At his house. I can't believe it. She's here with my wife and I now.'

At the house? But the police had searched that. She'd been there. Someone would be for the high jump for missing that. 'Can I speak to her?'

'She's not really up to it at the moment, I'm afraid, Ms Blain. She's been kept in a locked cellar for day after day. She's very traumatised.'

'I understand. But we would like to interview her. And you of course. And take photos. I hope you'll honour our agreement. Remember we were the only newspaper to take a real interest in your case. We were the ones who ran your interview before.'

'Of course, Ms Blain. I intend to honour my side of the bargain.'

'And people will be offering you money for Marie-Louise's side of the story, I'm sure of that. Please let us know of any offers you do get and allow us to match them.' Blain wished now she'd got the man to sign something about exclusivity when they'd run the original interview — she'd just been so pleased to get it, she hadn't really thought things through properly.

'I promise I will. Look, as you can imagine it's all a bit chaotic at the moment. Could you ring me in a couple of hours, and we'll work something out?'

Blain knew she needed to get on to Tanaka. Find out the exact details of how Marie-Louise had been discovered, and what her incarceration had been like. But before she could, her mobile beeped again. A text from Brett:

My girl has some info. Ring her. She's expecting your call. Will forward her contact number. And thanks for last night. Let's do it again soon. Bx

A few minutes later, Blain was torn when — as promised — Brett's Japan Airlines contact came through. Really, she should get down to the Tokyo Metropolitan Police Department headquarters, get hold of Tanaka, and get as much as possible on the freeing of Marie-Louise, before trying to nail down the interview with the girl herself and her father. The police would have to hold a press conference about it soon. But Marie-Louise being found safe and well was only half the story. A killer was on the loose. Brett's contact might be a long shot, but she was worth a try.

Blain had made her decision. She rang the young woman at Japan Airlines.

The story that emerged almost had Blain laughing out loud. Against all odds, and almost unbelievably, Brett's wild hunch seemed to have paid off. Sakamoto had indeed been booked on to an early morning flight to a far-flung part of Japan. Not just any far-flung part, either. To exactly the same island they'd been talking about in the live bar the previous night: Ishigaki — the stone-wall island, one of the most southerly in Okinawa — nearer to Taiwan than the part of Japan generally considered the 'mainland', in other words Honshu.

But he hadn't turned up.

Kelton Sakamoto was a no-show.

He must have seen Blain's story and realised that — even if he managed to get on the plane — by the time he arrived, the police in Ishigaki would have been alerted, and he would have been arrested as soon as he stepped off.

He had foiled them again.

Blain thanked the woman for all her help, then, as an afterthought, posed one last question. 'Could you perhaps send me the full passenger list for that flight — just so that I can have a look for myself?' It would be useful additional material for the next day's story — illustrating the man's plans to flee. The fact that his chosen bolthole was the same as the Sarin gas attacker all those years ago would give it added traction. She wondered if that was where Sakamoto had got the idea from. Maybe he was planning to commandeer a boat for the short crossing to Taiwan and escape Japanese territory that way?

Brett's contact agreed to email it through to the reporter as soon as she was off the phone. 'Please tell Brett-san I have done this for him. I am taking a big risk. And please tell him I would like to see him again soon.'

Blain was just about to leave the office to track down Tanaka at the TMPD when the email list came through.

She scrolled through it idly as the lift descended, speeding down the thirty-three floors. Sure enough, Kelton Sakamoto was marked as a 'no-show', just as Brett's Japanese conquest had said. Well, that's the end of that, she thought.

As she exited the lift, her route took her past the main despatch office for the building. Normally, if anything arrived for her an email would be sent to the newspaper's offices. Something — some nag in the back of her mind — made her stop, go to the front desk, and ask if there had been any more deliveries for her.

Perhaps she asked the question more forcefully than she

intended. Whatever, the despatch clerk hurried to the back office, after giving a deep bow — as though they had failed her in some way. After a few moments, the clerk was back, looking embarrassed and again bowing apologetically. A package had indeed arrived. Their system to alert the addressees must have failed. He bowed low in apology once more, before handing the parcel over and getting Blain to sign for it.

Even before she took it, two-handed, from him — much in the way the Japanese liked to exchange their *meishi*, or business cards — there was a prickling in her neck, as though someone was holding a stem of nettles against it. She'd still failed to tell Tanaka about the two other deliveries. Now, here was an identical-looking third. Same shape, and — as she held it in her hands — same weight.

She headed straight for the women's toilets in the lobby and found an empty cubicle. Lowering the seat, she sat down on top, breathing deeply to try to calm her heartbeat. Then she went through the same ritual. First trying to prise the plastic apart, then — when she failed — pulling and tearing at it until she could get inside.

Once again, a small white cardboard box, and what looked like another piece of photographic paper. She simply lifted the lid of the box this time to look inside, without taking it from the parcel. Another flower — but this time jet black. *Painted, surely?* Blain was no botanist, but as far as she knew black flowers just didn't exist. Very dark purples, perhaps, but never as black as a *geisha's* hair, as this was.

Gingerly, she pulled out the piece of photographic paper, and turned it over to see the image.

What she saw didn't surprise her, though it set her heart hammering again. Somehow it seemed a logical next step.

Once more, the photograph of the woman dressed in traditional *geisha's* clothes. The same pose.

Once more, the face obliterated.

And — as with the second package — not by scratching out the facial details, but by covering them with someone else's face.

Her own.

CHAPTER FORTY-SIX

The message was obvious. She was meant to be next. So why had Sakamoto even booked that Ishigaki flight, no-show or not? Was it a decoy, meant to lure the police to Okinawa while he struck against her, back in Tokyo?

She got out her phone again, opening the email from Brett's airline contact once more. Again, she scanned the list of passengers. Other than the 'no-show' against his name, nothing stuck out. But, just as she was about to close out of the email, the last name on the printed list — presumably the last to book — caught her attention.

JONASU KASHIWADA

At first, she couldn't understand why it interested her. Then she played the sounds and syllables on her tongue and came to the conclusion that it almost sounded slightly western.

'Jonasu' might well be the Japanese equivalent of the English 'Jonathan'.

John, Jonathan, Johnny.

Johnny! That was it.

Johnny Kashiwada. Sakamoto might be a killer — but he still had a warped sense of humour. He'd obviously realised — having seen his photo in the morning papers — if he carried on with his Roy Orbison lookalike guise, he was on a fast one-way trip to jail.

The newspaper hadn't printed a photo of what he looked like without shades — so if he just travelled with his bare, normal face, that was enough of a disguise.

That, and changing his name to Jonasu Kashiwada.

Blain very much doubted he was still wearing his black clothing, or indeed the heavy sunglasses — but with his choice of name, he was still very much The Man In Black.

She quickly closed her phone down and slipped it back into her pocket. Then carefully began to put the latest photograph Sakamoto had sent back into the parcel. She slipped it between the plastic covering, but something was preventing it from sliding smoothly down. At first, she thought it must have caught on the side of the cardboard flower box. Blain put her hand back in to free it, then found she was touching another — smaller — piece of photographic paper that she hadn't initially seen.

She pulled it out and found herself looking at the confirmation that she'd cracked Sakamoto's strange puzzle.

In case she hadn't worked it out from studying the passenger list, he'd sent her the solution.

A sombre-looking young man, with black hair piled high in a flattened quiff. At first glance, almost Japanese in appearance, staring out to the left of the photo, while writing on a sheet of paper — presumably the lyrics to his latest hit.

*Jona*su *Kash*iwada.

Jona Kash.

Johnny Cash!

Blain immediately abandoned her plans to go to the police headquarters — Yamamoto-san would have to assign another reporter to follow up the Marie-Louise Durand angle. The real story was flying south — in fact had almost certainly already arrived. Blain needed to follow him — and find him. If he persisted in using his Jonasu Kashiwada alias, then it might not be too difficult. It was after all — judging from the final package he'd sent her — exactly what he wanted her to do. To go along with his plan, she knew, was reckless in the extreme. But if she simply alerted Tanaka, he would without doubt prevent her from getting near to The Flower Arranger and, in doing so, thwart her scoop. In any case, she was confident in looking after herself. Her old martial arts training from back in the UK would be her defence — she'd reached a black belt in Aikido. Despite her size, her wrist locks and throws were up there with the best.

She got out her phone again and looked at the plane timetables from Haneda. If she was quick, she could get a midday flight and still arrive on the island in daylight. Sakamoto would, however, have a few hours' start, and she had no idea where on the island he'd be planning to go.

She left the toilets, returned to the lobby, and rang Yamamoto, rather than get the lift back up to the office.

'Yamamoto-san. I need you to assign someone else to the Marie-Louise Durand end of the story.'

'Why, Holly-san? I don't understand. You've been getting all the best lines. What's the matter? Are you ill? You were here in the office a moment ago. I saw you, but you dashed off before I could talk to you.'

'No, I'm not ill. I'm still on the story — of course I am. I've just got a new lead about where the killer might be. I'm going after him.'

'Where to?'

'If I tell you, you'll only try to stop me.'

'Have you told Tanaka yet?'

'No. But then he didn't tell us about finding Marie-Louise.'

'Are you sure you haven't had any missed calls?'

'No.' She answered first before checking. Then she put Yamamoto on speakerphone and looked in her recent calls folder. There *was* one. Early this morning, when she was still asleep. Why hadn't that shown up as an alert? Still, just the one call — and no message or text. He hadn't tried very hard.

'Well,' continued Yamamoto, 'if he rings the office looking for you, or asks the other reporter I assign to the story about you, I need to be able to tell him where you are — especially if you have information about where the killer might be. Information you haven't shared with the police. Otherwise this newspaper could be accused of putting people's lives in danger. So, I'll ask you one more time. Where are you going?'

'He was on an early flight to Ishigaki, under an assumed name. So that's where I'm going.'

She ended the call without waiting for his reply. She knew he would be yelling down the phone that the newspaper couldn't afford to send a reporter all the way to Ishigaki just based on a hunch. He would be saying they should leave it to the Okinawa stringer. But the Okinawa stringer would be in Naha on the main island — it was still a one-hour flight away. Hardly on the doorstep.

In any case, whatever Yamamoto was saying, she didn't want to hear it. If he didn't refund the trip on expenses, fine. She would pay out of her own money. It was worth it — to chase the story to its end.

CHAPTER FORTY-SEVEN

Tiredness was now weighing down on Tanaka like one of the sake barrels they loved to stack up at the entrance to shrines. The exhilaration of finding Marie-Louise had been replaced by a heavy cloak of administration and form filling. He'd tried popping a couple more caffeine pills and had drunk numerous cups of coffee. But what he really wanted was a long, long sleep. Yet now they had to face another press conference. The reporters had all gathered in the press club, and he and Yoshitake were about to go on the podium. They had hoped to present Marie-Louise at the press conference — but her father had insisted she wasn't well enough yet, and both he and his wife also refused to attend, saying they needed to stay with their daughter after her terrible ordeal. Tanaka had some sympathy. Family always ought to come first. But he had never fully trusted Durand from the start. His seedy activities had turned out to be nothing criminal, but they still left an unpleasant taste in Tanaka's mouth. And now he suspected some sort of news management was being undertaken. The fact that the Durands were staying away from the press conference, the fact that Holly Blain hadn't returned his call and wasn't here yet either, all signified to him that the *Tōkei Shimbun* had in all probability signed up the Durands for an exclusive. Blain was probably holed up with them in some swish Tokyo hotel, fielding all calls to make sure other journalists didn't get the chance to talk to Marie-Louise.

'Are you ready yet, Tanaka?' asked Yoshitake. 'I must say you look like shit warmed up.'

'I can assure you, whatever I look like, Yoshitake-san, I *feel* even worse. Give me a couple of minutes more.'

He got out his mobile. He tried Blain's personal number again. No answer. Then he rang the *Tōkei Shimbun*'s newsdesk.

'Is Blain-san there? It's Inspector Tetsu Tanaka here — we were expecting her for the news conference on the freeing of Marie-Louise Durand from captivity.' He could see Yoshitake rolling his eyes. The superintendent obviously didn't think it was worth delaying things just to wait for Blain — but Tanaka felt he owed her something. He wanted her to be there.

He waited while someone went to fetch the news editor. Blain wasn't in the office — perhaps she was on the way to the news briefing and had simply been held up.

'Hello, Inspector. It's Yamamoto here, the news editor. I've sent another reporter to cover the news conference. As far as I know he's already there.'

'Has something happened to Blain-san? Why isn't she on the story?'

'She is, but she's pursuing another lead. She has some information about where Sakamoto has gone. She's gone after him. I believe she tried to ring you, but you were busy.'

Tanaka frowned. He'd had no missed calls — he'd checked. So that was a lie. Why on earth hadn't she told him? It was a very serious matter to deliberately withhold information from the police — journalist or not.

'Where?' he demanded, his heart rate suddenly increasing. 'And what was the lead?'

'Apparently, he was on the early flight to Ishigaki this morning — under an assumed name, she said.'

Tanaka abruptly ended the call without thanking the news editor. It wasn't just the thought that she had got a new lead about Sakamoto. He felt a sudden overwhelming need to go after Blain, to protect her.

'What is it?' asked Yoshitake.

'You'll have to do the press briefing on your own, Yoshitake-san,' said Tanaka, picking up his raincoat.

'Don't be ridiculous, Tanaka. You were the one who worked out where the girl was — and who rescued her. They'll want to hear all that in your own words. You're the hero of the hour.'

Tanaka wasn't waiting to listen. He needed to catch up with her. If they were lucky, Izumi and he still might manage to catch the last afternoon flight.

On the way to Haneda in their taxi, Tanaka went through some of the same processes Blain had done a few hours earlier. He knew Japan Airlines were affiliated to Japan Transocean Air — the main airline involved in scheduled flights to Ishigaki, though there were also some budget options. He rang them to try to get their passenger lists for the early morning flight and the afternoon flight. The details from the later flight would tell him if Blain was really on her way there — or if the news editor was spinning them a line. From the passenger list on the earlier flight, he hoped to work out what the assumed name was that Sakamoto was travelling under. If Blain had worked it out, he — as a detective — ought to be able to as well.

The administration staff weren't terribly helpful, though. At least not initially.

'I'm sorry, Inspector,' said the official on the other end of the line. 'The passenger lists are subject to privacy rules. You would need a court order before we could hand them over.'

'Don't be ridiculous,' thundered Tanaka, causing the taxi driver to peer in alarm in his rear-view mirror. 'I am the head of a homicide inquiry. I'm led to believe your airline or one of its affiliates carried a murder suspect from Tokyo to Ishigaki today. I need the passenger lists now, otherwise I can charge you with obstructing a police inquiry. If you can't do it, get me your superior on the line — but I will be having strong words about your behaviour.'

The bullying seemed to do the trick. The official asked for Tanaka's email address and promised to forward the relevant details in the next few minutes.

When the documents arrived, he checked the afternoon flight first. There was Blain listed, as the news editor had said. The details for the early flight were more confusing. He saw Kelton Sakamoto's real name — but no obvious alias, although against his real name was the designation 'did not show'.

He scanned the list again. Then he saw it. What Blain had seen earlier — a little black humour from their suspect. Just to double check, he showed it to Izumi, next to him on the back seat of the cab.

'Look at this passenger list for me, Izumi-kun. Ignore the no-show against his real name but see if you can tell me which is his assumed name.'

His sergeant took Tanaka's phone and scrolled down the list.

He didn't see it at first and started the process again.

When he reached the end of the list for a second time, he pointed to the name.

'This one, Tanaka-san.'

'Correct, Izumi-kun. Why?'

'*Jona*su *Kash*iwada,' said Izumi, putting an irregular emphasis on the initial parts of each name. '*Jona Kash*. Say it quickly, and it sounds like how a Japanese person might pronounce Johnny Cash.'

'Excellent, Izumi. We might make an inspector of you yet.'

'I don't think I'd want to be one, thank you, Tanaka-san. Not if it meant I'd have to deal with Yoshitake on a daily basis.' Then he frowned. 'But why pick something so obvious? It's almost like he's sending us a message. That he wants us to catch him.'

'It's not meant for us, Izumi. It's meant for Blain. But yes, it *is* obvious, and I think he *wants* her to follow him, just like she has. I think she's his next intended victim. That's why we need to get on that plane and warn her.'

Izumi frowned. In his eyes, Tanaka saw a strange look — almost one of fear. 'Does it make sense for us both to fly to such a far-flung place, Inspector?'

'If our murder suspect has gone there, then yes, of course. Why?'

Instead of answering immediately, Izumi dropped his gaze, making a play of glancing down at his watch. 'No reason, Tanaka-san. Whatever you think best. But you might want to get on to your friends at Japan Airlines again. Or go to Japan Transocean directly. There's no way we're going to make it unless they agree to delay the plane.'

CHAPTER FORTY-EIGHT

The plane seemed to be waiting for ages to take off. Blain checked her phone — already twenty minutes late. Minutes where Sakamoto could be getting further and further away from her — he'd already had a head-start of several hours by catching the early morning flight. Now she was falling further and further behind.

The cabin staff had already asked passengers to turn their devices to flight-safe mode, but as they hadn't actually even started to taxi yet, Blain turned hers back on and just made sure it was silent so no one else knew.

Then Yamamoto's number flashed up on the screen. Blain rejected the call. Instead she texted her news editor.

On plane. Can't talk. Can you text instead pls? HB

She waited a few moments for Yamamoto's reply.

Important info from Botany Dept at uni about flower pix

**you sent them. All are varieties of sakura except one —
an orchid. It's v rare.**

What is the orchid's name?

Where can you find it?

**It's the Okinawa Sekkoku, the Okinawan Orchid. They
think these specimens were taken from the botanical
gardens in Tokyo. They reported damage to a plant.**

Blain could hear the motors increasing in speed, feel the
brakes being released. She'd have to stop texting soon. She
could see the stewardess approaching.

But where do you find it in Okinawa? Does it grow on
Ishigaki?

No. Mostly on Okinawa Island itself

But also, in rainforest in Iriomote.

Where is...

Blain was interrupted before she could finish her question
by the stewardess leaning over to her window seat.

'I'm afraid you'll have to turn that off now, madam,' she
said, pointing to the fasten seatbelts sign, as though it was
somehow relevant.

Blain obeyed, but, just as she was switching off, she noticed
another missed call from Tanaka. Oh well, he should have
tried harder to get hold of her earlier. And he should have
been more on the ball. She hadn't been privy to any special

information. The police should have done their own checks on flights earlier. They would have flagged up Sakamoto's initial booking.

She glanced out of the window. Even if she didn't find Sakamoto, she was looking forward to the trip. She'd been in Japan three years, but this was the furthest south she would ever have ventured — she hadn't been anywhere in Okinawa before.

The plane was turning as it started to taxi away from the stand. Then she saw them. Two figures waving their hands frantically, as if to try to get the plane to stop and let them on. Thankfully, security staff were preventing them getting any closer; she didn't want any further delays. Then she recognised who the two figures were: Tanaka and Izumi.

'Did you manage to warn her?' asked Izumi.

Tanaka looked at the ground, wringing his hands in frustration. 'I thought we were going to make it. The airline agreed to delay the flight by twenty minutes — they said that was the best they could do. When I realised we weren't going to make it, I tried to ring her.'

'You should have texted, Tanaka-san.'

'Izumi. Sometimes I could happily throttle you, which wouldn't be a very good career move for a detective. How the hell could I have texted when we were running full pelt to try to catch the plane? It was hard enough phoning.'

'Sorry, Inspector, of course, you're right. How long do we have to wait until the next flight?'

'There isn't another flight. Not till tomorrow morning.'

For an instant, there was a flicker of relief on Izumi's face, almost as though he was pleased. Then he frowned. 'Couldn't we charter a private plane?'

Tanaka snorted. 'On TMPD budgets? Pull the other one, Izumi. No. We'll book on for tomorrow morning. To be honest, I'm shattered. We'll liaise with Ishigaki police and see what they can do to try and find our Jonasu Kashiwada before we get there. But after that, I'm off home. I haven't slept for thirty-six hours, and we've another early start tomorrow.'

CHAPTER FORTY-NINE

A wall of humid, muggy air hit Blain as soon as she emerged from the plane at Ishigaki airport. It was a bit like being slapped in the face by a warm, wet flannel, and she immediately realised she was overdressed in her black working suit. Here, Hawaiian-style shirts were the order of the day, even in April.

She didn't have any baggage — so she didn't have to wait for any. She'd try to find some cheap clothes in the supermarket or market, although that wasn't as easy in Japan as it would have been in Europe.

She'd already worked out, while she was waiting to board at Haneda airport, that she'd hire a car — the smallest, cheapest one possible, hoping Yamamoto might approve it — and then head for Ishigaki town. It was the centre of activities — and also the port for speedboats and catamarans to neighbouring islands.

When she was waiting for the paperwork for the hire car, her phone started to chime.

Tanaka.

'Blain-san, I've been trying to get hold of you all day.'

'I'm sorry. I've been on metro trains, aeroplanes. In mid-flight there's no reception as you know. I heard about Marie-Louise Durand. Well done! Great result.'

'Hmm,' grumbled Tanaka. 'I was surprised you didn't want to come to the press conference to get the full story.'

'We sent another reporter. I think you know why. I saw you at Haneda on the tarmac.'

'Couldn't you have asked the cabin staff to stop the plane?'

'Have you ever known that to happen, Tanaka-san? I'd have been wasting my breath.'

The car hire official passed her a form to sign. Blain cradled the phone between her shoulder and cheek, and mouthed a '*sumimasen*' accompanied by a small bow.

'Anyway, there is a reason I believe that Sakamoto made his alias so easy to identify — to you and me at least,' continued Tanaka. 'He *wants* you to follow him, Holly. Don't. I believe you could be his next victim. Just leave it all to the Ishigaki police and us now. We haven't released any of this part of the story to the rest of the press yet, so you'll still be ahead of the game. And you're in situ — you'll still get your scoop. At the very least, wait until Izumi and I get there tomorrow, then you have some protection.'

'I hear what you're saying, Inspector. But as you know by now, I'm perfectly capable of looking after myself.'

She heard Tanaka give a long sigh. 'Well, I've tried to warn you. Let me give you another strong warning, though. If you do anything that jeopardises this inquiry, anything that under-mines our attempts to catch this man, I will not hesitate to press for criminal charges to be brought against you. Do you understand?'

'I understand, Inspector. You've made yourself very clear.'

. . .

As Blain drove away from the airport, she turned the air conditioning in the car up to maximum and began to relax for the first time for days. There was little she could do until she tracked down Sakamoto. There might be little she could do when she did. But the more knowledge she had, the better equipped she would be to confront him — whenever and wherever that happened.

Her enjoyment of the countryside was suddenly spoilt when a shrill female voice erupted from the satnav system. In the politest Japanese possible, the robotic-voiced woman told her she was several kilometres per hour above the speed limit and had to slow down. Yet she was on an open road, in the countryside, without another car in sight — and only doing the equivalent of what would have been about 35mph.

Driving in Ishigaki town was considerably more relaxed, however, than in Tokyo. She'd chosen a cheap hotel — by Japanese standards — right by the side of the port. So she found a parking area nearby, parked the car, and went to check in.

The landlady welcomed her profusely, amazed by Blain's proficiency in Japanese. Then she became apologetic, amid much mutual bowing and embarrassed smiling. 'I thought at first you were European. But now I see you're not. You *are* Japanese.'

'No, Ojōsama. You were correct first time. I am English. I look a little Japanese, I admit. But thank you for the compliment about my spoken Japanese. It needs to be good — I am a journalist working for a Japanese newspaper in Tokyo.'

This led to more bowing and embarrassed smiling.

'I've come to Okinawa as I'm trying to locate the site of the

293

very rare Okinawan orchid. I gather they grow on some of the islands.'

The woman nodded. 'Mostly on Naha, the main island. There is a related species, though, that is said to grow in the rainforest on Iriomote.'

'And Iriomote is where?'

'There are regular fast catamarans from the port just behind us.' She handed Blain a leaflet. 'Here's the timetable and prices. It's too late to get there and back today. Maybe it's something you can do tomorrow. How many nights are you staying?'

'Can I book in for two nights to start with?'

The landlady retreated to the back room, presumably to check the register.

'Yes, that's fine. Do you want breakfast?'

'How much is breakfast?'

'A hundred yen. It is very simple.'

A hundred yen? Less than seventy UK pence! 'Yes please,' said Blain. 'Breakfast each day.'

Once she'd dumped her bag, Blain immediately made her way to the passenger boat terminal round the back of the hotel on the quayside. She needed to find whether Sakamoto had already left Ishigaki — if it was simply a transit hub — and if so, which of the other Yaeyama islands he'd travelled on to. And if it was indeed Iriomote, when he'd gone.

She used plenty of bowing and tried to be as polite as possible at the passenger ferry reception.

'I'm trying to find my boyfriend,' she lied. 'I was due to meet him in Ishigaki before travelling to Iriomote, but I missed the plane from Tokyo and had to get a later one. Unfortunately, I can't seem to get him on my mobile. He was planning to visit the rainforest in Iriomote so that may be why. Could you perhaps check your passenger lists to see if he got one of your boats earlier today?'

The ticket assistant returned Blain's politeness and bows — but said she couldn't release any passenger information without the authority of her manager.

'I understand,' said Blain, bowing again. 'Could I perhaps speak to the manager?'

The woman rose from her chair and knocked on a door at the back of the room. A few moments later, a man in a short-sleeved white shirt and dark tie came to the counter. He lifted a flap in the counter and beckoned Blain through, and back to his office.

'What is your name, please?'

'Holly Blain. But it's my boyfriend's name I want you to check on the passenger list. His name is Jonasu Kashiwada.'

The man handed over a pen and paper pad, indicating Blain should spell the name out. She did so — in *kanji* and *romaji*, the Romanised form of Japanese script, knowing that was what was usually inputted into computers and word processors.

'J-o-n-a-s-u K-a-s-h-i-w-a-d-a.' The man repeated the name in elongated fashion as he typed it into his keyboard. He waited a few seconds, then nodded to himself, as though the computer had given him an answer. 'You realise, madam, that I'm not supposed to release this information?'

'I do realise, Tenchou-san. But I hope you understand my difficulties.' She got out her phone for effect. 'I cannot get through to him on the phone.' She effected a catch in her voice, as though she was about to burst into tears. 'And I'm supposed to be meeting him.'

The man nodded, solemnly. 'He took a boat to Iriomote around midday.'

'And just a one-way ticket?'

Another nod.

'And he hasn't booked a separate return?'

'Not yet, no, and the last boat for today has now left the island. He will be there at least until tomorrow morning.'

Blain ended the conversation with profuse thanks and said she would like to book for the earliest possible service the next day.

'The ticket assistants will look after you at the front desk.'

'Thank you so much, Tenchou-san.'

On the way back to the hotel, Blain diverted to the town's only dedicated shopping arcade, the Euglena Mall — two parallel streets covered by a domed roof. Most of the outlets sold souvenirs — with a similar range in each shop. But she managed to find a light-coloured t-shirt, shorts, and plimsolls which would serve as her sub-tropical uniform for a couple of days. Plus some clean knickers decorated in Okinawan flowers. They wouldn't normally be her — or Haruka's — choice, but fashion was the least of her concerns.

Hunger had kicked in too. In the excitement of the chase, she hadn't eaten properly since breakfast. She found a cheap *izakaya* with a few seats outside in the mall and ordered a couple of plates of fried chicken and squid and a beer to wash them down with.

At the neighbouring table were a couple of local men. They began talking to her in Japanese — obviously thinking she was a Tokyo-ite, not realising she was European. Her first impression was they were trying to chat her up. But then she realised they were simply being friendly. They were waiters from a restaurant on Takatomi — one of the smallest islands in the archipelago, and the nearest to Ishigaki — just a 15-minute boat trip away. The younger of the two had the usual black Japanese hair. The other was lighter brown-blonde — bleached in the *Chapatsu* style, once banned in Japanese schools. He was in his late thirties or early forties, though. Too old for teenage rebellion.

'What brings you to Ishigaki?' he asked, offering Blain a piece of fish from his own plate. She politely declined.

'I'm from a Tokyo newspaper. I'm trying to track down a rare flower that apparently only grows on Iriomote. Or rather, this variant only grows on Iriomote.' She got out her smartphone and showed them a photo of the flower. 'Somewhere in the rainforest. But I suspect that might not be too easy to find.'

'I've heard of it,' said the man. 'But couldn't tell you exactly where to go.' Then he started writing a telephone number on a paper napkin. 'When you get to Iriomote, ring this guy. He runs tours of the rainforest. If anyone knows where it grows, he will.'

Blain turned in early, after sharing several beers with the two waiters. She slept deeply until the clanging and crashing of daily life of the port woke her. Then she realised she'd slept through her alarm. She rushed to get dressed. The previous night's shower would have to sustain her on the cleanliness and personal hygiene front. That and a longer than usual spray of deodorant. Then she grabbed her bag and, on the way out of the hotel, explained to the owner she'd have to forego the 100-yen breakfast that day as she'd miss her ferry. The owner looked at the clock.

'One minute,' she said. 'You have time.'

She headed into the back room and then quickly reappeared with a small plastic bottle filled with cold tea, a banana, and a hard-boiled egg with two pieces of toast wrapped in a napkin.

'You have paid for it,' she bowed. 'I must provide it.'

Blain bowed in thanks and ran out of the door.

As the catamaran passenger ferry sliced through the water, Blain decided to ring the contact the off-duty waiters had given her the previous evening. The answer the man gave her — combined with Tanaka's warning the previous day — left her both excited and nervous.

'The orchids only grow in one particular part of the island,' he said. 'I can take you there, but it is off the beaten track. It will take several hours to reach — hiking and canoeing. A private tour like this is expensive.'

The man quoted a price. High enough to leave Blain wondering if she should simply strike out on her own. But then she'd come all this way. If the orchids only grew in one place, and if — as she strongly suspected — that was where Sakamoto was headed or had already been, then she would have to pay — and hope the story was good enough for Yamamoto to allow her to claim it on expenses once she was back in Tokyo.

'We need to set off as soon as you arrive at Uehara port from Ishigaki. The rainforest is safe enough during the day — but the *habu* snakes and wildcats come out at night. You don't want to be stuck in the jungle then. The cats are timid enough usually, unless you threaten a mother with her young. The snakes... well, they're vicious and killers.'

The guide — Wakui Shinichi — negotiated the first part of the Uehara river in a small motor boat, towing a double kayak behind. As they travelled deeper into the jungle, Blain found herself continually wiping her brow — the humidity increasing, it seemed, every few metres. She was thankful she'd invested in her lightweight clothing the previous evening. Shinichi, though, had frowned at her plimsolls. His own daughter, who ran a shop in the port, luckily had the same size feet as Blain: he insisted the reporter borrow her walking boots.

After a few kilometres, the tourist boats that had accompanied them at the start of the journey started to thin out. A few hundred metres more, and Shinichi cut the motor and dropped anchor.

He pulled the kayak alongside the vessel, then held it steady as Blain climbed in. He handed her a double paddle to match his own, but, once they set off, he was the one doing most of the work in the front of the double kayak, with Blain almost going through the motions in the rear.

'Where we're headed is too shallow and narrow for the motor boat, I'm afraid,' explained Shinichi.

He found a tributary off the main river artery and darted down it. Now they were deep in the jungle, hidden under a thick canopy of trees, with little of the bright sunlight penetrating down to the forest floor.

Then Shinichi was tying the kayak to a tree stump and helping Blain from the tiny craft.

'We have to do the last bit on foot.'

After a climb up a steep bankside, tangled with roots, the trees seemed to thin out slightly. Blain could hear the thunder of a waterfall nearby and even feel the cooling mist of water droplets on her face.

Then they saw it.

A makeshift camp. A v-shape of plastic or canvas stretched across a rope tied between two trees. Underneath, a flattened mattress roll — its Day-Glo pink highlighted against the greens and browns of the forest floor, announcing itself like a vibrant tropical flower. To one side, the charred remains of what looked like the previous night's campfire. On the other, a partially open bag — containing plant specimens, including a beautiful white orchid.

Shinichi knelt down next to the bag and rubbed one of the orchid's petals softly between his finger and thumb, as though he was examining its quality.

'Someone got here first,' he said. 'But they shouldn't be picking the flowers. They are a protected species. Very few specimens are left.'

He stood up and looked around, as though he was expecting to see the culprit. Blain had a very good idea who the flower picker was — Kelton Sakamoto. Damaging rare plant species was the very least of his crimes. But she had renewed hope. The fact that the camp was still here, the flower specimens were in the bag — waiting, presumably, for more — meant that Sakamoto was almost certainly still in the vicinity.

Shinichi seemed spooked by the discovery that someone been there before them. He became more alert, his head darting left and right every few moments as he scanned the forest ahead, turning with each rustle of a leaf or branch.

Then the forest thinned still further. A small clearing, letting a single ray of sunlight through the canopy. And there — on the edge of the clearing, highlighted in their brilliant virgin whiteness — the orchid blooms themselves.

Shinichi laughed. 'Their beauty always takes my breath away. It's a joy to bring you here to admire them. But please, in any article you write, do not give the details of how to get

here. They can probably survive one person picking them —
as long as he or she doesn't take too many.'

Blain moved forward, knelt down, and took her phone out
to photograph the specimens. They were like a series of white
six-pointed stars, each with one petal missing — the space
between the fifth and first petal lending an asymmetrical
beauty. As though the space, what wasn't there, was almost as
important as the waxy white petals themselves.

Then she heard irregular footsteps, turned, and saw
Shinichi staggering like a drunk, some sort of a white mask
over his face. His hands were trying — in slow motion — to
get the mask away from his nose and mouth. As she ran
towards him, he staggered forward, slumping to the ground
with a thud. Blain knelt down, cradled his head, and ripped off
the mask.

As she did, he tried to speak.

Then she felt her own head being yanked back, a cloth or
rag over her face, and a sweet nutty smell that she knew she
didn't want to breathe in. But she couldn't fight it and couldn't
fight whoever was holding the rag. And then she knew she
wasn't meant to fight. She was just meant to let go.

CHAPTER FIFTY

Tanaka did sleep, but only for a couple of hours. A dream about leafing through photo albums, seeing his own parents transform into those of Sakamoto, then hearing his father tell his mother he was sorry — that he wanted to get back together with her — had him wide awake in hope.

A hope crushed by consciousness. It was too late now. News had reached them a couple of years previously that his father had died — a hopeless and lonely alcoholic, who'd been living out his days on a trailer park near the nondescript town of Hattiesburg in Mississippi. Similar dreams had come to Tanaka most nights since hearing of his death.

Each time when he woke, his heart was raced as it was now. With the adrenaline surge, he knew he wasn't going back to sleep any time soon. He could hear Miho and the boys watching their favourite reality TV show downstairs, something Tanaka would have excused himself from anyway. As he began to get dressed, he rang Izumi.

'Izumi-kun. Where are you?'

'Still at the office, Tanaka-san, running errands for Yoshitake.'

'I want to go through Sakamoto's photograph albums again, but I don't want to run into Yoshitake. Can you book a room in the basement and take them all there? And I mean all of them, Izumi.'

'There are lots of them, I warn you.'

'Well, just load them on a trolley. Get a uniformed officer to help you if necessary. Text me which room. I'll be there within half an hour.'

Tanaka knew the basement routes through police headquarters that he could use to make sure he didn't stumble across Yoshitake or anyone else he didn't want to see. A warren of corridors and doors with interlinking passages few people used on a daily basis.

He half-ran towards the room number Izumi had texted him, but then opened the door so quietly that his deputy only noticed him once he was sitting down alongside — in front of the piles of photo albums.

'Any luck yet, Izumi-kun?'

'Nothing leaps out at me, Tanaka-san. I've been concentrating on the ones pre-1992, when they were supposedly a happy little family. If we think he's doing some sort of nostalgia tour — recreating happy moments from his childhood — then I thought that was the best place to start. But there's nothing relating to Ishigaki — or indeed anywhere in Okinawa. Unlike the other destinations he's been visiting, it doesn't seem to have been a family favourite.'

'So which ones haven't you done yet?'

'Well, I've still got plenty of the pre-1992 ones to go

through. Why don't you make a start on the ones *after* the death of his parents?'

'Did you do this one — 1992 itself?'

'No, not yet.'

Tanaka decided to start there and opened the album — but he could tell immediately that it was different to the ones in Izumi's pile. They were all much thicker — almost as though they'd expanded in the damp of the cellar, sucking up the moist air like blotting paper. Tanaka knew that wasn't the reason — it was simply that with several prints attached to the cellophane under each leaf, they really were fuller volumes. The year 1992, however, was virtually unused. A handful of prints for *Hinamatsuri* — the doll festival for girls, celebrated on March 3rd. It looked like Sakamoto and his mother had visited this alone. Unusual for a boy to want to go, thought Tanaka. Sakamoto seemed to be carrying his own doll in the photos taken, presumably, by his mother, a candy-coloured clown placed by him next to the more traditional displays, and a toothy grin for the camera.

The rest of that year's album was completely blank.

The next year — 1993 — didn't even seem to have a photograph album devoted to it, unless they'd failed to retrieve it from the cellar. Tanaka couldn't believe that.

But he could see from the thickness of the next volume — 1994 — that it definitely contained some prints, though nowhere near as many as in the albums Izumi was ploughing through at his side.

The first entry was for April. The landscape, the vegetation, and the light summer clothes Sakamoto and the other children in the photograph were wearing immediately had Tanaka tapping his feet underneath the desk in anticipation. There was no caption to indicate where it was taken, but it was somewhere in a hot climate. And the faces were all

Japanese. In the background of the outside shots, an azure sea. All the caption said was:

My new school. I hope I will be happier here.

But Sakamoto's own face — with a few classmates — was unsmiling, a shadow of fear across his features.

Tanaka flicked quickly through — trying to find clues to the location, other than the lush vegetation, and Hawaiian-style dress, which pointed to somewhere in Okinawa.

Then he found another caption from later in the year:

Thank you to the Kaihin Ryūgaku *programme for bringing happiness back to my life.*

It showed Sakamoto as a gangly-looking eleven or twelve-year-old, in what looked like a family group — an older couple and three children: an older boy, and a younger girl, with Sakamoto in the middle. This must be significant, thought Tanaka, and it must be somewhere in Okinawa. From his own childhood spent on Ishigaki, the name seemed familiar. But still there was no location.

He quickly flicked through the rest of that album, then the next, then started on 1996, when Sakamoto must have been thirteen and fourteen. And here he found his answer. A series of photographs captioned: *'1996 Typhoon Herb Disaster'*. Here, the photographs showed the lush vegetation flattened, buildings damaged and destroyed. And in one photo, an image of a school name sign, blown to the ground by the storm.

Hatoma Island School.

'Here it is, Izumi!' shouted Tanaka. 'Hatoma — that's his link to Okinawa. He seems to have been sent to school there after his parents' suicide.'

Izumi peered over his shoulder. 'I've never heard of Hatoma.' Tanaka met his sergeant's gaze. Again, there seemed to be a strange look of fear in his eyes.

'I have,' said Tanaka, wondering what it was that had spooked Izumi. 'And that's where I think he's heading.'

Just before he replaced the album, he quickly leafed through. The typhoon photographs were the last entries, until one in October. The photograph was depressing; a gravestone with a woman's name on it. Alongside, her picture — and Tanaka realised it was the same woman from the earlier family shot.

The accompanying caption was heart-breakingly sad:

Typhoon Herb's legacy for Hatoma. I shall always remember you, Mama. I was lucky enough to have two mothers, but both were taken away. I am truly sorry. It was all my fault.

CHAPTER FIFTY-ONE

Tanaka tried to get a few more hours' sleep before their dawn flight south, but too many thoughts raced through his brain. He kept on imagining parallels between his own life and that of Kelton Sakamoto — how both of them had lost their fathers at too young an age. The difference: Tanaka had been brought up by a loving mother he still doted on, and who was still very much part of his and Miho's family. Sakamoto's life had been wrecked by three tragedies in relatively quick succession: the double suicide of his mother and father and then the death of his second — foster — mother at the hands of a devastating typhoon.

He'd looked up the *Kaihin Ryūgaku* programme. It had been an ingenious way the islanders on Hatoma — now numbering just sixty — had kept their only school open when it had been threatened with closure. It was a programme offering schooling and foster homes on the beautiful Okinawan islet off Iriomote's north coast — specifically aimed at children who couldn't attend regular schools on the mainland because of stress or emotional difficulties. After his parents' deaths,

Kelton Sakamoto was one of those offered a new start in life. One that had ended again in 1996, when Typhoon Herb robbed him of his second mother.

Tanaka had alerted the Ishigaki police, and he and Izumi were met at the airport by a local detective. Then, with blue lights flashing and sirens wailing, they raced through the island of Tanaka's birth — the half-American, half-Japanese son whose own family had been torn apart, but not as devastatingly as the man he was hunting.

At Ishigaki port, two police launches and an ambulance boat were waiting. A rare outing in armed riot gear for the island's police force, more used to giving directions to lost tourists than tackling a potential serial killer.

As soon as he and Izumi stepped on board, the boat cast off, turned, and accelerated out of the harbour, followed by the other two vessels in convoy. The two Tokyo detectives were ushered below deck.

A square-faced, heavy-eyebrowed man in police uniform rose to greet them from the large-scale map of the islands that he'd been studying. Tanaka could tell he was of Okinawan ancestry from his darker skin and more open-eyed face. Tanaka — though born and raised here, and only half-Japanese — knew he probably looked more Japanese than this man — his mother had come to Ishigaki from Tokyo.

'Inspector Tanaka and Sergeant Izumi. My name is Superintendent Orimitsu Naagusuku.' Tanaka attempted to bow but then had to brace himself as the boat was buffeted by a wave. 'We thought it prudent to wait for you two before heading to Hatoma.'

'You seem to have assembled a strong squad of officers, Naagusuku-san,' said Tanaka. 'Thank you very much for this.'

'We're worried from what you said, Tanaka-san. The other schoolchildren on Hatoma could be at risk from this madman. And we have some more information for you.'

Tanaka bowed again. 'Thank you, Naagusuku-san.'

'The first is that this journalist you mentioned — Holly Blain — she may be being held by him.'

Tanaka felt his heart rate quicken. 'How do you know this, Superintendent?'

'A tour guide in Ishigaki made a report to the local police there. He had been asked to show the journalist some rare orchids only found in a remote spot near one of the island's waterfalls. He doesn't know what happened exactly, but he was attacked by someone. A chloroform-soaked mask was attached to his face, rendering him unconscious. When he came round, Blain had disappeared. We can only assume the same attacker used the same method on her.'

'Did anyone see her with Sakamoto?'

'They may have. Some tourists on a boat trip reported seeing a man and a woman in a small motorboat. The woman seemed half asleep or ill. They asked the man if he wanted any help. He declined.'

Tanaka braced himself again as another larger wave struck. He felt his stomach lurch.

'Where was he going?'

'Back downriver from the waterfall. Towards the north coast. But also towards Hatoma.'

'But we don't know he's there?'

'No. But the school has an outward-bound hut on another islet — an even smaller one a few hundred metres from Hatoma. It's an old fisherman's hut which was abandoned when the bottom fell out of the skipjack tuna industry. They use it for weekend camps, things like that, but normally just in the summer, not this early in the year.'

'And why do you think Sakamoto might have taken Blain there, Naagusuku-san?' asked Izumi.

'The staff at the school reported lights on at the hut last night. A teacher was planning to go and investigate — we told her not to. That it might be dangerous. Instead we asked her to evacuate the children temporarily to Iriomote itself — just in case Sakamoto did something stupid. All the children are now safe.'

But, thought Tanaka, Holly Blain most definitely wasn't. Even though she'd ignored his instructions not to chase after Sakamoto, even though by doing so she had jeopardised the whole police operation for the sake of her 'story', Tanaka felt bound to do everything he could to save her.

Just as he would for Miho, his wife. Or for his sons. His thoughts crystallised at that moment. The feeling had been growing over the past few days of what Blain represented to him. Now it was clear. Like an adult embodiment of the baby daughter he and Miho had lost, Blain was his errant, surrogate daughter and she needed to be protected.

CHAPTER FIFTY-TWO

He hoped he'd got the dose right for the girl — just enough to keep her soporific and unable to escape. But not enough to render her unconscious, or worse. He would deal with her in a moment, drawing enough blood to get her skin tone exactly right to offset the beauty of the orchids. First, he wanted to perfect the flower arrangement — it would be his most extravagant, his best so far. He wanted this to be a proper tribute to his mother. The *maiko* had been nearly perfect — but not quite. Too much blood taken from her. Just like the Swedish girl.

The other two had seemed frightened of him. The French girl too. But this girl — who'd followed his every move so faithfully — he didn't think she was afraid. Her brown-black eyes, eyes that almost looked Japanese, were dulled by the Rohypnol. But in them, he saw a fire burning. A defiance, even through the haze of the drugs. He liked that.

It excited him.

It excited him in the same way the slivers of red on his mother's eyelids used to excite him, when she dressed for their private tea ceremonies. It excited him in the same way that his mother's powdering of her chest used to excite him. In his core, his very being.

This old fisherman's house — with its simple, traditional Japanese rooms — was exactly right for his final flourish. His final arrangement.

He checked the way he'd dressed the *tokonoma* alcove, snipped off another leaf from the orchids he'd collected near the waterfall on Iriomote. Very few people knew they were there. His nature teacher at the school here on Hatoma had been one of them. He still remembered the joy and excitement of that expedition to find them — they felt like real explorers, adventurers, hacking through the jungle. Those few short years of happiness until mama died.

He once again assessed the *Ma*. Of course, he'd always known he was going to fill it. That was why he'd lured the girl here. He was only surprised that it had been so easy.

This would be an end for him. In the place where his dreams died. But it wouldn't necessarily be an end for her. He just wanted to capture her for one beautiful split second. He was sure that was what his mother and father had intended. They had simply wanted to take a beautiful photograph for him but hadn't known when to stop. He couldn't believe they would have been selfish enough to deliberately take their own lives and leave him alone. No one would abandon a nine-year-old only child like that, surely? However desperate they had been feeling.

As he worked, he sang. The haunting, exquisite song that was his father's favourite. His father could never hit all the high notes, but he could, both as a boy and, now, as a man.

He'd made sure no one could get to them.

He'd surrounded the *tokonoma* with a wall of crates the fishermen had abandoned. Inside the channel between the crates, two creatures he'd collected from the jungle at the same time as the orchids. Luring them, just like he'd lured the girl, who now lolled semi-comatose, strapped to a chair.

A pair of deadly *habu* snakes.

So, when he heard the police megaphone, he simply ignored it.

'Armed police. Kelton Sakamoto, this island is surrounded. You will not be harmed if you release the woman and come out with your hands raised.'

He wouldn't be doing that.

His work here was nearly done.

The flower arrangement was ready.

Now, he just needed to get the girl's skin tone exactly right.

He made the incision in her neck, inserted the catheter, and watched as her blood began to drain.

CHAPTER FIFTY-THREE

Blain felt like she needed to wake herself from a fevered, heavy sleep. Like she was fighting her way out from the back of a wardrobe, but each time she pushed one set of clothes aside, she was confronted by another. And the light in front of her was getting dimmer. She was slipping further back.

Something at her neck was wet.

And she couldn't remember where she was or why.

Only that there was someone who would come looking for her. Someone that would try to save her. She'd ignored his advice, but she knew he was kind. He was a friend. He wouldn't let her go.

He just needed to get here in time.

Because her life was running down her skin, running down her neck, like the sand grains of an hourglass, and already the top of the timer was down to its last few grains.

She'd looked at that photograph Sakamoto had sent in his third package. Her own face superimposed on a *geisha's*. Now she knew that somehow this was it — she had become the photograph. Fulfilled his destiny. Shaped herself as the last piece in his jigsaw puzzle.

Somehow, she had to cling on. Somehow, she had to tip that timer over the other way.

Despite her situation, she managed a wry inward laugh at her naivety in chasing him down in Okinawa, thinking her black belt in Aikido would defend her. Against whatever drug he'd injected her with, it was useless. Utterly useless.

The truth was, she was weak. So very, very weak.

And the song was nearing its climax.

CHAPTER FIFTY-FOUR

Tanaka stood with Izumi in the cockpit of the police boat, willing Sakamoto to respond to the warning. If the armed officers were forced to go in, he knew this was likely to end badly. There was no response, no sound, other than the gentle slapping of the waves on the side of the police boat, as though the sea was counting down the remaining seconds of Blain's life.

They had to do something. Otherwise, Blain faced the same fate as Elin Granqvist. The same fate as the *maiko* at Fuji Five Lakes.

'He's not responding, Tanaka-san,' said Superintendent Naagusuku. 'What do you want us to do?'

'Let me go ashore with my sergeant and talk to him.'

'I can't allow you two to go alone.'

'We'll take one armed officer to cover us. Let me at least try to talk to him from close quarters. I know a little about what makes him tick.'

'Very well, Tanaka. That would not be my advice, but it's your investigation.'

. . .

Tanaka prepared to jump from the boat to the rocky shore. Then he realised Izumi was hanging back — the fleeting look of fear Tanaka had noticed on his sergeant's face before had now become manifest.

'What's wrong, Izumi?'

His sergeant simply shook his head, cradling his arms round his body. 'I can't go, Tanaka-san. I'm sorry.'

Tanaka had never taken his Number Two for a coward. But there was no time to lose. He would have to do it alone. He found a handhold on the rocks and hauled himself up. The other armed officer followed.

They crept towards the fishermen's hut, crouching low to the ground. As they drew closer, the music grew louder. Tanaka recognised it as one of Roy Orbison's most famous songs. He wondered if he'd ever be able to listen to it in the same way again after it had been sullied like this.

When they got to the door, Tanaka whispered to the officer to stay back.

'I don't want you opening fire, coming in, anything, unless I give the order. Do you understand?'

The man nodded.

Tanaka drew his gun, released the safety catch, and then slowly opened the door.

The sight that greeted him was shocking.

An exact replica of the crime scene photo taken of Sakamoto's parents' double suicide twenty-five years earlier.

The only difference: Sakamoto was still alive, but Tanaka wasn't sure about Blain. He ran towards the *tokonoma* alcove — his gun hand pointing directly towards Sakamoto.

He was about to move the crates to get through, then Sakamoto shouted out.

'I wouldn't do that, Inspector. Take a look inside first.'

Tanaka looked down. Then immediately drew his head back.

The *habu* snake's eyes had met his — it looked ready to strike with its deadly fangs.

He knew he had to get to Blain and quickly. Her apparently lifeless form was strung up in the middle of Sakamoto's latest arrangement.

CHAPTER FIFTY-FIVE

That day flashed in front of his eyes now.

Now that it was nearly over.

Really, he'd known something was wrong. Having to move to the smaller house in a neighbourhood much further from the centre. His father being at home all the time, drinking all the time, the fact that he was never bought toys anymore, the way all his usual favourite brands of food had been replaced with cheaper supermarket alternatives, and how there didn't seem to be much left even of those. But it was the sadness in his mother's eyes that hurt him the most.

But that afternoon had started with him in a joyous mood — as though all the troubles and anger in the family home might be banished for good. His flower arrangement had been judged the best in his class. He'd put so much work into it, collecting the flowers, finding later blooming varieties of *sakura* in the parks so that everything looked fresh and new. His teacher had ruffled his hair.

'You see, Kelton. This is what it feels like when you really work hard at something you're good at. When you really put the effort in, you get the rewards. I'm so pleased for you. It's going to be the main display at the parents' evening tomorrow night. I'm sure your mother and father will be really proud of you.'

The other boys in the class teased him, of course. Flower-arranging is for girls, they told him. Even some of the girls were mean, spiteful, jealous of his success. But he let all the teasing wash over him. The teacher's words of praise still left a glow inside him.

He ran home through the narrow residential streets of Oizumigakuen-cho to the new house they'd moved to. He didn't particularly like it and hadn't made any new friends here. But that didn't matter today.

'Mama, Mama,' he shouted as soon as he was through the front door, taking off his school shoes and sliding into his house slippers. 'Guess what. I won the flower-arranging prize.'

He didn't hear an answer, and his mother wasn't in the kitchen where she'd usually be at this time, preparing the evening meal. And his father's music, that same damn song by the American singer, was even louder than usual — as though it was coming from downstairs.

When he ran into the lounge, he stopped dead.

'Mama! Mama! Wake up!'

She was suspended on some sort of wire contraption, as though she was a display item in an exhibition — surrounded by one of the most beautiful, elaborate flower arrangements he'd ever seen.

Brilliant white orchids matching her pure white powdered skin.

The pinks of the *sakura* complementing what little bare flesh was on show. Dressed in her traditional *geisha*-like clothing and make-up. But something had gone wrong with the red. She'd spilt some on her neck, and it had run down and stained her kimono. But not the bright red that excited him — this was duller, bluer.

He touched it. It was wet.

And her skin was cold.

Then he looked at his father, his head slumped forward, one arm suspended from the ceiling like a puppet with a broken string.

The music playing, over and over.

The same song, again and again.

Never reaching a chorus.

And then he realised. His parents wouldn't be coming to the parents' evening. They wouldn't see his prize display.

Everything had come to an end.

And then he screamed. He screamed, for minutes, for hours. And that was how the police found him. Screaming at the feet of his dead mother and father, clutching his candy-coloured clown doll.

The next couple of years were a blur of blackness, hatred, and loneliness. Foisted from one relative to another. Kicking out, screaming, biting, hating everything and everyone. Thrown out of school after school.

Then it had all changed. At first — arriving at the school in Hatoma — he'd been scared, frightened, withdrawn. But slowly, he opened up, and started to live. The beauty of the sea, of nature, on his doorstep. Excelling in biology — particularly botany — coming top in the class for the first time. And embraced by a new family who loved him. With a brother and sister who were damaged like him, but who were repaired by a new Mama, a new Papa — his loving, giving foster parents.

Their own children had left the family nest years before — heading in the opposite direction, to find their fortunes in Tokyo. He and his brother and sister had helped fill a void in Mama and Papa's lives — and helped to justify the continued viability of the island's school.

The warmth of the Okinawan climate thawed the ice in his heart.

Field trips to neighbouring Iriomote to discover the beautiful flowers, exotic and rare animals — all of it brought him to life. Even the ones that scared most people, like the *habu* snakes. Kelton Sakamoto bloomed — just like every year the *sakura* bloomed all over Japan. He found his forte — could see a future.

When the blackness returned, it was his own fault.

Most of the islanders and schoolchildren had watched the weather forecast with growing fear. Hatoma hadn't been evacuated because Typhoon Herb hadn't been predicted to make direct landfall.

But then it changed course.

While others were frightened, he was excited by the power of nature. For Christmas, Mama and Papa had given him a simple hand-held anemometer, and this was a chance to use it in earnest.

As the storm grew in power, he braved it. Bracing himself against the side of Mama's simple dwelling, marvelling as the meter reading climbed and climbed, exhilarated by the typhoon's destructive power.

But he hadn't told Mama. She'd come to look for him. He saw her struggling along the side of the house, one step at a time. Beckoning him in. But he ignored her. He just wanted a few more seconds to see how far to the right the meter would go, how high a speed he could record.

He saw the roof tile almost in slow motion, although it happened in an instant. Flying off the roof, hitting her square in the forehead. She slumped slowly to the floor. He staggered towards her as quickly as he could, abandoning his precious wind-speed meter to the elements. Kneeling down over her, asking if she was alright, not getting an answer.

Another roof tile flew off, arrowing into his knee. Shattering it instantly. He didn't know it then, but it would leave him with a limp — an awkward gait — for life.

He crawled using his hands, his one good leg, to try to reach Papa — to get him to save her.

But it was too late. The ice was back in the centre of his heart.

Now he would melt the ice again by going back to where it began with this tribute to his first Mama.

The girl looked like her — had her same ethereal, slightly androgynous beauty. The others had been nearly right, but not quite.

She was the one.

And now it could finally be over.

CHAPTER FIFTY-SIX

Tanaka looked around frantically for something to cover the channel between the crates. To prevent the *habu* snakes from leaping up as he crossed. On one side of the room he saw an old blackboard.

As he rushed to get it, he saw a flash of silver in Sakamoto's hand. A hypodermic needle.

'Don't do it, Kelton. To her, or you.' Tanaka had to keep him talking. If he'd already administered anything lethal to Blain, he had to know what it was to give the medics half a chance of finding an antidote. 'I understand what happened now — how you lost two mothers. It must have been awful for you.' He placed the blackboard across the makeshift snake pit, tested his weight, then ran across.

As he did, the Orbison song was reaching its climax, and Sakamoto sank the needle into his arm.

But Tanaka only had eyes for Blain.

He used a handkerchief to stem the bleeding from the vein.

Then felt for a pulse in the wrist of her suspended, stretched-out arm.

There was one, but it was only faint.

'It's safe,' shouted Tanaka to the armed officer outside. 'Get the medics in. Two casualties. One may need an urgent blood transfusion.'

'Will do, Inspector.'

Tanaka frantically searched for something to cut the ties that were suspending Blain in the middle of the flower arrangement. He spotted the retractable-bladed knife Sakamoto had obviously used to trim the flowers and plants, made a grab for it, and then slashed at the cords holding up Blain, supporting her weight at the same time.

She felt so fragile, so light, so small.

He laid her down, then heard the paramedics entering.

'Take care near those crates. Use the blackboard to climb over them. There are snakes inside the channel.'

The two paramedics gingerly made their way across, as Tanaka, for the first time, truly turned his attention to Sakamoto. He had suspended one of his arms from the ceiling to hold his weight, but his head and upper chest had slumped forward lifelessly.

Tanaka pulled the syringe from his arm. But it was empty.

He felt for a pulse. And couldn't find one.

Kelton Sakamoto had — finally — joined his mother and father in death.

There was nothing more that could be done for him.

He wouldn't pay for his crimes — he'd chosen the same way out as his mother and father.

Tanaka looked across at Blain being tended by the paramedics.

'This one is dead,' he said. 'But do everything you can to save her.'

When he looked in their faces, he realised they thought they might be too late for Blain too.

. . .

Tanaka ran alongside the stretcher, holding Blain's hand.

He tried to think of something to say to her, something to make her cling on.

'You got the story, Holly. You were there — you got the story. You have to fight. You have to be able to write it.'

There was no response.

He stayed with her, clambering aboard the ambulance boat after the paramedics. He had done all he could in advance. Checking her blood type with the *Tōkei Shimbun* before he and Izumi had set off for Ishigaki, making sure the ambulance boat had plenty of supplies of the exact match on board. He had tried to warn her. He'd known what had been likely to happen.

And that was what they were doing now.

Desperately trying to replace the blood that Sakamoto had drained out of her.

Hoping it would be enough to save her life.

CHAPTER FIFTY-SEVEN

In those few moments, running alongside the stretcher, Tanaka's life flashed before him.

He was back to the day, seventeen years ago, when his and Miho's life caved in.

Misaki had been three months old, their most beautiful gift. Even at that young age, you could tell she had inherited Miho's delicate looks. They joked that she was their Japanese flower, their very own blossom from a cherry tree. The percentage of her genes from Tanaka's non-Japanese side was nowhere to be seen.

She didn't seem to have a fever, but she just wouldn't stop crying. She would only calm down if Miho held her close. They'd tried settling her in her cot by the side of their futon, but the crying just went on and on. Both Tanaka and Miho were exhausted. Finally, Tanaka had suggested letting Misaki sleep between them. It seemed to do the trick. Misaki calmed, and both Tanaka and Miho fell — at last — into a deep, deep sleep.

Tanaka had woken first. It was the coldness he noticed. Not ice-cold, but lukewarm, like a hot water bottle that had lost all but its last couple of degrees of heat.

He tore back the bed covers. Screamed at Miho to wake up.

Began shaking Misaki, then desperately trying to give her mouth-to-mouth resuscitation.

But it was too late.

Her little spirit had gone to another world.

Miho was inconsolable.

Tanaka had tried to bury himself in work. To try to forget, even though he didn't want to forget.

The births of his sons — Takumi and Sora — were some consolation. They had tried for another child, even having IVF sessions, but it was no good. Misaki had been their gift of a daughter, and Tanaka — in suggesting the baby share their bed just so they might get some sleep — felt he had as good as killed her.

They were never blessed with another.

As each year passed, Tanaka would look longingly at the daughters of friends, watching them grow, trying to share his friends' joy. But all the time, every minute of every day, he was imagining whether those girls were how Misaki would have turned out.

And then he met Blain. Suddenly, in her unrelenting, persistent spirit, he felt she was the embodiment of his daughter. That — in some way — she *was* his daughter, his second chance.

He didn't want another daughter wrenched away.

. . .

As he sat by her stretcher on the boat, there was a flicker from her eyelids.

'Her pulse is recovering,' said one of the medics. 'But we're not out of the woods yet.'

Tanaka was immediately at her side, whispering into her ear. 'You're going to make it, Blain. You have to make it.'

Then he realised she was trying to move her lips.

He put his ear close to her mouth.

'Take... a... photograph... for... me,' she rasped. 'Of... his... last... arrangement. Need... it for... my story.'

And Tanaka knew he would do just that. He would give the police photos ahead of all the other press, he would ensure she got the best coverage.

Because they had worked as a team. Together.

True, they had been unable to bring Sakamoto before a court of law. They had been unable to make him pay for his crimes. But they had put an end to his reign of terror.

Now he was back where he wanted to be. With his mother and father. They had abandoned him, but he had gone back to them.

And they were together.

In Dreams.

CHAPTER FIFTY-EIGHT

With Blain safely in hospital, Tanaka took Izumi to a café in Ishigaki town centre for a heart-to-heart.

He now knew what was wrong with his deputy, why he hadn't wanted to go to Ishigaki in the first place, and why he seemed even more reluctant to set foot on the rocky islet off Hatoma. Something had clicked in Tanaka's brain, and he'd found the answer amongst the phone snaps he'd taken of Sakamoto's photo album pages.

It was the 'happy family' shot of Sakamoto with his surrogate family on Hatoma that triggered the recognition. And Tanaka swiped to it now and held it in front of his deputy's eyes.

Izumi tried to look away.

'I didn't recognise you at first, Izumi. You were a good-looking boy.'

'I was happy then, Tanaka-san,' mumbled his deputy.

Then Tanaka's tone turned serious. 'I very much hope, Izumi, that you haven't been deliberately withholding information or undermining this inquiry.'

Izumi held his hands up in horror. 'Of course not, Tanaka-san. I only realised at the last moment, when we were about to travel to Ishigaki.'

'That the man we were hunting was your adoptive brother?'

With shaking hands, Izumi took the proffered smartphone, and reverse-pinched his thumb and finger, enlarging the photo. Tanaka could see the tears glistening in his eyes.

'Does this mean the end of my police career, Tanaka-san?'

Tanaka creased his brow in puzzlement. Clearly, he hadn't yet pieced this all together. 'Why should it, Izumi?'

His sergeant gave a long sigh, then furtively looked round the café to make sure no one was observing them. Then he took off his jacket and rolled up his left sleeve. 'Because of this.'

The tattoo was a thing of beauty but could also — Tanaka was well aware — inspire fear. It was nothing that should ever be seen on a Japanese police officer's arm. A permanent inking, a permanent sign, of membership in a Yakuza gang.

'It's not what you think, Inspector,' said the sergeant, letting his sleeve fall back, the secret sign covered once more. 'I have had this since I was a boy of twelve. I have never, ever, been a member of the Yakuza. I despise them. I have more reason to despise them than most.'

Tanaka found himself clenching his fists, hoping Izumi's explanation was a good one. Hoping that he wouldn't have to report him. That it wouldn't be the end of their partnership. 'If you're not a gang member, Izumi, why do you have one of their tattoos?'

'My father was in the Yakuza. He was a heavy drinker. One night, when, as usual, he'd had far too much, he pulled me from my bed. And took me to the tattooist.' The tears now were slowly falling down Izumi's cheek. Tanaka laid his hand on the man's other arm. 'When my mother found out, she was livid. There was shouting, screaming, I think my father hit her although I didn't witness it. Next thing I knew, my mother had taken me away from him. We went on the run. To a safe house. But always she was afraid he would catch up with us. That is why she sent me away, to safety.'

'To the school in Hatoma?'

Izumi nodded. 'And I was placed with the same family as Kelton Sakamoto. But I swear to you, Tanaka-san, I did not know that was his name. I didn't recognise him from the photographs, what with his dark glasses and everything. I had no idea that the boy who — at that time — I looked upon as a brother, would end up being a killer. It fills me with shame.'

Tanaka tried to reassure his sergeant as much as possible that — as long as his story was verified, as long as they could prove the tattoo had been forcibly inked on at the behest of his estranged father — he had nothing to fear about his job. They would continue to be able to work together, of that Tanaka was sure. But when he looked into his deputy's eyes, he wasn't entirely convinced the other man believed him.

With Izumi finally on the plane back to Tokyo, Tanaka managed to get permission from Superintendent Yoshitake for a couple of days' leave on the island of his birth. He had no connections here now, but he still had memories. Like Sakamoto, he wanted to do his own little nostalgia tour — but he wasn't planning on anyone being killed as a result.

His first stop was the *nana-san-maru* — the 730 — monument, at the main road junction in the centre of Ishigaki. He didn't remember the day — in 1972 — when the Americans handed back control of Okinawa, including the island of Ishigaki, to the Japanese. He had only just been born. But it didn't mean the Americans pulled out immediately — his father, an American army officer, was by that time the only representative on the far-flung island, initially working for the US Civil Administration. The main bases were on Okinawa island itself. Nowadays, here on Ishigaki, all that remained were a couple of army training ranges.

Six years later, in September 1978, the officer had taken his six-year-old half-Japanese son to the monument's unveiling, and Tanaka remembered holding his father's hand with pride — yet still half aware of mumblings of discontent from the locals.

A white arrow snaking from right to left on the stone monument flagged its significance: commemorating the day, some two months earlier, when the roads on Okinawa had switched overnight to driving on the left. The Japanese way, not the occupying American way. Tanaka could remember that day too, going out before breakfast with his mother and father just so that they could make the switch — at exactly 6am on the 30th of July. 7/30 in the Japanese date system — hence the 730 monument.

He dabbed away a tear. The monument was just as he remembered, except for the two stone Okinawan lion dogs flanking it, an addition from later years.

His father must have known what was about to happen. He must have planned it, just like Sakamoto's parents must have planned their set-piece double suicide.

The day after the ceremony, his father returned to the United States, without Tanaka or his mother, and filed for divorce. Tanaka never did find out why.

Tanaka hailed a taxi to take him out to the north-western edge of the town. He watched the concrete buildings pass the car's window — unremarkable slabs of cement-grey, and the same sort of businesses you'd get in any provincial Japanese town.

After a couple of kilometres or so, the driver dropped Tanaka at the apartment blocks which looked like they'd been lifted wholesale from East Germany and dropped in the middle of a subtropical paradise.

Each block had a number painted on its end. He headed for Number 9.

He climbed the open, concrete staircase to the second floor and then found the entrance to apartment 215. No doubt a Japanese or Okinawan family lived there now. He wasn't going to disturb them.

Standing on the communal walkway, he looked out over the East China Sea — the *higashishinakai* — towards Taiwan. Far beyond that lay Vietnam — scene of such conflict involving the Americans in Tanaka's early years.

He understood, now, why he'd never felt at home here in Ishigaki. Why he always got the feeling other pupils — and indeed the teachers — had looked down on him at school. It was partly because he was half-American. That was obvious in his facial features. But the real reason was that his other half wasn't Okinawan. His mother was from the mainland, from Tokyo, and that was where she'd chosen to go that fateful day after his father walked out.

Tanaka had gone with her, adopting her maiden surname as his, and helped her to build a new life.

And he'd never seen — or heard from — his father again.

CHAPTER FIFTY-NINE

B lain wasn't about to let a little thing like a near-death experience stop her from filing her story — the one she'd fought so hard to get, chasing Kelton Sakamoto to the very end.

She only had a vague, blurry, drugged-up idea of what had actually happened in those final few hours after finding the rare orchids in the forest. But she'd got Tanaka to fill in the blanks when he visited her, and she'd insisted he send some of the official police photographs directly to Yamamoto-san to illustrate her piece. Now Yamamoto had emailed through the front-page splash that had appeared in this morning's *Tōkei Shimbun* and, even now, was being followed up by the rolling news services. In thirty minutes' time, a reporter from one of them was coming in to interview her from her hospital bed — she'd brushed off the doctors' concerns that she wasn't yet well enough.

What the doctors had said, though, was reassuring: the drugs she'd inhaled and been injected with were — hopefully — not in sufficient quantities to cause lasting damage to any organs. Her neck wound was healing, and the blood transfusion had saved her. It seemed as though Tanaka's insistence that an ambulance boat and paramedics should accompany the police operation was the only reason why she'd survived.

Blain reverse-pinched her fingers on her phone screen to enlarge the news story and began to read.

'OTAKU KILLER' IS DEAD:
POLICE RAID SAVES FINAL VICTIM
OUR REPORTER WOUNDED BUT FREE
WORLD EXCLUSIVE

By *Tōkei Shimbun* Crime Staff

She was immediately annoyed by the fact it was an anonymous group by-line, but perhaps it was a necessary corollary of her being such an integral part of the story. Further down the text, and in accompanying pieces, she was given due credit.

The so-called 'Otaku Killer' — Kelton Sakamoto — killed himself by self-administered lethal injection as police raided his Okinawan island lair.

But his last victim — Tōkei Shimbun crime reporter Holly Blain — was rescued and is recovering in hospital.

Sakamoto, also known as 'The Flower Arranger' because of the strange and beautiful floral arrangements surrounding each of his victims, was hunted down to a remote islet off the coast of Iriomote.

There, he had drugged our reporter, made her the centrepiece of his final flower arrangement, and left her to bleed to death. Only the quick intervention of police, led by Tokyo Inspector Tetsu Tanaka, saved her life.

During his reign of terror across Japan, Sakamoto was

responsible for the deaths of two young women — a maiko and a Swedish teenager — and abducted and drugged or wounded two more, including our reporter.

He liked to dress up as the late American singer, Roy Orbison, wearing all black and trademark sunglasses. He died listening to a loop of one of Orbison's most famous songs, 'In Dreams'.

Ms Blain, aged 25, is currently recovering in hospital on the nearby island of Ishigaki after undergoing an emergency blood transfusion. She is expected to make a full recovery with no lasting ill effects.

Only now can the full shocking story of the Otaku Killer be told. How he:

- *lost his parents in a tragic double suicide and how the 25th anniversary of that double death made him 'snap'*
- *felt responsible for the death of his foster mother, when she tried to rescue him from a typhoon*
- *'bled' his victims — including our reporter — to try to match their skin colour to his bizarre flower arrangements*
- *guarded his last arrangement with a 'pit' filled with killer habu snakes*

INSIDE TODAY'S NEWSPAPER

P2 — Inside the mind of the 'Otaku Killer' — what turned Sakamoto mad

P3 — Exclusive interview with police hero Tetsu Tanaka

P4 — 'How I was a victim of The Flower Arranger but survived' — exclusive report by the Tōkei Shimbun's Holly Blain.

In that final page four background feature, for the first time, she'd revealed how she'd received the three packages. It was clear now that the woman whose face had been obliterated, replaced with her own in that final, third parcel, had been Sakamoto's mother. The last package, she'd brought with her to Ishigaki and had — finally — handed it to Tanaka. He didn't remonstrate or complain. There was just the slightest flicker in his eye. An unspoken message that, in that small way at least, she'd let him down.

Blain scanned through the remaining stories which Yamamoto had also attached to his email. She didn't need to read them in detail — she'd written them all, dictating them over her mobile from her hospital bed. Not only had she written them, she'd lived them.

Then she noticed a few extra sentences of text at the bottom of the email. They gladdened her heart.

It goes without saying, Holly-san, that you are now confirmed as our crime reporter. Not only that, you will carry the title Chief Crime Reporter. You'll get a bit more money too — we can discuss that. We're very proud of you.

Congratulations, and get well soon! Yamamoto

EPILOGUE

The guitarist — who until now had seemed semi-detached from the group — stepped forward and began to strum and sing at the same time. The song started gently, in total contrast to the loud indie-rock that preceded it. Before the notes of her voice began to fill the club, the audience might have wondered if she was male or female — her androgynous looks almost marked her down as neither one nor quite the other.

She sang of the Sandman, a candy-coloured clown, and falling into a dream-filled sleep. The purity of her voice, the sparkling clarity and jangle of the guitar, almost seemed to be trying to claim the song as her own, even though some would know it was by the other Man in Black. The Big 'O'.

It was a song that never repeated, never reached a chorus.

It was unique and utterly beautiful.

There was an older man in the audience. He felt out of place, as he had on his previous visit a couple of weeks earlier. But this time, he listened intently, and he felt the emotion and marvelled at her courage, so soon after she'd almost died.

He'd been part of the team that saved her. But he was only doing his job. It was doing her job that had led her into danger.

He knew what she was doing now. Not claiming the song for herself — no one could do that. But reclaiming it.

Reclaiming it from evil — transforming it back into the beautiful piece of art it was.

When she'd arrived in the hospital, the staff had asked for details of her next of kin. He'd tried to find it from her newspaper without success.

Like Kelton Sakamoto, she didn't have a next of kin. Like Tanaka, she no longer had a father. All three of them — Sakamoto included — had endured terrible loss.

But Sakamoto had let it poison his mind — that was the difference, thought the police inspector. The girl singing now hadn't.

But that was where he was wrong.

The girl on stage — singing so beautifully — she had a dark and hidden past too.

It was just that Inspector Tetsu Tanaka of the Tokyo Metropolitan Police Department's Gaikoku-jin Unit didn't actually know that yet.

And, perhaps, that was for the best.

LOVE AGORA BOOKS?

JOIN OUR BOOK CLUB

If you sign up today, you'll get:

1. A free novel from Agora Books
2. Exclusive insights into our books and authors, and the chance to get copies in advance of publication, and
3. The chance to win exclusive prizes in regular competitions

Interested? It takes less than a minute to sign up. You can get your novel and your first newsletter by signing up at www.agorabooks.co